A TAXING DEATH

ALEC PECHE

GBSW PUBLISHING

Text Copyright © May 2015 Alec Peche

Published by GBSW Publishing

Cover art: Vila Design

Author Photo: Rachael Paulsen Photography

ACKNOWLEDGMENTS

Many thanks to my first reader and my editor for improving the quality of the story and my writing!

PROLOGUE

*I*f Manuel had known this was his last hour on earth, it is doubtful that he would have spent it at his desk reviewing Burgundy Mountain Corporation's audit results. All who knew him would have insisted that this was not his last hour, that he deserved many hours more; most of all, they would have insisted that he spend his last hour in the arms of Anna, his beloved wife and the center of his world.

CHAPTER 1

*P*eople were walking on the sidewalk in front of the Capitol Building. Some had lanyards with government identification hanging down to their chest, while others had the strap of a camera around their neck taking pictures as reminders of their California vacation. The sky looked ominous: dark clouds were filling up with rainwater, ready to unleash fury on those below in a rare summer storm.

Workers and tourists alike paused at the sound of an approaching siren heralding an ambulance and turned to look. Soon enough it pulled up to the front entrance. Two men jumped out in uniform--a paramedic and an emergency medical technician—and they quickly moved to the back of the van where they extracted a gurney, placing equipment on top of it, and adding gloves to their hands before moving swiftly up a ramp entrance where they disappeared inside the entrance. On the sidewalk outside, those that had paused to gawk at the noise and the vehicle soon resumed their activity as there was nothing left to hold their attention. Too bad the emergency was inside the building; otherwise they could have stood and watched the men care for someone on the sidewalk.

Inside the large building, the ambulance crew proceeded to the elevators. A California Highway Patrol officer approached and asked, "Where are you going?"

The first technician pulled a clipboard off the gurney and said, "Third floor, Room 347. 911 dispatch received a call that a man was having a heart attack."

"I'll escort you so you won't waste time getting lost along the way," said the officer. "I am surprised that we didn't receive notification of the emergency so we could assist."

"We appreciate your help. We don't know what happens with the 911 dispatch calls; we just received the order to come here for resuscitation and transport to St. Matthew's Hospital."

By then the elevator doors had opened onto the third floor and the trio exited the car. Moving fast down a long corridor, the officer soon brought them to Room 347. The nameplate on the wall said this was the office of Manuel Valencia, Chief of the Audit Division, Department of Revenue.

The paramedic said to the officer, "Why don't you stay out here to answer any questions staff may have?" and he smoothly closed the door in his face.

Inside, a receptionist looked up with an alarmed look on her face. "May I help you?" she said quickly while standing up, intending to block their entry into the inner office.

"Ma'am, step aside. We received a call from the man inside that he was having a heart attack."

With that, the two men moved into the inner office, this time closing and quietly locking the door in the face of the worried receptionist. The man inside looked up, surprised at the interruption.

"May I help you? Do you have an appointment with me?"

Then, taking in the stretcher and the men's uniforms, he added in a confused voice, "Is someone having an emergency? Can I direct you to the right office?"

Moving forward, the man dressed in the paramedic uniform

said, "Mr. Valencia, you have been reported as having a heart attack. If you would just lie down on the floor, I'll transmit your heart waves to the base station so they can decide what to do next."

"I'm fine. I have a pacemaker and my heart is working just fine; you must have the wrong office. I didn't call."

The paramedic was pulling the chair out and helping Mr. Valencia to the floor while he was putting up baffled resistance.

"Maybe your pacemaker transmitted a problem with your heart. All I know is 911 dispatch received a call that your heart was having problems. Like I said, we'll transmit to the base station and if nothing is wrong, they'll verify that."

Reluctantly, Manuel Valencia stretched out on the floor of his office. The paramedic brought a portable defibrillator and cardiac monitor over to his body as he unbuttoned his shirt and placed electrodes on his chest. Soon heart waves could be seen on the monitor; they looked perfectly normal. Suddenly the paramedics declared, "You're going into ventricular defibrillation – we're going to have to convert you."

"I feel normal; my heart isn't racing. Let me see your monitor. It must be reading my heart wrong."

The paramedic took a quick look around to make sure that Mr. Valencia's body was not touching any metal. He then pulled out the defibrillator paddles and said "all clear" to warn his partner to step away from the target.

Soon Mr. Valencia's body jumped from the jolt of electricity that had just been delivered, killing his pacemaker, his heart, and electrocuting him from the inside out. And then Manuel really did need the services of a real paramedic as all visible signs of life were quickly departing his body. The door could be heard rattling behind them as they worked on Mr. Valencia.

A moment later, the paramedic stood up and went to the door, opening it. Affixing a tragic look on his face he said to the receptionist, "I'm sorry, he is gone. We couldn't restart his heart. The base station has notified the medical examiner and they will be sending someone out to collect Mr. Valencia's remains."

The receptionist began weeping so loudly that the officer who had escorted the emergency crew opened the door to the hallway and stuck his head inside. The two men from the ambulance had packed up and were exiting the office, pushing the empty stretcher. The officer stepped back, holding the door open. The crew exited the office, heading toward the elevator, and soon disappeared from view. The officer turned his attention back to the office, not sure what he should do next. He called for backup and his supervisor soon arrived.

The ambulance crew reloaded the ambulance and left the scene in a much quieter manner than they had arrived in. As they pulled away, the driver gave the passenger a fist bump and a smile.

"That went smoothly; it was worth the weeks of planning. That bastard won't be around to screw with anyone else's taxes," said Allen Frost in the driver's seat. Today he was wearing the uniform of a paramedic, complete with a stolen badge from Sacramento County sewn on his sleeve.

"I got such satisfaction putting the paddles to his chest knowing that he wouldn't be able to mess with anyone else's bank accounts. That's three targets down and three to go." Jerome Taylor smiled in satisfaction.

"Our work is done for today. Let's drive this ambulance back to the auto auction lot and head home," Frost replied.

Allen Frost and Jerome Taylor had met online in a chat room devoted to the subject of tax resistance. Both had been active in the chat room for years. Manuel Valencia and five other employees of the Department of Revenue had managed to enrage both men within a month of each other. Once they had discovered their common misfortune, they became united in doing something about it and met in person to discuss their options. They were enjoying the satisfaction that three employees were dead and no one had a clue that they were behind it. With each murder they had listened carefully to the news and monitored the internet, but so far no one had connected the three deaths. Not one of their victims was thought to be a suspicious death.

Today, the two men left behind puzzled workers and a grieving receptionist. The leader of the Capitol Protection Section had made his way over to the office and notified his supervisor in the Protective Services Division. By this time, the ambulance had departed an hour ago, and still Mr. Valencia's body lay on his office floor. The officer's supervisor had called Personnel and Mr. Valencia's supervisor. Someone needed to tell the family about his demise and someone needed to remove his body from the premises. It was a question that had never arisen before, because no one had died in their office. Finally someone contacted the Sacramento Police since they could come up with no answers on their own.

The Sacramento Police arrived and listened to the story of what had transpired that day in the office. They had no reason to be suspicious, but under the law it was clearly a coroner's case. A call to the Coroner's Office resulted in the removal of Mr. Valencia within the hour. It was decided that the police would join Mr. Steward, Mr. Valencia's supervisor, in a visit to meet with his wife. Mr. Steward had never met Mrs. Valencia as she was an agricultural lobbyist and busy with her own work. They located her and departed the Capitol Building to walk to her office. Lobbyists tended to have offices close to the Capitol Building as they were frequent visitors, and hers was just a block away.

Mr. Steward and the officer were shown into Mrs. Valencia's office by a receptionist who indicated that her boss was in another office for a meeting. The receptionist then went off to notify Mrs. Valencia of their presence.

A small, smartly dressed Hispanic woman in her fifties soon appeared in the office doorway. She looked at her visitors with worry, as it was never good to be greeted by a policeman under any circumstances.

"Hello, I am Anna Valencia. What's this about?" she asked, puzzled by the two men standing in her office.

"Hello, Mrs. Valencia, I am John Steward, your husband's supervisor at the Department of Revenue, and this is Officer Greg Gould. I regret to inform you that your husband passed away in his office today."

She looked confused and sank down into her visitor chair. "What? Um...how?" she managed to get out as the tears began flowing down her cheeks.

Officer Gould had been scanning her office; he retrieved both a box of tissue and a glass filled with water and put them within her reach.

"Mrs. Valencia, it's rather a confusing story at the moment, but let me tell you what we know. Your husband experienced a malfunction of his pacemaker this morning and either called 911 or whatever monitors the pacemaker called 911 for him. According to Amanda, your husband's assistant, the paramedics arrived and she heard him say that he was feeling okay. They laid him down on the floor of his office and connected him to the base station at the hospital. They said he was having an irregular heart-beat and he needed to be converted by the defibrillator paddles, which the paramedics did, but then his heart never started again. He is with the Coroner's Office at the moment as they are required to do an autopsy since he died outside of a hospital. Mr. Steward and I arrived on the scene after your husband was pronounced, so that is why we have so little information for you," explained Officer Gould.

"Are you sure he is dead? Did you see him before he was moved? Maybe it wasn't my husband," said a hopeful Anna.

"I am sorry, but his receptionist was there during all of this activity this morning and she positively identified your husband," Mr. Steward replied.

"What do I do now?" Anna sobbed.

"Is there someone I can call for you, a friend perhaps, or one of your children?" Mr. Steward offered.

"Oh my God, what do I say to my children? They loved their father. What do I say to them?"

"Why don't you give me their names and numbers and I'll call them," offered Officer Gould. "Is there someone from this office that will take you home and stay with you until your children arrive? Is there someone you would like me to call?"

"Please have my assistant call my sister, Leticia. She has the number. She'll meet me at my house. My assistant will take me home and stay with me until my sister and children arrive."

"Mrs. Valencia, on behalf of the Department of Revenue and I am sure the Governor, we are so sorry for your loss. When you're ready to talk, give me a call and we'll talk about benefits," said Mr. Steward handing her his card.

Officer Gould stepped out to an empty conference room and after getting the number from Mrs. Valencia's assistant, made the calls to her children. Their son was an attorney in New York City, and a daughter was a pediatrician in the El Dorado Hills. The son would make arrangements to be there in the evening and the daughter would meet her mother at her home within the hour. Both children were devastated by the news.

Mr. Steward and Officer Gould were soon departing the lobbyist building to return to Mr. Valencia's office. Officer Gould's partner had chatted with Capitol Police while awaiting his partner's return.

"How is Mrs. Valencia?" asked Officer Gould's partner, Kenny Olsen.

"About what you would imagine - she was shocked by the suddenness, devastated by her loss. I also notified her children and they are on their way home at the moment. This was a strange case as there seemed not to be a hint by those closest to Mr. Valencia that he was having heart problems or even feeling sick."

"None of his co-workers thought that Mr. Valencia was feeling poorly here either. They all thought he looked healthy and well. I guess this proves to you that life is short," Olsen observed.

The two officers headed out to their patrol car to write up their report and head back out on assignment.

The Capitol Police department was also somewhat mystified. They couldn't remember when the 9-1-1 dispatcher had ever failed to notify them of an emergency. Maybe it was a new operator who didn't understand that this was one of the most important buildings in the city. What if it had been the Governor that had taken ill? It had been strange that the paramedics had left the dead body for the coroner, and then when they called the Coroner's office they had no record of being contacted by the paramedics. It was rare that you had both dispatch and the paramedics failing to do proper notification.

They had an intern in their department and she would be assigned the job of running down those answers when she worked next. Both men returned to work with their thoughts split between what else was waiting to be done and the tragedy of Mr. Valencia.

CHAPTER 2

*A*nna Valencia sat on a sofa bewildered by the unexpected death of her husband. Her sister Leticia was there as well as her daughter, Christina. Her son, Michael, would be arriving in a few hours. More family members were expected as well. There was confusion, denial, and anger in the living room. There was a funeral to plan. Mostly though, mother and daughter wanted answers.

"Mom, are you sure that dad was not having heart problems? You didn't notice that he was short of breath, tired, or felt his heart racing?" asked Christina, her physician's brain at work in the background.

"No, he was feeling good. He was looking forward to our annual visit to Yosemite next month. He purchased new hiking shoes that he was walking around the house in so they would be broken in for the hike. The fact that you and Michael could join us this year was even better. We love the Ahwahnee Lodge in Yosemite Valley. Now I have to remember to cancel that reservation."

"Mom, don't cancel it yet. I'm sure that dad would love for us to hike the falls and remember his joy of the park. Maybe we could bring his favorite single malt scotch and toast him. You have time to change your plans, but I am sure Michael and I will still plan to be here even if you don't want to go to the park."

"Yes, you're right. Your father loved that park," Anna agreed as she reached for more tissue while contemplating a life without Manuel.

"Do you remember what dad's assistant's name was? I would really like to talk to her. This whole situation is weird and I would like to speak with her to understand what happened this morning."

"Oh honey, it won't change anything. It's not going to bring back your father."

"I know Mom. It won't bring Dad back, but what happened this morning doesn't make sense from a medical perspective and I am sure if I know more details, I'll understand this better."

"Well okay. Your father's assistant is Amanda Hopkins. I'm sure you can call his number and she'll pick up if she hasn't gone home for the day."

Christina looked at her Aunt Leticia's eyes and found what she was looking for. Her aunt had conveyed that she would take care of her mom while she left the room to make the call.

From the large kitchen decorated in shades of grey and light green, she made the call to Amanda.

"Hello, Department of Revenue, Amanda speaking."

"Hi Amanda, it's Christina Valencia. Would you have a moment to talk about the events this morning?"

"Of course. I just got my tears under control about an hour ago. So I give you fair warning that I will turn into a watering pot. I'm so sorry about the loss of your father. I loved working for him."

"He also spoke highly of you. If I asked if he was free mid-week for dinner, he would always preface it with 'let me check with the efficient Amanda just to be sure I am free'. Then he would get back to me if you gave him the go-ahead."

"That sounds like him. Even though he had both a paper and electronic calendar, he would check with me to verify he was available. He knew sometimes that I might be working on an evening event for him and it wouldn't be on his calendar yet. What do you want to know about this morning?"

"As you know, I am a physician. I'm a pediatrician, but I did do adult medicine while I was in medical school. The explanation provided to my mother seemed inadequate so I am looking for more details. Can you walk me through this morning step-by-step?"

"Sure I can walk you through. Let me just switch to another phone to make sure we are not interrupted," Amanda said as she moved to an empty conference room to continue her conversation with Christina.

"Okay, I'm back. Your father seemed fine this morning. It was just another normal day at the office. At about eleven, two ambulance drivers arrived at this office escorted by our Capitol police force which is a division of the Highway Patrol. They told me that there had been a 9-1-1 call that originated from your father's office."

"Did you hear my father complain in any way of not feeling well this morning?"

"No, I was shocked by the arrival of paramedics. I had left your father's office about twenty minutes before they arrived. He was working on a speech for an event later this week and wanted thirty minutes of quiet. He said that "taxes were boring, and he would have to write an exciting speech not to put the audience to sleep.""

"That sounds like Dad."

Amanda sniffled and continued, "The paramedics opened the door to your father's office and I heard him say something like 'May I help you', and 'I feel fine it must have been a mistake' and then the door closed and I could only hear murmurs not actual words."

"Dad said he was feeling fine and he didn't call 9-1-1?"

"Yes, and then I sat transfixed at my desk trying to hear through the door, worried about your father. Then about ten minutes later the door opened and they said that Mr. Valencia had an abnormal wave and the base station had him converted, at least I think that was the word, but then his heart never restarted. Then they left saying the coroner would come for your dad. That was strange because the coroner had no record of being notified by the paramedics or the base station that they were to pick up your father."

"This whole episode sounds strange. I didn't think that patients with a beating heart would ever convert outside of a hospital unless it was a dire emergency and this doesn't sound like one. Amanda, pardon me for thinking out loud and thank you for telling me what happened. I'm going to do a little more research on my own about these paramedics. It won't bring back my father but at least I'll feel better understanding the situation better."

"Please convey to your mother that my thoughts and prayers are with her and your family. If I can do anything to help, don't hesitate to call me."

"Thanks again and I'll tell my mom that you're thinking about her."

With that, the conversation ended and Christina leaned against the marble counter-top thinking about the events of the morning. Frankly it sounded to her medical mind that they took a good heart and killed it. Her father had had a pacemaker for nearly thirty years having been diagnosed with a minor congenital heart defect in his thirties. She wanted more investigation into his death and wasn't sure where to start. Then she remembered a story in the news about a year or so ago. She did an internet search on 'young man murdered by infection.' She clicked on one of the thousands of suggested articles to read.

She scanned through the article and came upon the physician that led the investigation. She did a further search on her and found she'd had several high profile cases in the year since the murder by infection case. She then decided she would start an investigation without her mom's knowledge. Mom had enough to worry about at the moment, and likely she was wrong about the death being suspicious. After all, the police were not involved and her father's office was not considered a crime scene. She made another call, this time to Dr. Jill Quint, MD, Forensic Pathologist. She got her answering machine and left a message. The greeting on the voicemail sounded like she would return the call shortly. Christina stood there in a trance, thinking about good times with her father, countless ways that she would miss his presence when she felt and heard her cell phone indicating that she had a call.

"Hello, this is Christina Valencia."

"Hi, Ms. Valencia, this is Dr. Jill Quint, you left a message earlier for me concerning your father."

"Yes thank you for returning my call. My father passed away this morning and something seems just a little off. Dad was 62, healthy and had a pacemaker for over thirty years. Two paramedics showed up at his office this morning in response to a 9-1-1 call that no one admits to making. Dad said he was feeling fine, but the paramedics ran roughshod over him and the base station agreed he was having a weird arrhythmia and he needed to be converted on the spot and he didn't survive that cardio-version. I should mention that I am a pediatrician but I did do adult medicine in medical school. What would you do with a situation like this?"

"Dr. Valencia, I'm sorry for your loss. This does sound unusual. Why did your father have a pacemaker?"

"Thank you. He had a congenital heart defect that showed up in his early thirties as bradycardia. Since he got the pacemaker, other than model updates, he has had no problem with his heart. He and mom regularly hiked major strenuous trails in National Parks with no heart problems. When I spoke with his assistant at his office, she said he seemed well, and even told the paramedics that he was doing fine and didn't need their services. They asked to check his heart and now he's dead," Christina said the last words on a sob.

"You're calling from a Sacramento number, is that where your family and your father are located?"

"Yes my parents live in the Arden area of the city. I live in El Dorado Hills."

"Is your father at the Sacramento County Coroner's Office?"

"Yes."

"He is in good hands there. Let me explain what I typically do and we can move on from there." Jill proceeded to give Christina a synopsis of her background and training, her contract terms and fees, and some of the additional services she could offer beyond just the autopsy. She also mentioned that in order to do the most for her father, then her mother, as spouse, would need to sign forms to give her access to records.

Christina verbalized her agreement with Jill's terms as well as her comment about her mother's agreement. "Dr. Quint, I had hoped to spare my mom some grief in following up on my father's death. Now I see I need to have her agree to your engagement because it is respectful of her wishes and legally you would need her authority to move forward. Let me talk with her and I'll call you back."

Jill sat for a few minutes in her kitchen thinking about the call. It sounded like an interesting case. It seemed like those paramedics had forced care upon a healthy man and it had caused a terrible outcome— his death. She wondered what the mother would do in this case. Often people thought that an autopsy expert meant that she needed to slice and dice a loved one's body up in order to get answers. Sometimes that was the case, other times she could get answers in other ways. Regardless if there were suspicions about his death by Mr. Valencia's family, then for their own peace of mind, she hoped they would hire her.

Jill Quint, MD was a full-time vintner and a part-time consultant providing second opinions on the cause of death. Her vine-yard was within an hour of Sacramento in California's central valley. She had been a forensic pathologist with the state crime lab, but had left after fifteen years, tired of paperwork and legal testimony. Now she had the luxury of pursuing both of her passions – making the perfect Moscato wine and providing second opinions on the cause of death for grieving families. Best of all she had the help of her three best friends when the research for a case went beyond the autopsy. Jo Pringle was her financial wizard and could always follow the money to a motive for murder. Marie Simon could create a profile on anyone using the internet and social media to compile a complete picture. Angela Weber was her resident photographer and interviewer, and given the opportunity, she could squeeze the truth out of a CIA opera-tive. As friends, they had known each other for over fifteen years and they had worked together on Jill's cases part-time for the past five years. They all loved their day jobs, so it was doubtful that they would ever pursue chasing murder suspects on a full time basis.

Jill gathered up her gloves intending to return to her vineyard and had one foot out the door when her telephone rang.

"This is Jill Quint."

"Hi Dr. Quint, this is Christina Valencia. I spoke with my mother and she is onboard to hire you. How soon can you start?"

"If I email you my contract and privacy forms, will you have them signed and returned to me today?"

"Frankly, if you send them now, we'll get them back to you in five minutes!"

"Great! As soon as I get your mother's signature, I'll call the Sacramento Coroner's Office to arrange a private autopsy. I will likely want to visit you and your mother before or after my visit to the Coroner's Office today."

"We would like to meet with you as well. Let me get the forms signed and I'll get them back to you and we can make arrangements from there."

"Great!" said Jill after she wrote down Christina's email address and they ended the call.

Jill walked over to her computer and hit the send button with the attachments she needed signed. Then she went out to her car just to confirm the presence of her ready-to-travel autopsy kit. Everything looked good in her car trunk, so she left the garage, returning to the house, Mr. Valencia on her mind. She would have to find out where his pacemaker transmitted to and see if she could get the record of its performance. It was an interesting case. She looked over at her in-box as she passed by her computer and saw a new email from Christina. She looked at the forms and they were all signed by Anna Valencia. Good, now she had the means to contact the Coroner's office to arrange for the autopsy. She used to know many of the medical examiners in the Sacramento office, but she hadn't kept in touch after she left the state crime lab. Looking up their number, she dialed the general information number as that was usually all they handed out to the public.

"Sacramento Coroner's Office."

"Hello, my name is Dr. Jill Quint. I am a forensic pathologist. I would like to speak with your supervisor of forensic pathology."

"One moment please."

Jill listened to elevator music from the 1970's, the coroner's on-hold selection, while she imagined the conversation that was occurring between the person who answered the phone and the person she actually wanted to speak to. Depending on their availability, she thought she would be on hold for two songs or about four and a half minutes. She knew she had misjudged her estimated hold time when the music ventured into the third song; fortunately she didn't have to wait for the fourth one.

"Hello, this is John Garcia, Supervising Deputy Coroner, am I speaking to the Jill Quint that once worked for the state crime lab?"

"John, thanks for remembering me. Yes, this is that Jill Quint."

"I heard you were famous now, doing autopsies all over the country, if you're calling me, we must have a body that you're interested in. What's the deceased's name?"

"John, I always enjoyed the rapid pace of your thoughts, not to mention the quality of your work. Glad to hear that you have been rewarded with the supervisor position. The deceased's name is Manuel Valencia. Your office retrieved him late this morning or early afternoon from the Capitol building."

"Ah yes, I remember hearing about that one. He is scheduled for autopsy tomorrow morning. Sadly we had four teens that drowned in the American River last night in addition to our usual spate of gang shootings, and dumb people choosing to get themselves dead, so we were not able to get to him right away."

"Sorry to hear about the teens, that must be rough for the staff, especially those with teens of their own. I have Mr. Valencia's wife's authority to conduct a private autopsy. I wondered if I might do that this evening at your facility and then you could accept my report or choose to repeat the autopsy tomorrow as scheduled. I've maintained my license in the State of California."

"Why does the family want a private autopsy? Why are they suspicious about his death? I thought I heard he had a bad heart and he couldn't be resuscitated?"

"That is partially true. He had a pacemaker for some thirty years due to remnants of congenital heart disease. He was active and according to his receptionist, he wasn't feeling bad and had not called 9-1-1. He even told the paramedics that he was feeling fine."

"Hmm that all sounds interesting. Can you complete the autopsy in less than two hours? Or now that you do boutique autopsies have you slowed down?"

"John, I can promise you that even in my 'boutique autopsy' practice as you called it, I have never spent more than two hours on an autopsy. Sure there is time beyond the actual examination when I am running information down, but the physical examination will take less than two hours."

"Okay then if you can be here by five this evening, I'll supervise you doing the autopsy, so we both get what we need from Mr. Valencia. Sound like a plan?"

"Sounds perfect, thank you."

"Thank my wife for being understanding about me getting home late tonight. At least it will ease the burden on my pathologists who have had a rather rough day with those teen autopsies."

"Appreciate your help, see you at five," Jill responded and they ended the call.

She called Christina Valencia next, "Christina, this is Jill Quint. I wanted to update you on my progress."

"Wow that was quick, I feel like I just sent you the contract."

"I'm used to moving fast as I don't want evidence to disappear. I have made arrangements to jointly conduct your father's autopsy with the Sacramento County Coroner tonight at five. I expect I'll be done about seven and wanted to have a sense if you and your mother would be available to meet with me between seven-thirty and eight-thirty tonight? I can easily come back tomorrow morning and speak with you then if you think that is better."

"No, please come by at that time. If you have found something we would like to know immediately. My brother will have arrived by that time, and the house is full of relatives right now, so there may be a few extra family members that want to hear about your examination."

"I am making no promise that I will find anything at all wrong. You need to understand that."

"I do, we do," Christina corrected herself. "If you find that Dad threw a big blood clot shortly after the paramedics arrived then I understand the outcome. Regardless your examination will not bring Dad back alive, but it may provide the answers for my mom."

"Okay, I'll give you a call at the end of the autopsy, so you will have a sense of when to expect me. From the Coroner's Office to Arden should be about a fifteen to twenty minute drive. Do you or your mother have any questions before I begin?"

"My mother is an attorney by training, so all she knows about autopsies she's learned from watching CSI on television, so she won't have any questions nor will she want to imagine the actual process of an autopsy. I have no questions, rather just as a reminder, we would like you to focus on his heart and his pacemaker."

"Of course, I've examined other pacemakers during the autopsy process and this will be no exception. Both the coroner and I will want to see the records that were transmitted to the hospital as well as speak to the paramedics that treated him this morning. We likely won't get to talk to them today, but we will speak to them at some point."

"Thank you and we look forward to speaking with you this evening."

After Jill ended the conversation, she went over in her head any possible supplies that she needed and she couldn't think of anything unique that she needed for this case. She had two things left to do - leave Trixie, her Dalmatian, with plenty of treats, and call Nathan, the love of her life.

Trixie gave Jill her best pout knowing her owner was racing off, planning on leaving her alone. Since Jill knew the dog planned to sleep anytime she was away from her house, Jill was aware that the dog's pout was a performance. Still Jill left her a few treats and fresh water.

Soon she was traveling down the road in her 1956 Thunderbird convertible, on her way to Sacramento. Often she would have the top down, but this was summer and temperatures could reach one-hundred degrees during the day. While her car had not originally come with air conditioning, she had had a mechanic add it to the car. The air-conditioning could not overcome high heat, which while great for the Moscato grape, was uncomfortable if you were just driving down the highway. She put her headset on and called Nathan.

"Where are you driving to?" Nathan asked.

"How do you know I am driving?"

"I know you love that car but it really was not built for a quiet drive, I can hear lots of road noise in the background."

"Oh, I should have known. Hey, I'm going to have to cancel dinner. I caught a case a few hours ago and I am on my way into Sacramento to perform an autopsy. I won't be back until ten tonight, so I'll just sleep at my house."

"What's the story on this case?" Nathan asked.

The first year they had dated, Nathan had gotten used to her disappearing on cases about once a month. It was inconvenient, but really nothing more. This past year's cases had caused Nathan chest pain every time she picked up a new case. In four of her cases over the past year she had attracted the murderer. Jill and her friends, and even Nathan had been the targets of murder attempts. Nathan had been paralyzed when he was shot by a murderer's dart gun dart containing a paralytic drug. Angela had been grazed in the arm by a bullet in her last case. At least this investigation was close by and he could protect her if he saw the investigation heading in that direction.

"It's an interesting case. The guy was feeling fine when an ambulance crew arrived and told him he was sick. Then his heart went into a mysterious rhythm and he died."

"That is a weird story. Sounds like the ambulance crew killed the guy. Did he have a bad heart?"

"Yes and no. He had a heart defect that he was born with and for which he was treated with a pacemaker for over thirty years. So his heart wasn't perfect, but he led an active lifestyle and exhibited no symptoms of a bad heart."

"Wow, what a bummer. Have you heard of anything like that before?"

"Frankly no, which is why I am itching to start his autopsy. I got a break there with the Coroner's office. I have an old friend there and they are overloaded at the moment, so the plan is for me to do the autopsy supervised by them. I like being the first and only person to perform an autopsy for a client, but I respect their legal requirement to rule on a death. So we are all going to win with this process."

"Jill, can I just say that it's weird to be excited by doing an autopsy? I mean I understand why you're excited, but it's still weird."

With a laugh, Jill replied, "Nathan, that's okay. I might be offended if you were excited about me performing autopsies. I am excited for any scientific discoveries that I make and for the opportunity to bring justice to the deceased. You shouldn't feel those same emotions. Okay, can I just say that this is a weird conversation? Let's move on and talk about your day."

Jill could hear the smile in his voice as Nathan agreed they should move the conversation along, "I've been contemplating a wine label featuring an artistic rendering of Arthur."

Besides being the love of Jill's life, Nathan was a world class wine label artist with his designs featured on the bottles of at least five hundred different wineries. Arthur was his cat and the nemesis of Trixie whenever the two were in the same room.

"Arthur? Oh my, Trixie will never forgive you making him a star and not her."

"You forget that Trixie has been a beer dog for Budweiser for decades. Her calling is beer, not wine."

"I can't argue with that line of reasoning, she is more of a beer dog. Is this for a winery with a cat in the name, perhaps Cat Napped winery, or Catnip Winery? Or is he in the background of say a garden?"

"Hey, you're pretty creative there - it's your second option. When I met with the owners, they wanted a lazy summer after-noon garden scene for their brand. So for lunch, I sat on my own patio looking around for inspiration and there was Arthur, watching bees and butterflies around the edge of my patio garden. I snapped a picture of him including the flowers and butterfly and sent it to the client, who sent it back to me within five minutes saying I had nailed their vision. I just need to turn the picture into a sketch. This has been one of the easier brand designs to create from scratch."

"How cool that Arthur served as such inspiration!"

"It's hard to tell if he is impressed with himself since he is always impressed with himself. Cats are quite egotistical. I'll have a mock-up for my client by tonight. Most of my designs aren't created that fast. Of course, it helps that I won't be seeing you tonight."

Jill could hear the smile in his voice as he said that and added, "Far be it for me to interfere with creative genius. Sail forth and create, and I'll talk to you tomorrow."

"Why don't you call me on your way home? Talking to me should help keep you awake if you're driving at a time that is late for you."

"That's a great idea. I'll do that, talk to you later," and Jill ended the call, smiling.

CHAPTER 3

*J*ill was on the outskirts of Sacramento, her GPS guiding her towards the Coroner's Office. She was trying to remember if she had been there before, but she couldn't remember when she had that opportunity. She had spoken by phone to John Garcia and she had had lunch with him at a professional meeting, but she didn't think she had been to his office. Soon she was turning into a parking lot. It was a white, two-story government-looking building with nice mature landscaping around it. Of course it could have several floors below ground level, invisible to the eye from the parking lot, and suited to metal refrigerators that contained the dead. From looking at their website, she knew they processed about fifteen-hundred deaths a year as Coroner's cases, and the building looked capable of fulfilling that duty.

She exited her car, extracted her autopsy kit from the trunk and was soon entering the lobby where she was greeted by a receptionist who likely doubled as a records registrar. Budgets were usually too tight now to afford the luxury of a pure receptionist anymore.

"Hi, I'm Dr. Jill Quint here to see John Garcia, the Supervising Deputy Coroner."

"Yes, just a minute please," the receptionist said as she dialed a number to connect with John. She quickly ended the call and said, "He's coming over to reception to meet you."

Jill waited no more than a few minutes, when a tall Hispanic man in scrubs and a lab coat opened the door into the lobby.

"Hey, Jill, let's head over to the autopsy room," John said as he unlocked the door and held it open for Jill.

They walked down a series of corridors and then took the elevator down one floor to the autopsy suite. Staff had weighed Mr. Valencia, x-rayed him upon entry to the morgue, and kept him refrigerated awaiting his autopsy.

After applying the protective apparel of a gown, gloves, booties, and a mask, Jill and John were ready to begin. She left her kit closed for the time-being as she thought she would only need it to collect duplicate specimens as the Coroner's Office would collect their own to analyze. They decided that Jill would perform the primary recording of the autopsy with John adding comments where necessary.

Jill provided the words for the dictation software to turn into the autopsy report. She would turn the microphone off and on at different points to discuss her findings with John. Just over ninety minutes later, they were joined by Detective Stan Chang of the Sacramento Police. Jill and John had preliminarily ruled the case a homicide.

Jill pointed out the marks on the body of Manuel Valencia, "These marks on his chest are from the defibrillator paddles. You can see these red burn marks are the likely source of his electrocution. The jolt destroyed his pacemaker, burned his lungs and skin, and completely ended all electrical conduction of the heart."

"How do you know that isn't a side effect of being resuscitated?" the detective asked.

"EMS and hospitals throughout the U.S. converted to biphasic defibrillators over a decade ago," Jill explained. "They don't use paddles - instead pads are placed on the chest, which do a better job of conforming to the body, present less danger for health care personnel, and damage the heart muscle less than a monophasic system that uses paddles. We checked with Sacramento EMS and indeed none of their units uses paddles on a defibrillator."

"Okay that is a new way to murder someone. I've never handled a case of death by electrocution," observed Detective Chang looking at Jill. "I guess there is a first time for everything. Talk to me some more about how you got involved in this case, Dr. Quint."

"Detective Chang, I am a licensed physician in the State of California and at one time worked for the state crime lab. For the past five years I've provided private autopsy services for families desiring a second opinion on the cause of death. In this case Mr. Valencia's daughter is a physician and she had suspicions about his death and the sequence of events this morning. I am due to meet the family as soon as I finish here; would you like to follow me there? I assume you'll be notifying them tonight?"

"I had planned to do just that so I'll follow you to their house. Do you know this family?"

"I only know the daughter through conversations on the phone. The spouse is an attorney, and she lobbies for the agricultural industry. The daughter is a pediatrician and the son, who was flying in from New York, is an attorney working for an investment bank. A policeman visited Mrs. Valencia at the office this morning to notify her of her husband's death."

"Okay, thanks. Let me make one call to the California Highway Patrol to get tapes of that ambulance crew's arrival at the Capitol Building. I've also got someone working on getting data from 9-1-1 dispatch and St. Matthews to determine if any contact was made between them and anyone regarding Mr. Valencia."

A few minutes later after making his call, Jill, with Detective Chang following in his car, made the short drive to the Valencia house. Soon they parked down the street from a stately one-story home in an impressive neighborhood. There were cars in the driveway and on both sides of the street in front of the home. It was ablaze with lights perhaps a reflection of friends and family who had come to offer comfort to Mr. Valencia's immediate family. Jill and the detective looked at each other as they walked up the driveway, each possibly contemplating how to handle a conversation with a large extended family. The detective had briefly debated leaving Dr. Quint out of his conversation with the widow, but in truth she likely could better explain the autopsy's findings than he could.

As they stood at the front door, Jill said, "Why don't I introduce myself and then you. If you like, I can deliver the news to the family and we can both answer questions. I won't answer any police procedure questions and you stay away from the autopsy. Deal?"

"Sounds like a plan. We should offer to speak just with Mrs. Valencia, but I'm guessing she'll want the entire family in on our discussion."

"I would agree with your guess," Jill said as she rang the doorbell.

The door was opened by a petite Hispanic woman in her late 20s to early 30s, red-eyed with bags forming under her eyes from swollen tear ducts. She said, "Hello, I'm Christina. Are you Jill?" and then she looked with puzzlement at Detective Chang standing to the side and behind Jill.

"Hello, Christina, and yes I'm Jill. This is Detective Chang. Is there somewhere private we can speak to you and your mother?"

"Detective Chang? That must mean that there is something suspicious with Dad's death," Christina said as a new round of tears began slipping from her eyes. "Damn these tears, I should be too dehydrated to cry anymore today. Mom will want the entire family to hear her news with her, so come on in to the living room."

They entered a lovely home, with marble floors in the entry and mahogany woodwork apparent in the built-ins and crown moldings. Sculptures that looked like they had been created by Degas were displayed on an entryway table. They followed Christina into a well-lit living room that was filled with ten to fifteen people seated on a variety of sofas, armchairs, and mismatched chairs brought in from other areas of the house. Christina walked across the room to a woman who was obviously an older version of herself.

"Mom, this is Dr. Jill Quint, and Detective Chang. They have some news for us. They wanted to know if you would want the conversation in private and I thought not."

"My daughter knows me well, Dr. Quint, Detective. Michael, please get our guests some chairs. Would you like something to drink?"

"No thank you," Jill replied.

The detective gave a negative shake of his head as well and they were soon both seated in the tight circle of the family.

"Mrs. Valencia, I had several conversations with your daughter so I assume you know that the Sacramento Coroner's Office did a joint autopsy with me on your husband. I'll provide you with my own report of the autopsy and the Coroner will file the official report, but your husband's death will be declared a homicide. Detective Chang joined me at the Coroner's office when we determined the mode of death. To be more specific, whoever provided the defibrillator shock to your husband this morning, did so with equipment not in use by EMS squads in this area and likely modified it to deliver excessive electricity to his heart damaging both his pacemaker and heart muscle."

Jill stopped here knowing the family would need time to digest her words and to answer the questions that would soon start. For a few moments, there was silence in the living room except for a few sniffs. Then brains started working, and the questions started flowing, like a train slowly gathering steam, sometimes one on top of another until there was a fast moving locomotion of words and questions aimed at Jill and the Detective.

"Whoa, slow down folks," said Jill over the noise. "I'll stay as long as long as you need to answer questions and the Detective has time as well," at least Jill hoped that was true since she had just volunteered him.

"I'll answer a few questions that I heard and then I'll pause for the Detective to answer his. First question I think was why didn't you know this earlier in the day? Why wasn't it recognized as a crime scene?"

"The detective is pulling surveillance video, but from what we heard, a real ambulance pulled up to the Capitol building and two real-looking first responders took a stretcher and equipment into the building looking for your husband. He was the target. No one had any reason to question the actions because under normal circumstances, if it was a true emergency, you would not want to delay treatment while you verified someone's credentials. When Christina spoke with Amanda, your husband's receptionist, she said she overheard your husband say that he was feeling fine and this must have been a mistaken call. Whomever these fake first responders were, they knew in advance that your husband had a pacemaker and said that it had signaled an alert for heartbeat problems. Those words were a heads up to your daughter and I as we have never heard of a pacemaker calling out to a remote computer to report heart problems."

"Detective Chang, from what Dr. Quint has explained, my husband was the target. Do you have a motive? Who would possibly want my husband dead?" asked Mrs. Valencia.

"Mrs. Valencia, we are just beginning this investigation so we don't have a motive yet. We'll need to start the case by interviewing everyone in this room. Those interviews will give us clues to follow up on. We've already requested the recordings from your husband's office building security cameras to see if we can identify the first responders. Also just to close the door on the question, we'll check with 9-1-1 Dispatch, St. Matthews, and the first responders groups that operate in this region. Those activities will give us more information about our suspects, but won't fill in the reason for motives. As you can imagine we have just begun the investigation, so I don't have a lot of information for you just yet."

The detective answered a few more questions, took the names, phone numbers, and family relationships of the people in the room with a promise to schedule interviews the next day, and left the house, perhaps an hour after he had arrived.

Jill was left inside with the family. She saw her role as likely ending, but wanted to get any questions answered before she left.

"Do you think that the Coroner would have discovered the problems if Christina hadn't been suspicious?" Michael asked.

"Probably, but it's hard to say. The evidence on the surface seemed appropriate to the description of medically what occurred with your father's heart. Frankly I noticed the problem right away because I had renewed my advanced cardiac life support certificate last month and part of my continuing education contained a section devoted to the latest technology in defibrillators. So I was alerted by the burn marks on your father's chest. Are there any other questions I can answer for you?"

"What are the next steps for us as a family?" asked Mrs. Valencia.

"There are a couple of things I would recommend. You should expect to be contacted by the media tomorrow as word of this homicide gets out, so appoint a family spokesperson and think about what you might want to say. Secondly, as the police are involved in this case, I would suggest that you have no need for my services. I do provide a broad range of investigative services but I believe you should rely on the police as your first level of investigation. Certainly it is easier and legal for them to obtain copies of video feed. If you would like to retain my services down the road, I would be pleased to help.

"The coroner should release a final report and your husband's remains to a funeral service, so think of who you want to use. If you're planning on a cremation, I would suggest waiting until the police finish their investigation in case Manuel's body contains any clues. A mortuary can store his body indefinitely for a price."

"I would plan on the entire family being individually interviewed tomorrow. This is because some sixty percent of deaths are at the hands of family members. I would just say that this doesn't feel like it was directed by a family member. It's too well-planned for starters. The sooner you are all cleared, the sooner the police will move on to someone else."

"Did Manuel suffer this morning?" asked a tearful Mrs. Valencia. Her daughter reached over to place a hand on her arm while she croaked out, "oh Mom."

"Mrs. Valencia, that kind of jolt of electricity would be so quick, that I think Mr. Valencia would have felt little pain," Jill offered. On one hand she had a real desire to comfort Anna Valencia, and yet in the small recesses of her brain, Jill was thinking, how long do you retain consciousness after your heart stops? It seemed like the two would go hand in hand, but it was the kind of question that you couldn't study and so she let it go.

Jill felt like she had reached the end of the conversation with the family. They needed her to leave so they could get on with the grieving. She rose and said to Anna and Christina, "I'll have a final report for you tomorrow. Here is my business card and don't hesitate to call or email me with any questions that I can help with. I am so sorry for your loss and Mr. Valencia was lucky to have this large supportive family." Jill left the room and headed for the door, one of the family members escorting her.

CHAPTER 4

*S*he looked at her watch and noted that it was close to ten. She would hopefully be home by eleven, but at least she didn't feel like she might fall asleep while driving. The family had been one of the best that she had ever interacted with and she always felt a little drained when the deceased seemed to be such a good guy. Oh well, life was a crap shoot and one never knew what the day would bring.

After starting up her car, she made a series of turns to reach the interstate highway. Once there and with nothing but relatively uncrowded traffic miles in front of her, she used her headset to dial Nathan so they could chat.

"Hey babe, this is a little later than I would have expected you to call, did you run into problems with the autopsy?" asked Nathan upon answering his phone, and seeing who the caller was.

"Yes and no. It wasn't a complicated autopsy, but I could relatively quickly identify the mode of death as homicide. That meant a different kind of conversation with the coroner and discussion with a detective before driving to the family to discuss the findings with them."

"Sounds like you have had a tough evening. How did the family conversation go?"

"It was a very nice family, devastated widow and adult children. I told them I would send them my final report tomorrow and that my services were basically at an end as the police were active and involved. I offered them an explanation of what to expect tomorrow and going forward. It was really quite sad. Sort of reminded me of the same feeling around Henrik when we discussed Laura's death."

"I remember that feeling in Germany; it was sad seeing the impact on the survivor. What did you think of the detective?"

"He seemed quick enough and was cooperative, but time will tell how good he is at investigating. Did you finish your design for the English garden concept?"

Nathan glad of the conversation shift replied, "Yes, I finished. It took me a while to warm up to this design request as the owners explained their ideas up front when they hired me. However having worked with them on the design, toured their vineyard, and understood their varietal focus, I've come around on the design. I like what I have created and it suits this vineyard from a brand prospective."

"You'll have to show me tomorrow. I'm planning on working in the vineyard throughout the day and then Trixie and I will drop by your house for dinner."

"You won't be tied up with this new case?"

"It will take me an hour to complete a final report and prepare a final invoice. I advised the family to end my services as the police are involved in the case."

"You have stayed involved in lots of cases where the police are involved, what is different about this one?"

"I'm not sure the family needs my services at this point and until they do, it's best if I just sit on the sidelines waiting for them to call."

"Sounds like you think they will re-engage you."

"Actually I do. They are an intelligent family, with drive and ambition. I think they likely have the funds and probably a boat-load full of impatience. I think in under a week, they will engage me for investigative services. In fact I'll bet you a pepperoni pizza on it."

"That's no bet; you win either way since you love pizza so much."

"Am I that transparent?"

"You forget how many pizzas I have seen you devour in the two years we have been together," Nathan said. Jill felt comforted on her drive, imagining Nathan leaning back in his design studio chair, smiling over their conversation. She really had found a wonderful man to partner with.

"Well yes, but you love me anyway despite my pepperoni breath."

"Pepperoni breath? Hmmm, that's true that I have smelled pepperoni on your breath, but fortunately I stuck with you anyway."

"Hey, there are night-time construction cones up ahead. I'm going to end this call and concentrate on being a good driver. Talk to you later."

"Have a good night and be careful!"

They ended their conversation just as Jill was required to slow down to merge into a single lane. California highways were so congested all the time, that repairs and construction had to be done at night. It was a common sight to see bright lamps focused on a particular highway section in the dark. The Highway Patrol often participated in the projects keeping the workers safe by either using their emergency lights to alert approaching traffic or by chasing down speeders who didn't take care and drop their speed in a construction zone. Regardless, she never wanted to have a role in injuring a highway worker because she was a care-less driver. She had seen a few bodies on her autopsy table that had been crushed or hit by a vehicle and it was never pretty.

Shortly she exited the zone and drove another half an hour to home. Trixie greeted her with an air of no doggy worries, which was good. Jill had learned that the Dalmatian was very sensitive to strangers on her property. She had saved Jill's life a number of times by alerting her to danger on her property. Soon the car was put away in the garage, and she and Trixie were both having a late snack to make-up for their respective disrupted dinners. Jill was eating yogurt, fresh berries and pita chips, washing it down with a glass of her own premium Moscato. Trixie had dog food followed by stinky duck treats and a rawhide bone.

Jill took a minute to go through her email. John Garcia had sent her a copy of the official Coroner's report. Christina Valencia had dropped her a note of thanks. Angela had sent her an article on the Green Bay Packers' training camp. All of the emails could wait until the morning. She watched an episode of a home buying show and went up to bed, Trixie in tow. It had been a long day and she was looking forward to her bed.

The next day, as planned, she finished off her report of the Valencia case and was soon out the door to her vineyard. She was perhaps a month away from harvest, so checking that all of the branches containing her grape clusters were appropriately supported was her priority. She continued her schedule of vine-yard maintenance during the day, spending most evenings and nights at Nathan's. Her forensic consulting business was such that she could go an entire month without a call to discuss a new case and she wasn't disturbed by the lack of calls for any other suspicious deaths during that week.

However it was now the morning of the seventh day and she would be losing her pizza bet with Nathan if the Valencia family did not call today. Morning passed into afternoon and still there was no call. It was the end of the day and she was cleaning up after spending the day with her hands touching sticky grapevines, when the telephone rang. She saw the Sacramento area code and knew this phone call would mean she had won the bet.

Picking up the handset she said, "Jill Quint speaking."

"Hello, Dr. Quint. This is Anna Valencia. Is this a convenient time to talk?"

"Yes, give me a few seconds to grab pen and paper. Okay, go ahead."

"It has been a week since my husband was murdered and there are few leads that the police are investigating. I reviewed the original contract you provided me at the start of your engagement and I would like to hire you for additional investigative services. I feel that the police are not moving fast enough and that evidence may disappear with time. May we set up an appointment for tomorrow morning at my house? This time it will be just me and my children meeting with you."

"I would be happy to meet you at eight or nine in the morning to discuss where you are with the case. I think after I hear what the police have given you as an update I will be able to formulate a plan to accelerate this investigation."

"Dr. Quint, you don't seem surprised that I have called. In fact you sound prepared to jump right into this case. Why is that?"

"Please call me Jill. When I met you and your family last week I found you to be loving, intelligent, and ambitious, or perhaps a better word is an aggressive family. I was fairly sure you would lose patience with the speed of a police investigation. Whether you would reach out to me or another investigative company remained to be seen. From the little exposure I had to Detective Chang, I thought him competent and I was also pretty sure this was not his only case and so progress might be slower than was acceptable to your family."

"I did discuss another private investigative company as you don't have a license and your team seems casually committed. However when we did further research into the previous cases that you have worked on, you have an impressive track record in solving some unusual murders and frankly I liked the fact that you advised us not to retain your services shortly after my husband's death was declared a homicide. I'm not worried that you'll take any direction motivated by money rather than a desire to see justice. I'll expect you at eight at my house in the morning and since that is such an early hour, anticipate that breakfast will be served. I like to cook and we can have the conversation as easily in my kitchen as in my living room."

"Thank you, Mrs. Valencia. I don't enjoy cooking so I appreciate whenever someone cooks for me. See you in the morning."

"Yes, and please call me Anna."

They ended their call and Jill went upstairs to shower away the dirt and grime of her vineyard. She dropped a note to her team giving them notification that she might be enlisting their skills and a synopsis of the case. She decided that she would spend the night at Nathan's as she could leave Trixie with him in the morning. She would have a long day in Sacramento and Trixie would actually prefer being snubbed by Arthur rather than the dead silence of Jill's home if she was gone twelve to fourteen hours. Nathan usually shared some treats with Trixie during the day and human food while he was cooking which always sat well with the dog.

Jill was up at six and on the road before seven, coffee mug in its beverage holder in her car. She would hit commuter traffic approaching Sacramento and gave herself extra time to reach Anna Valencia's house. Jill was dressed in a business casual pantsuit, an elegant ivory, with low heeled sandal shoes in anticipation of a warm day wherein she expected to do a lot of walking. Jill's pale skin and blonde hair made her highly selective when it came to shades of ivory. Some tones could suck the color out of her complexion and give her a look of someone battling the flu. She was short of stature at five feet three inches tall, given to wearing higher heels to appear taller, a lifelong ambition of hers, but alas those high heels were incompatible with any distance over a football field on hard concrete. Given she wasn't sure where she would be driving to during the day, she left her vintage

Thunderbird at home, driving her sedan instead. Her briefcase containing her iPad and a yellow legal pad to take notes was the final accessory.

Right at eight she was parking at the curb in front of Anna's house. There were several cars in the driveway, and that made Jill wonder who else might be in on the interview other than Anna. She soon had her answer as Michael Valencia opened the front door after Jill rang the doorbell.

"Hello, Dr. Quint, please come in to the kitchen; Mom is in there cooking up a massive breakfast. I hope you're hungry."

"Good morning Michael, please call me Jill. I love when other people cook and I am sure your mother is a wonderful cook."

They moved to the back of the house where the beautiful kitchen was located. It featured white cabinetry, a light colored granite countertop, double ovens and a six burner stove. Whenever Jill saw a six burner stove, she knew she was in the house of a master chef. Personally she very rarely used more than two burners, let alone six. The light colors and morning sun streaming in served to make the kitchen look very large. Anna was moving between the stove and the countertop, and there were four place settings in a cheery breakfast nook. Christina was also in the kitchen and paused to ask Jill what she wanted to drink offering her a wide array of choices.

"Even though I had a large coffee on the way here, I'd love some more with fake sugar and a little milk if you have it."

"I can do that. Looks like Mom is almost ready to serve, why don't you have a seat while I help her bring everything to the table?"

Jill took a seat, pulling out pen and paper. She wanted to be ready to take notes as soon as the conversation drifted into areas that were relevant to the case. Anna cooked a phenomenal scramble that included eggs, cheese, sausage, and vegetables, as well as hash browns, fresh fruit, and toast. Jill wondered how the woman stayed so thin. Over the breakfast she got to know a little more about Michael and Christina. Both had taken leaves from work to support their mother and were ready to assist Jill with sleuthing if she needed their help. Jill, over the course of the entire conversation, learned the strengths of each child. Michael, a tax attorney, would be able to help her with reviewing any financial documents with his combined legal and financial education, while Christina's skill set seemed to duplicate Jill's. She filed the information away for the time being and began the conversation about Manuel Valencia in earnest. The children were smart and had the looks of both parents. They were both much taller than their mother, had green eyes, light olive complexions, and were long legged and short in the torso. Michael had thick black hair while Christina had auburn highlights in hair long enough to make into a ponytail.

Jill started with, "What exactly did your husband do as Chief of the Audit division for the Department of Revenue? Did he audit a branch of government, or perhaps taxpayers, or corporations?"

Anne replied, "His focus was taxpayers - both individuals and corporations. Manuel's staff reviewed all tax returns for accuracy, but also reviewed large corporations in the state. He was really bugged by some of the larger Silicon Valley companies, hiding their cash overseas to avoid corporate taxes. He also, on occasion, recommended legislation to tighten loopholes in the tax code. From my attorney's point of view, it seemed like pretty boring stuff, but he loved numbers, and said 'they told a story'."

"I agree with Dad, numbers do tell a story and he had some fascinating stories of financial irregularities that he or his unit discovered," Michael countered. "He also had some real boring examples of taxpayers simply trying to cheat. I inherited Dad's love of numbers, but not of working for the government."

"Did he ever mention that anyone threatened him for being the subject of an audit?" Jill asked.

Mother and children looked at each other appearing to examine years of shared dinners wherein work was discussed.

They all seemed to arrive at a moment of remembrance of such discussions. Anna went first.

"I would say he got threats maybe once or twice a year. In the case of corporations, they would hide behind tax attorneys and were very polite. Individual taxpayers might behave irrationally at times. Any threatening letters or calls were turned over to the Highway Patrol as they handled security for him. I can't recall Manuel making any comments about what happened after the threats were turned over to law enforcement. We never had anyone stalk us at home in any way."

Anna then looked over at her children seeking their recollections about their father's comments.

Michael added, "Dad often tried to make light of how crazed people got about the notices from his office. He was very sympathetic to people who described the dire financial situations they might be in, but he could get some bizarre letters from anti-tax people."

"What is the difference between anti-tax people versus someone that doesn't want to pay their taxes?" Jill asked, thinking of how much she hated paying taxes.

"Anti-tax people are sort of a revolutionary group." Michael explained."They feel their state and federal tax burdens are taxation without representation and they follow some of our Revolutionary War heroes and speeches. There is also a side group of anti-government people, sort of anarchists that believe we should have no government and let the people rule themselves. They are against taxes as it is used by the government to fund itself, so they figure if they refused to pay taxes, the government will eventually close. What they don't take into their calculation is that they are far less than one percent of taxpayers. For the anarchy strategy to ever work they would need to gain far more followers."

"I'm going to note these threats and move on to an update of what the police have told you so far with this case. Anna, after you called me last night, I wrote a series of questions related to what I learned from the autopsy and the entire ambulance saga. My first question was I assume by now the police pulled the video of the exterior and interior of the building. Were they able to do anything with that video? Were they able to identify the two attendants? Were they able to watch the two attendants from arrival to departure, in the elevators and corridors of the Capitol building?"

"You know Jill, I wish I had you with me for all the calls we have had with the police in this last week. I asked none of those questions and just passively accepted what information they fed me not asking any questions - that's embarrassing considering that I am a highly trained argumentative attorney. All I can say is that I'm glad we hired you because I didn't think to ask the simplest of questions of the police."

"Anna, don't beat yourself up. I bet you were having conversations with the police in-between planning a funeral and being a strong female leader to this large, loving, clan of yours," Jill asserted, placing her hand on Anna's. "You likely have respect for the police with your legal career and somehow figured that they were giving you one-hundred percent of what they know. Detective Chang was also probably trying to spare you the emotions of the investigation. I don't think he willingly withheld something from you."

"I do have to agree with you that Detective Chang seems competent and so maybe you're right that he sensed I was already overwhelmed by Manuel's death and decided not to bother me with details. So where do we go next?"

"After you called last night, I called the detective and set up an appointment today to go over the evidence so far. I also made an appointment with your husband's supervisor, John Steward. I would like to better understand Manuel's department and get his recap of what happened to Manuel. I'd like his perception about threats made to employees in that division. Basically, I plan to explore the work angle first, then the family angle, and finally sort of a history angle - look far back in Manuel's background."

"You will not find Manuel's killer within our family," Anna said forcefully. "He was loved by every member of my family; no one even disliked him, let alone hated him enough to kill him."

"Anna, my gut feeling which nearly is always accurate in predicting the direction of a murder case, is telling me it's not your family, which is why I am not focusing there first. But I would be a bad investigator if I found nothing at his place of employment, then failed to look at your family. Twenty-five percent of victims are killed by a family member and another fifty-four percent know their killer; maybe it is a friend, a co-worker, or a neighbor. Are you asking me to not investigate your family if I don't find clues elsewhere?"

Anna paused for a moment, shifting through all of their family members, unable to pick a killer out of the bunch of them and so said with resolve, "If you must investigate my family, do so. I need to find Manuel's murderer."

She looked at her children as if seeking their agreement and nodded when she saw it.

Jill looked at her watch and said, "I need to get going to meet Detective Chang. Michael and Christina what are your schedules for the remainder of the week? Are you going to be here or are you returning to your homes?"

Michael replied, "We both took a leave of absence from work for three weeks. So we'll be staying with Mom for another two weeks. Why?"

"I'll want to interview you more as I gather more material on your dad and so I wanted to know if I could contact you here. It just makes life simpler. If this is a good time, I would propose we meet here tomorrow at the same time to go over what I have found," Jill suggested as she stood up and began replacing her notes in her briefcase.

"That works perfectly," Anna agreed. "Expect breakfast and coffee when you arrive."

"I would tell you not to bother, but I know what it is like to be near a great cook, you can't resist cooking for anyone that is a guest in your home. I don't enjoy cooking and my cupboards and refrigerator are relatively empty. My friend Nathan knows he has to bring all supplies when he plans to cook in my kitchen. I would rather experiment with organic moth killer spray than with food."

With a rusty laugh, Anna showed Jill to the front door and she departed in her car heading for the downtown area where the detective was housed. The Sacramento Police Headquarters were not in the area of the Capitol Building; it was about six miles south. A little farther than Jill wanted to walk on a day where the temperature might reach one-hundred degrees Fahrenheit. Instead she would look for covered parking to avoid her car baking in the direct sun. Once she arrived at the building and saw no covered parking, the best she could hope for was a tree to give her shade.

CHAPTER 5

*A*fter presenting herself at the front desk, she was escorted back to the cubicle area of the detective division. She had researched the police department before she set out this morning. She knew there was a total of 150 personnel working in the investigation unit - both detectives and forensic specialists. She also knew that this location was one of four police stations for the city. She wasn't sure how the forensic analysis was handled as there were both State and County crime labs in addition to the city of Sacramento Police crime lab. Some of the lab was likely a duplication among the jurisdictions, but there might be unique components to each as well.

After a journey of one flight up and perhaps half the length of the building, Jill and her escort arrived at a door announcing it as the Detective Division and she soon thereafter arrived at a space occupied by Detective Chang. Jill held her hand out and said "Thanks for meeting with me, Detective."

"Before we start, can you show me your contract with the family?" replied Detective Chang.

Jill quickly pulled out her contract wherein the language was quite clear that she was authorized to speak on behalf of the family, and examine any and all evidence. Furthermore, she showed the detective her shiny new private detective license. She had finally decided she should get the license and had taken the exam a few weeks prior.

"Great thanks for getting their written permission, saves us both time. I've worked with other private detectives over the years but you're rather unique in that you come from a medical examiner background. I have Mr. Valencia's file here and I'll go over it with you."

"Do you have a murder board set up for him? I would love to see that first if you have it."

"We keep our murder boards in a separate area so that visitors to this section are not greeted by the sometimes grisly pictures of a murder scene. Why don't you have a seat here," said the detective, "while I go retrieve that murder board and wheel it over here?"

Jill did as advised and looked around the cubicle in the short time the detective was gone. She saw no information on the case that she might take a picture of to look at later. He was soon rolling a white board into the opening of his cubicle. Jill took a first glance at it to determine if she thought the detective might have removed some information from the board. She didn't think so as there were no obvious spaces where a document might have been. He could have moved things around to cover an empty space, but she didn't think he had time. Regardless she asked him.

"Is this everything on your murder board? I mean you didn't remove anything thinking it would put me off?"

With a sigh the detective said, "No I didn't remove anything. I haven't hid anything from you or Mrs. Valencia."

"I didn't think you had removed anything but nevertheless, I had to ask. How many cases are you working on at the moment?" Jill asked in an absent-minded fashion while studying the board.

"I have four other cases besides this one."

"Are they all murders, or are some other felonies involved?"

"One other murder case and the remaining three cases are robberies."

"Which case is taking the majority of your time?"

"Mr. Valencia's murder, but only because there are so many agencies involved - the California Highway Patrol, the Governor's Office, the County Sheriff as they have a piece of the crime lab, and the State Crime Lab. I lose a fair amount of time working between the agencies."

"I can imagine the politics involved with all of these agencies. As I read your murder board, you have no suspects so far. Is that correct?"

"That's correct. That is good news for the family as none of them were a standout for the murder of Mr. Valencia. The bad news is of course how difficult it is to track down these two ambulance drivers."

"Will you show me the footage or better still can you email a file containing the specific time period?"

"The files are too big to email. Do you have a flash drive I can copy them onto for you?"

Jill searched her briefcase found the flash drive and passed it over to the detective. A minute later, after downloading the video clip he passed it back to her.

"Were you able to identify the men in the video? I assume given the distance they traveled from outside to Manuel's office, that several different cameras caught their activity."

"Yes we did have them on several different camera angles. Their uniforms were authentic although I doubt the ambulance was as it had no markings of an ambulance company owner and the license plates belonged to a 2005 Toyota Camry."

"Do you know where the ambulance went after leaving the Capitol? Were you able to see it on cameras around the city? Do you have cameras on the streets of Sacramento?" asked Jill. It seemed like every city nowadays had some degree of cameras focused on its streets.

"We do have cameras on some streets and in particular on streets around the Capitol building. We followed the ambulance on camera until it left the Capitol building zone. Once you get outside of that zone, cameras are sporadically placed, and it would take a lot of man hours to look at all of those cameras to determine a path and I'm not sure it would tell us anything in the end."

Jill was taking notes while the detective spoke. His last sentence sort of rubbed her the wrong way. She felt he wasn't devoting due diligence to all angles of the investigation by ignoring cameras that might tell the police where the ambulance went after it left the Capitol building. Perhaps Detective Chang's diligence into investigating the departure of the ambulance more reflected his total workload rather than a lack of desire to follow up on all possible leads.

Jill inquired, "Do you know who manages those cameras? I'd love to follow the ambulance on tape and I'll share the data with you."

"Sure, his name is George Fellows and he is at the street main-tenance yard over on 24th Street."

"Great, thanks for the name," Jill said. "Back to the question about suspects, have you finished interviewing the family?"

"No. It's a big family; he had six siblings and she nine, and three of the four grandparents on both sides are alive."

"Have you interviewed co-workers? Christina Valencia mentioned an 'Amanda', who was her father's assistant. I think there was also his supervisor at the Capitol that notified Anna Valencia of her husband's death. Have you had the chance to interview them?"

"I interviewed Amanda last week and what she described matched the footage on the Capitol cameras. The supervisor was on vacation and we're scheduled to meet this afternoon. I had a brief discussion with him and so I don't expect anything to come out of that interview."

"Do you know if the California Highway Patrol is following up on any leads separate from what you are pursuing?"

"They don't share with me everything that they're working on in this case so I'm not sure what leads they're following up on at this point. The officer working the case in their office is Detective Randy Banks."

Jill was running out of questions to ask Detective Chang. It felt like he ran into barriers in dealing with the California Highway Patrol on this case and for whatever reason did not push beyond those barriers. The situation brought up one more question for Jill.

"Detective, can you explain the jurisdictional boundaries with this case? Does the investigation belong to the California Highway Patrol because it happened inside the Capitol building and the Sacramento police are the secondary agency because the murder happened in the city of Sacramento? I'm just not sure who the lead agency is in the murder of Mr. Valencia."

"There is a problem with jurisdiction and each agency has a legal right to take the lead role. As you can imagine this leads to confusion and both agencies want their prospective detectives to solve the case. To the best of my knowledge, my counterpart in the Highway Patrol has never investigated a murder simply because there hasn't been one before in our Capitol building."

Jill's first thought was that Anna Valencia had made a great decision to hire her as these two very competent agencies were likely stymied by the role confusion in this case and the agency with seemingly the greatest number of facts about the case had little to no experience in investigating murder. Certainly this would make it challenging to collect information. Jill felt like she understood the position that Detective Chang was in but she would reserve judgment until she met with Randy Banks of the Highway Patrol. Once she and Detective Chang were done with their conversation, she stepped outside of the building and immediately placed a call to Detective Banks. It was the little things that could trip up an official investigation. She scheduled an appointment with the detective that afternoon. Checking her watch, she figured she had an hour before her appointment with John Steward and it was a fifteen minute drive to the Capitol building. She would have to think about a line of questioning related to Manuel's work. She hadn't eliminated friends and family as the source of the murderer, but her gut said it was related to work as usually murderous co-workers or customers did their killing at the workplace.

Given the equipment involved in this murder: an ambulance, a gurney, an old defibrillator, and the uniforms, Jill deduced that this was a well-planned, expensive, and well-executed scheme. It was not a crime of passion; instead someone went to a lot of trouble to kill Manuel while making it look like his own heart was the cause of his death. The killer made certain assumptions about the forensic evidence left behind. If the killer was a co-worker, then this might be his one and only target. If the killer was a customer, then there might be several targets on his list. She would ask Mr. Steward about any other employee deaths as part of her investigation.

Jill was soon pulling into a garage near the Capitol. She had about a two-hour break between the two scheduled interviews and she hoped to be allowed into Mr. Valencia's office and be able to speak to his assistant, Amanda. From what the police said, her earlier statement matched what was seen on the security cameras, but perhaps she might know about any threats made in the office. As she walked towards the Capitol, she looked around for a place to eat lunch between interviews. Looking at her choices as she walked down the street, she settled on returning to a little café that looked like it had excellent sandwiches and Wi-Fi. She wanted to do some research on the Highway Patrol's responsibility for the Capitol. Her stride soon had her arriving at the security station at the Capitol wherein, just like the airport, you had to pass your belongings and yourself through a metal detector and security scanner. From there, she was directed to the stairs to find Mr. Steward's office.

Jill presented herself to an assistant sitting inside the door marked Jon Steward, Head of Income, Sales, and Excise Tax. She soon found herself in the inner office.

"Hello, Mr. Steward, I am Jill Quint, a private consultant hired by the Valencia family to investigate Manuel Valencia's death. I appreciate you taking the time to meet with me today."

"Hello, Jill. Manuel's murder is about the strangest and saddest thing I have ever come across in my career. The day I had to tell Mrs. Valencia that her husband was dead in his office was the worst day of my work life. Finding out the next day that he was murdered was the second worse day of my work life. To have his life taken away from him when he likely had a few more decades left is terrible. What can I do for you? I have already provided information to Detective Banks."

"As I understand it, you arrived on scene well after the time that Mr. Valencia died?"

"Yes, that is true. He had been dead maybe thirty to forty-five minutes when I arrived to his office. I had been in a meeting elsewhere and between the time it took the folks in his office to call and for me to be located, and finally to walk over to Manuel's office, some time elapsed."

"I know you have probably been over the scene several time for various reports, but if you would, please tell me about the scene from the moment you began walking down the hallway towards Mr. Valencia's office."

With a sigh Mr. Steward began his description of the scene, "I approached Manuel's office door. There was a guard standing outside of the office who asked me what my business was. When I explained, he stepped aside and allowed me to enter. I entered the office to find Amanda, Manuel's assistant, inside with two other officers, my assistant was also there, providing comfort to Amanda. There was little conversation occurring;

rather there was an uncomfortable silence that came and went with the cloud cover of grief. I continued on into Manuel's office where he was lying flat on his back, shirt open, completely leeched of all color and to my untrained eye, dead. Someone in the room said that the paramedics had pronounced him dead and that they should wait for the medical examiner to come pick his body up. I really didn't know what to do at the time, how to be a leader. I asked Amanda when the coroner would be there to pick up Manuel. That gave her something to do and so she called the coroner's office to find out when they would be there. They looked through their logs and then told her that they had no notification about a Manuel Valencia at the Capitol building. Amanda passed the receiver over to one of the officers who said he was on-scene and that there was indeed a need for them to pick-up the body as it would be a coroner's case.

"My assistant was working with HR to look at next of kin notification. We all assumed that his wife Anna would be the emergency contact, but we needed to make sure that that was what we had on record. Amanda then verified that Mrs. Valencia was in the building that housed her firm's offices and an officer and I made arrangements to visit her and give her the bad news. Once her assistant took Mrs. Valencia home, we returned here and by then the coroner had come and gone and the room was empty. I sent Amanda home and worked with HR on some paper-work for terminating his employment. I know that sounds cold, but it was the most important thing I could do to assist Mrs. Valencia in getting access to any and all benefits that she was enti-tled to. I always observed Manuel to be deeply enamored of his wife, and I think he would've wanted me to attend to her needs first."

"Sounds like a very tough day and one that you don't receive training for as most of us will never have to do for an employee what you had to do for Manuel Valencia. At the time of the event, did anything get stuck in your head as being weird or inconsistent in the story of what happened to Mr. Valencia?"

"I thought the whole pacemaker thing was weird. Here was a guy actively doing his job, speaking aloud to his assistant and these paramedics arrive and in the next moment, he is dead. I know two other people with pacemakers and I told each of them the story and warned them to never let a paramedic get close to them. My friends thought the story was strange and each of them contacted their doctor the next day to find out if anyone was monitoring their pacemaker and they were both assured that their pacemakers were not transmitting to some central source. Perhaps because Manuel had had a pacemaker for so long, his was not the latest and greatest in technology."

"When I first heard of this case I thought perhaps I was not up to date on pacemaker technology and so I reviewed the most popular models on the market," Jill commented."None of them communicate with the central computer that monitors their heart waves; it was a creative excuse to get close enough to Mr. Valencia to do him grievous harm. As an aside several years ago there was concern that hackers could hack into Vice President Cheney's pacemaker and kill him. So the manufacturer made some changes to his pacemaker that prevented it from wirelessly connecting to anything. Was there anything else you thought unusual about this case?"

"Before I knew this was a murder investigation, we had begun to research how the paramedics arrived without advance notice to the Capitol police. We encourage our employees to call 9-1-1 dispatch for an emergency, and dispatch always notifies the Capitol police as we have automatic defibrillators in the hallways that they're trained to use. So we were researching the breakdown in communication only to find out that 9-1-1 dispatch was never in the loop. I think those are the only two things that stuck out as being unusual."

"Have the police kept you informed of this investigation?"

"No. I would guess that at the end when they find their suspect that they'll inform me but they are not updating me with their progress in capturing whoever killed Manuel."

"Has anyone asked you about threats in Manuel's department? I'm speaking to threats from customers or threats between co-workers."

"It's our policy that all threats be referred to the police, so I would expect that they had all the information they needed in their files and saw no reason to question me about threats. By the way we receive about seventy concerning threats each year which are referred for action through our police department in the building. Some customers have been assessed fines or serve jail time for making threats against this department, although that's a small number each year."

"How about his role as a supervisor; were there issues among the employees? Did Manuel ever receive threats for disciplining or terminating an employee? Was there an employee in his division that worried other people due to a temper or erratic behavior?"

"I don't remember hearing of any complaints, but I will ask HR to see if they have record of anything."

"Can you describe what Manuel did for the Department of Revenue? I know his title, but what was his interaction with the public?"

"His division was responsible for the accuracy of tax returns - both individual and corporate. His people review tax returns in which a computer simulator has indicated there is a problem. It could be something as simple as an addition error, or something more complex like a corporation with an extremely high charitable giving percentage. He supervised a staff of thirty and also worked with a data firm to design the algorithms that we use to evaluate tax returns. He personally reviewed some audits; in fact that was what he was doing when he was killed. He also handled some correspondence from customers."

"How long had he been in this role? Did he aspire to another job in your division?"

"He had been in this role for at least fifteen years. He was really well thought of in the department and had been offered promotions, but his passion was catching tax cheaters and the audits and algorithms were the tools of his trade. He felt he could be most effective by staying where he was."

"It sounds like he would have made enemies out of the cheaters."

"Yes indeed, this division did generate a lot of angry correspondence, probably eighty percent of unprofessional correspondence from the public was directed to this division out of the whole of the Department of Revenue. Some of the audits ended up as court cases."

"I did a quick internet search yesterday on the Department of Revenue haters, for lack of a better term. I noted you have been embroiled with one court case for more than twenty years trying to prove that the guy who invented the microchip was a California resident. I didn't read all of the information on the case, but it sounded like you sued Mr. Hyatt for forty-four million dollars in taxes related to income from licensing the patent he held for the microchip; but the most recent court case in Nevada had your department owing Mr. Hyatt over hundred million dollars. Was Mr. Valencia involved in that case?"

"No he was not involved in that case. His algorithms and audits were not focused on who was or wasn't a California resident rather it was about the tax code, tax rates, and the distribution of expenses and write-offs in corporations. I believe that case originated more than two decades ago as a plan created by the then head of the Department of Revenue and the State Attorney General. While both have since retired, their old departments continue the fight over this one tax case. Manuel did whatever he could to distance himself from that case after he had looked into the suit; his only comment was that it was not a tax code violation and therefore of no interest to him."

"Do you have a file of threatening letters? Who investigates these letters to determine if there is a threat to the department?"

"Like I mentioned, the letters go to our security force here - the California Highway Patrol which oversees the Capitol police who have responsibility for the safety and security of this building and others across the city as well as for the governor and other elected officers of the State of California. I can't say that I've ever heard back from security about a particular threatening letter so I really can't tell you what they do with the letters upon receipt."

"How about phone calls? Surely you get calls from angry customers from time to time. Who follows up on those phone calls?"

"I'm not sure. Let me ask my assistant because I would guess that those phone calls get dispersed all over this building as anger may come up in any conversation."

Mr. Steward left Jill sitting in his office while he left briefly to ask his assistant a question. He returned to his office and resumed his seat behind the desk. "My assistant indicated that as part of their emergency procedures for recording any bad conversations, they have a form which they complete and forward to security. If someone is escalating on the phone, they have instructions on how to get security on the phone. So it sounds like all roads lead to Detective Banks as the source of information."

"Who has taken over Manuel's job? It sounds like he had some unique qualities that aren't easily replaced."

"This has been a bad month for employees in his Division. I didn't mention that two other employees also died this month and while he was searching for replacement employees, he passed away. So I need to handle the hiring and find a way to carry on the workload of those folks," with a small grimace he added, "It's been a month full of tragedy. What are the odds of that happening?"

"That is unusual," Jill agreed. "What happened to the other two employees? Were they in an accident together?"

"No they weren't in an accident - they died from an underlying medical condition; I just don't remember what their underlying condition was."

"Mr. Steward, I've taken enough of your time and you answered all of my questions for the moment. I may need to ask you a few others in time. Would you mind if I corresponded with you by email if I do have new questions?"

"Yes that is fine. I tend to stay on top of email so it's likely the fastest way to get information. Do you know your way to Detective Banks' office?"

"No I don't."

"It's in the basement to the right of the stairway where you come in by security. Just take the stairs down."

Jill exited Mr. Steward's office intending to head out to the restaurant she had spied earlier and grab a bite to eat. She stopped on a bench perhaps a hundred feet down the hallway to make sure she had captured all that he said. She was especially curious about the other two employee deaths. It had indeed been a bad month for employees of the Department of Revenue. Sure she had captured all of his comments; she was soon striding down the stairs and out of the building into the intense heat of Sacramento in the summertime. It was a dry heat, but still she was glad to pop into the air-conditioned coolness of the café she had eyed earlier. With a quick thought for her grape clusters back home, she imagined them plumbing up with sweetness in the heat of the mid-day sun.

While at the café she did a search to see if she could find the names of the two employees who had died. She searched for obituaries that listed the Department of Revenue or the State as the employer in the past month. Of course, not everyone had an obituary published in the paper, but sometimes she lucked out. She found the names of two women ages forty-five and forty-eight with the same date of death and a note that they were State employees. She picked up her phone and called John Garcia at the Coroner's office.

"John, it's Jill Quint."

"Hey Jill, didn't think I would hear from you so soon after our joint autopsy last week. What's up?"

"The Valencia family hired me to follow up on the murder of Manuel Valencia, so I have begun investigating this case and a strange fact came to light and I wondered if you could help me with it."

"Depends on what you need, you're well aware of some of our privacy laws."

"Okay. So I just learned that Manuel Valencia was the third death in the Department of Revenue, Audit Division this month. That equates to about a ten percent mortality rate. I wondered if you could see if your office performed autopsies on the two women and let me know if there are any similarities to Manuel Valencia's death?"

"Normally I wouldn't share that kind of information with a private detective, but let me look into the situation and I'll let you know."

"Thanks, John that is all I can ask."

They ended their call after she gave him the name of the two employees. She always had the mantra that coincidence was often a precursor to a substantial clue. The world was a small place. She wrapped up her notes, finished her lunch and got ready to go back through the security routine at the Capitol before following John Steward's directions to security, Capitol Police, or California Highway Patrol as she looked for the various names she had heard this department called.

She located Detective Banks' office and walked in. A uniformed officer watching a bank of cameras looked up and then quickly returned to the monitors saying, "May I help you?"

"Yes, I'm Jill Quint, and I have an appointment with Detective Banks."

"Yes, he mentioned that on his way to his current meeting. He thought he might be a few minutes late returning to his office and asked that you wait in a visitor chair over there," said the officer vaguely pointing to a corner of the office.

Jill sat down, impressed with the officer's diligence to monitoring the camera screens. Then she thought of a question, "Do you have the entrances and hallways in that bank of cameras?"

"Yes, ma'am."

"Would you mind if I look over your shoulder at the cameras? It's one of several topics I am speaking to Detective Banks about."

"Sure, you can look. There are no private areas on these cameras."

Jill stood and asked the officer to point out the front entrance and the third floor cameras to her. She studied them a few moments, and then resumed her seat. The video had produced a very clear picture which suggested that she would be able to get a clear view of the ambulance drivers and that was presumably the file on the flash drive that Detective Chang gave her.

She was scanning email that had arrived in her in-box. She wished she could get off the list of whatever spam server was sending her Viagra emails. She was perfectly happy with her man and didn't need all these advertisements filling her in-box up. She would have to ask Nathan if he got those same ads or maybe the spam servers were only targeting female email addresses. Just as she finished pondering the Viagra spam mail question, Detective Banks walked into the office and strode over to her.

"Dr. Quint, I presume. I am pleased to meet you and apologize for making you wait."

"It's a pleasure meeting you, Detective Banks. I appreciate you agreeing to meet with me on such short notice. Everyone I have spoken to about this case so far seems to believe that you're the source of all information."

"I don't know about that, but let's get right to your questions."

"First, can you tell me about your involvement with the case - when you were notified and what conclusions or theories you're pursuing?"

"On the day of Mr. Valencia's murder, I was away at a conference and so it was given to me to pursue the next day."

"What did you think of the murder? I mean as far as organization and execution," Jill asked, trying and failing so far to have a feel for the detective.

"I thought the murderer was highly organized and executed a great plan. If Mr. Valencia's daughter had not been a physician and asked questions of Amanda, I'm not sure this would have been labeled a homicide."

Jill liked to think that the county Medical Examiner would have noted the burn marks, but she wasn't sure and it was not important that she figure out the answer to that question.

"Since you came on-board as the lead detective for the Highway Patrol, what have you learned? Do you have any suspects? Do you have a murder board set up somewhere?"

"We don't use murder boards in the Highway Patrol, rather we have a software package which we are trained on in the academy and periodically as changes are made to criminal investigation science. So I have reconstructed the crime scene that resulted in Mr. Valencia's murder."

Jill thought she would hope for the best out of Detective Banks. She had never heard of a homicide being investigated without some type of a murder board. She gave some thought to how to avoid having the detective turn defensive on her with his answers. He seemed genuinely interested in solving Manuel's murder, but his inexperience with a murder investigation could be the biggest problem. At least he was talking with her.

"I have not had experience with the process you are talking about. Can you take me through it - how you created it and what you learned?"

"We have a 3D printer that creates models of a crime scene."

"May I see that model?"

"I don't have it here at the moment. It is stored in our evidence room for use as we need it while the case is active, for use by our attorneys that may prosecute a case, and it becomes a part of our permanent archive if the case goes cold. We destroy all models if a case is closed with a defendant being found innocent or sent to prison."

"Why don't you keep it here in your office? The case is not cold yet."

The detective looked chagrined as he said, "I didn't find it useful after the initial reconstruct of the crime scene and it takes up a lot of room on my desk. The 3D model seems to be a lot more useful to solving the series of events relating to car crashes than to murders."

"The 3D model sounds like it would show you how the murder went down which is likely useful information for a defense attorney, but it would rarely help with identifying murderers," Jill noted.

"I'll have to agree with that," Detective Banks added, "I've investigated numerous car crashes and these models are critical to understanding accident causation. Perhaps if this murder had been a multi-person fight and I needed to understand who threw which punch, knife, or bullet, the model would be useful. In this case, having perfect recall of the murder doesn't help much to determine who actually committed the murder."

Jill decided she needed to take a different tack. Banks was smart and knowledgeable, a cop you would want at an accident scene or perhaps running the security of your building, but he seemed to be a fish out of water trying to search for a murderer.

"Were you able to track down the ambulance?"

"The plates on the ambulance were stolen. The paint job was not similar to any paint job used by any ambulance company within a hundred miles of here."

"Did you search for the ambulance in any salvage or auto auction lots?"

"We entered the license plate into our system which notifies those kinds of businesses that we're interested in a vehicle," Banks explained.

"Did you include a picture of the ambulance from the exterior cameras here at the Capitol?"

"No our system doesn't allow attachments such as pictures to go along with our notification."

Jill could see flaws in the system used by the Highway Patrol, but she let it go and instead asked, "How good is the resolution on the exterior cameras here? Would you be able to focus on the ambulance and perhaps see the vehicle identification number?"

"That's a good question. You can see the ambulance approach the building and that gives you a view of the driver side windshield where the VIN is located. I enlarged it but couldn't read the number."

"I'd like a copy of all of the original videos clips regarding this incident," Jill requested thinking about asking her friend Jack, a graphic artist, who might be able to enhance the film to read the number.

"I'm not sure I can release the video or any other materials to you, let me check with my command."

"I'll check back with you tomorrow morning," Jill said, wanting to say more, wanting to remind the detective that she was working on the family's behalf, wanting to remind him of the freedom of information act which would compel him to release the information to her, but knowing if she used that card it would likely permanently damage their relationship so she stayed silent for now.

"I need to go in a few minutes; do you have any further questions I can answer?"

"Just one, what do you think is the motive for this murder?"

"Honestly, I don't have enough evidence or clues to understand the motive. We are lucky to have their faces on video, but we have been unable to identify the two men masquerading as emergency services personnel. They are not in any of the databases available to law enforcement, but we are still looking for them."

"Thank you for your time Detective Banks and I'll be in touch with you tomorrow regarding obtaining copies of any reports and the video feed that you currently have in your possession."

Jill stood up and shook hands with the detective and soon departed the Capitol. She found a bench in the shade and sat down to jot a few thoughts down about the interview. She had debated telling the detective about the other two deaths in the Department of Revenue but decided that she would figure out if this was pertinent data first before bringing it to the detective's attention.

CHAPTER 6

*J*ill completed her notes and headed for her car as she was essentially done in Sacramento unless the medical examiner had come across something with the other two deaths in the Department of Revenue. She had not received an email or voicemail from John Garcia and so she dialed his number.

"John, before I leave the beautiful city of Sacramento, I thought I would check with you to see if you found anything on those two deaths. Have you had the time to research them?"

"Jill, you called about five minutes before I was about to call you. Why don't you drive over to my office so we can discuss those two deaths?"

Jill entered the medical examiner's address in her car's navigation system and was soon heading that way. She speculated on what story John might have for her once she arrived. She had spoken with key persons in this investigation and so far had come away with very little new information or leads to follow up on. Both Detectives Banks and Chang knew what they were doing but didn't seem to be moving the case forward with any great speed.

She presented to the receptionist and again waited for John in the lobby of the medical examiner's office. This time he took her to his office on the second floor of the building rather than to the autopsy area which was below ground and without outside daylight to cheer one up. He pointed to a chair on the opposite side of his desk and proceeded to turn his computer screen so they could both view what was on the monitor.

"I'm going to bring up pictures from the autopsy. I'd like your opinion of what you see in these photos," John requested.

"Can you tell me anything about these photos? I assume they are from the autopsy of the two people whose names I gave to you this morning."

"Yes they are and this is a picture of the chest of the first person," John noted as he brought the picture up on the screen.

After looking at the picture for mere seconds, Jill noted, "Those marks look remarkably similar to the burn marks on Manuel Valencia's chest. Did she also have a pacemaker?"

"No this person did not have a pacemaker, but she was being treated for atrial fibrillation."

"And her friend? Did she also have these burn marks on her chest?"

"Here are the pictures from the second person's chest. She had no history of heart disease," John said as they both sat there silently examining the picture.

"Did you perform the autopsy?"

"I did the first autopsy, and the second autopsy was performed by the Placer County coroner as she died in that jurisdiction. I called them to get the report and pictures of the autopsy"

"Did they die together?"

"No. They died about two hours apart, of likely the same cause of death—electrocution made to look like a heart attack."

"Tell me the circumstances of each death," Jill urged.

"Victim number one, was dining at a restaurant, when the paramedics arrived saying they had a report of a woman in distress. She dined at this same restaurant every week. She would have breakfast while her daughter was at swim practice for three hours each morning. An ambulance crew arrived with gear and walked over to her table saying that they had been called because she was in distress. She said 'no she was fine', then they asked her if she had been diagnosed with atrial fibrillation and she said 'yes'. They said to let them check her heart then they would be on their way. Perhaps she was looking fine, but her heart might be doing poorly due to a subtle atrial fib."

"Really! The woman bought that explanation?" Jill said leaning back in her chair.

"Yes. Remember she was an accountant by training. So they had her lay down on the booth bench and did nearly the same thing to her that they did to Manuel Valencia. When she arrived here, I was given the details of atrial fib and so the ambulance personnel story made sense. I had not realized that we upgraded our defibrillators and so the marks compared to what I have seen in the past twenty-five years. So I made a mistake with her autopsy. I checked our burial records and she was cremated so I can't go back and examine her again."

"John, do you remember if she showed signs of electrical burns in her lungs or heart from your autopsy?"

"I do remember seeing those signs but I attributed them to the resuscitation effort rather than to murder. I am in a quandary as to what to do with her death. The cause of death remains the same – she died because her heart quit beating. The mode of her death I believe I will have to change from 'natural' to 'could not be determined'. Would you agree?"

Jill could tell that John Garcia had suffered a severe hit to his professional confidence with this case. She liked him and had thought highly of him when she was working at the state crime lab. So she searched for something to boost his confidence or at least make him feel better.

"John, what do you think about the two of us putting together an educational tool on the physical evidence of a resuscitation specifically related to improved technologies and their impact on autopsy findings? I don't have time now but once this case is over I think it will do the field good to have this knowledge out there."

"Thanks, Jill, for helping me feel better, and I would like to put together an educational tool as you suggested. I'm going to notify detective Chang about this case even though I can't declare it a homicide. It might have some useful information for the Valencia case. He will also need to notify the family about the change on the death certificate."

"Let's move onto the second victim. She has the same burns on her chest, what were the circumstances of her death and what did the Placer County coroner list as her mode of death?"

"She was also in a café; this one was across the street from the Sierra Mountain Dialysis Center. Her husband had been getting dialysis for at least three years at that location. The victim waited out the husband's dialysis in a café where she always was found reading a book. According to the café owner, the victim had a known allergy to strawberries. Because she was a regular she always sat in the same booth which the staff saved in advance of her arrival, and would go over with extra heavy duty cleaner to make sure that any previous patron that ate strawberries left no residue in the booth. She started having an allergic reaction and before 9-1-1 was called, two paramedics sitting in another booth on break, noticed her distress and got their equipment out of their rig. She did not survive their resuscitation and the coroner ruled accidental death by food allergy."

"Wow these guys are scary. They're doing extensive surveillance on their victims to figure out where they can find them and what excuse they can use to move in and offer aid. They must've had some kind of aerosolized strawberry spray that they misted into the air around the victim. I'm guessing the coroner ruled the allergy as the cause of death and the resuscitation as a failure to revive her. If you don't mind, I think that I'd like to stay here until Detective Chang arrives to discuss these two cases. Did you call the Placer County Sheriff yet?"

"No I need to call the coroner first and have them agree that we have a suspicious death on our hands. We don't have enough details in the second case to know for sure that this was those rogue emergency medical services people. The second victim was not cremated so her body could be exhumed for another autopsy."

"Why don't you talk with the coroner first and explain the bigger picture here. She or he may be willing to change the death certificate to undetermined without an exhumation and down the road law enforcement may be able to get a confession from the killers once they have them in custody. This might save the family some grief."

"You're right especially since we know the victim's husband is on dialysis," John agreed. "It would be nice to avoid the grief of an exhumation for him. This has become a big scary problem. I worry my wife might have an accident and these two fake paramedics might show up and kill her. I'll have a talk with her at home tonight after I apologize for another late night as I think we will be here a while and you should stay involved in the conversation since you've been quickly putting the pieces together."

"If you don't mind, I'm going to call Detective Banks with the Highway Patrol and ask him to meet with us here as it seems to be employees under his jurisdiction that are the targets of these killers."

"Good suggestion Jill. I didn't know that the Highway Patrol was involved with Mr. Valencia's murder."

"I only learned that today when I spoke with Detective Chang. The Highway Patrol provides security for the Governor, major government buildings like the Capitol, and for key members of the legislation. Because the murder occurred in the Capitol building, the Highway Patrol has had a role in this case."

"Why don't you call the two detectives while I speak with the Placer coroner as that's going to be a longer conversation? I want to give people time to get here, see if the two detectives can be here in ninety minutes."

"Sounds like a plan John and thanks for looking those cases up for me. The city has a huge problem on its hands."

Jill had many things on her mind. She wanted to notify Nathan that she would get back late from Sacramento and just head to her house as she would need to be up early to head back into into the city the next morning. She debated grabbing a hotel and staying there, but really she slept much better in her own bed and it was only an hour away. She was also thinking about when and what to tell the Valencia family. This one murder was exploding into a case with two killers who seemed to have a targeted list of people related to the Department of Revenue to kill. The scariest question was how many people were on the list? As much as she wanted to tell the family the news right now, she was fairly certain that none of them were at risk and her energies could be better spent in moving the case forward tonight. She also had an edge of anxiety about her knowing that the real and sanctioned detectives could close her off from the case. She hoped in her meetings that day and with the solid finding of these two additional victims that it would be enough to keep her involved. She would still investigate regardless of law enforcement's inclusiveness, but it would be so much easier and she could bring real value to them if they included her in the investigation.

She looked at the clock and it was getting close to the time that the detectives might be going home. She would take a chance that she could get the two of them on a conference call and tell them both the news at once. She had the added benefit of the caller ID saying this was the coroner's office which might make them more likely to answer the phone call.

She dialed Detective Chang first, "Detective Chang this is Jill Quint. I'm at the coroner's office speaking to John Garcia and we have a new lead in the Manuel Valencia case. If you'll hold for a minute, I'll try and conference in Detective Banks," Jill requested, and she soon had both detectives on the line to explain the latest finding and the request that they come to the medical examiner's office.

Jill looked over her shoulder at John who was still speaking with the Placer Coroner. She motioned that she was stepping outside to make a phone call and entered a hallway to call Nathan.

"Hey babe, when are you going to be home for dinner?" Nathan asked as soon as he saw who was calling.

"I'm not going to get home for dinner. The case here has taken a strange new twist. It looks like we have discovered two additional cases that may be connected to Manuel Valencia and now we're bringing in law enforcement personnel to discuss the case."

"Are they going to let you stay in the conversation?" Nathan asked, aware of the police excluding Jill as a private consultant from their conversations and investigations. From case to case, it was her biggest fear and greatest insecurity.

"So far I'm in because I've likely discovered two additional murder victims that escaped their attention so keep your fingers crossed. I'm glad I left Trixie with you today. I knew it would be a long day, I just didn't guess how long. I have to be back here by eight tomorrow morning, but I am guessing that I'll be back in my home office by noon. I'll keep you posted."

"Okay, I'll see you when I see you and meanwhile Trixie is enjoying my cooking so all is well. Love you babe."

"Love you back and thanks."

Jill ended the call and returned to the suite that contained John's office. She walked in and asked, "How did your conversation with the coroner go? Did you know him or her prior to today?"

"The call went about as expected - denial, anger, and then acceptance that there might be more to the picture than expected. I didn't know this coroner, but she indicated at the end that she would notify the Placer Sheriff of our meeting in an hour. We have a conference room in this suite that we can occupy to discuss the case. Have you said anything to Mrs. Valencia?"

"No I debated giving her a call, but I have a face to face meeting with her at 8:00a.m. and I thought it would be better to tell her then. It's a huge finding in the case, but let's see if everyone else thinks it is a big lead."

"I guess I have to agree with you there. Since we have another hour before the two detectives arrive, do you want to work on that presentation on recent advances in CPR?"

"Sure," Jill agreed and by the time the detectives arrived, they had completed most of the presentation.

Detectives Banks and Chang were joined by Deputy Williamson from the Placer County Sheriff's department. Despite the fact that the Coroner had been upset with a probable change in a death certificate, she still had the foresight to call her Sheriff to make sure they were in on the investigation to solve these murders. After introductions were made and Jill's credentials discussed, they got down to business. John and Jill took different turns presenting the evidence gathered in the case.

"We believe these three cases are likely connected," Jill described the unusual facts of the case. "We are afraid of how long the murder list is for these two killers as they may have killed three members of the Department of Revenue." She continued with an explanation of the autopsy findings and the story of the emergency medical service personnel. After a long conversation with the detectives, there was general agreement that there was substantial evidence that the three cases were connected. Further-more, their attention quickly moved to the protection of other Department of Revenue employees. Jill could see the snowball starting to roll downhill gathering snow as it went. Each revolu-tion of conversation of the group gathered more leads and actions needed by the group. Jill would keep the family informed about the investigation. Deputy Williamson was going to explore exhuming the second victim's body. Despite Jill wanting to hold on that for the husband's sake, the others wanted solid evidence of a connection between the murders. The Deputy asked Jill if she would serve as an expert civilian consultant to his own coroner once he got the body exhumed and she agreed.

Detective Banks had requested his superior join him at the Coroner's office to discuss the issue of protecting staff. Knowing his boss, the detective thought he would be on-board quicker, believe in the threat, and work tirelessly tonight to develop a plan to protect the employees. Detective Chang's Lieutenant had been informed and was waiting for an update on the direction the three separate law enforcement agencies planned to take. Deputy Williamson left to go speak with the spouse of victim two to see if he could get his voluntary agreement to exhume his wife's body.

It had been a busy and fulfilling day. Jill thought they were making good progress in first identifying and second collecting more evidence to find and convict the two fake emergency services personnel. Jill wanted to stay involved in the case and so she decided to lay her cards on the table while they were waiting for the head of the Capitol Protection Command to arrive.

"Gentlemen you have a choice going forward whether to include me or not with this investigation. Not to be a braggart but I have uncovered several critical pieces of information related to this case. I hope that you will continue to include me in your major conversations."

There was an uncomfortable silence as they all looked at each other.

Jill added, "I am a former officer of the State and I am quite capable of keeping my mouth shut. I don't need any publicity from this case; you can take all the credit for solving this crime. I do need to do well for my client, Anna Valencia, and I can do that by contributing to solving her husband's murder and," Jill said with all the emphasis she could put into her voice, "I can best do that by being included in your conversations."

Again there was silence, and then Detective Banks stated, "You have put together a case I couldn't, so I am going to recommend to my Lieutenant that you be included in our conversations."

"I would also suggest that we need to keep this problem with fake ambulance staff out of the press," Jill urged. "Imagine the public's panic if the public loses faith in emergency services."

Everyone nodded and silence again returned to the room which was broken a few minutes later with the Lieutenant's arrival. Introductions were made and he was brought up to speed. Lieutenant Moss quickly grasped the threat to the Department of Revenue's employees. He was so satisfied with the connection between the employees that he scheduled an emergency meeting that night with personnel and Mr. Steward to develop a plan to protect the employees. In the back of Jill's mind was fear that Anna Valencia and her family members were on the target kill list. In the end she knew she could not sleep on the information and texted Anna to see if she was available to meet in under half an hour. She agreed and Jill started wrapping up her belongings after collecting contact information from everyone in the room.

The meeting broke up at that point and John Garcia was the lucky guy who got to go home, Jill moving on to the Valencia house, Lieutenant Moss and Detective Banks returning to the Capitol to develop a protection plan, and Detective Chang returning to Police headquarters to formulate a plan to find this ambulance and its killers. Everyone was thinking about the panic and hysteria that could come from the general public not being able to trust their emergency services personnel. Would non-targeted people die after refusing the aid of legitimate para-medics? It would be a scary situation until these killers were caught.

Jill made the quick drive to the Valencia house, parking in the driveway. Her push of the doorbell was quickly opened by Michael Valencia who invited Jill into their living room. Anna was offering tea and cookies which Jill enjoyed having missed dinner that evening.

"I had some major breakthroughs in this case today that I wanted to discuss with you now rather than our scheduled time as it is not clear to me if the three of you are at risk," Jill declared.

"What! Why would we be at risk?" asked Michael. "What is going on with this investigation?"

Jill took a moment to recount her day including the off-hand mention of two other employee deaths in Manuel's division that started the ball rolling and what the various law enforcement agencies were planning for that night.

Jill concluded with, "These two killers have a list of people that they are targeting. So far as we know, all of the victims have worked in Manuel's department. The problem is that we may not know about other deaths out there. These two fake emergency medical technicians know medical information about each victim which is an angle I'll explore, but they are good at getting people to submit to their care before electrocuting them with defibrillator paddles. Employees that work in Sacramento may live in any of the surrounding counties, and therefore would be autopsied by different coroners. It was just a chance question that alerted me to the two additional deaths which were before Manuel's. John Garcia of the Sacramento Coroner's Office is taking the lead to notify the other counties and we'll see if anyone else was a potential victim of the killers. Since I'm not in the head of the killers, I don't know if they were planning to move on to family members. I'm inclined to think not as these murders are focused on the Audit Division of the Department of Revenue. However, I wanted to alert you of that distant risk tonight. We can talk at length tomorrow about all the details going on with this case and next steps. My only advice is if you have a medical emergency tonight, drive whichever family member to the hospital, and don't call an ambulance."

Anna was holding a hand of each of her children, tearing with a combination of fear and anger for these killers, fear that she couldn't lose either child after losing her husband, supreme anger of the terrible damage these two killers had inflicted on her family and others. As bad as her situation was, the tears began running down her cheeks thinking of the child that never got to see her mother alive after swim practice, or the husband facing his own health problems losing his wife while he was receiving his dialysis treatment. She would make plans to contact these other families; Manuel would have wanted her to do that as he cared for his employees while alive. Michael saw Jill to the door and as she was driving away, the Valencia family was making plans to protect themselves from an unknown pair of killers.

Jill arrived home late, hungry, and itching to do some research before heading to bed. Normally she liked to be in bed and asleep at this time, but she was so wired with the discoveries of the day. She had been taking notes all day to look up this or that, but really she knew she needed a plan going forward as she could waste time chasing those things top of mind rather than having a planned approach. She knew it was also time to send her team a detailed email and with a good plan she could parcel out the work among her friends. She thought she would need the most hours from Marie as there were going to be a fair amount of internet searching for the killers.

She sat down and started to do her plan, then changed her mind thinking that it would benefit from input from her team. She worked on crafting an email to them with the facts they knew so far and where she thought they might search and asked for both input and volunteers to do the work. Sometimes they could all do some of the internet searches and it was a matter of parceling out the work. Other times searching required knowledge of some rare databases that Jo or Marie knew about, and sometimes in was simply not a convenient time in their lives to give her hours of investigative work.

She also wanted to see if Jo's boyfriend, Jack, could do anything with the video surveillance that she had on her flash drive, and if he could not, then maybe her friend Henrik, might be interested in running it through his facial recognition software which was generally more powerful than anything available in the United States. Henrik Klein, who they had met on a previous case when they solved his wife's murder, was a brilliant software and security guru based in Germany. Living in a country with an excellent reputation for engineering had allowed him to design more sophisticated software than might be available in a law enforcement agency. As he was always looking for new clients and the United States was a large target audience and he was grateful for Jill's help on his wife's case, he was usually eager to help.

Wrapping up her email, as she munched on a leftover piece of pizza washed down with a bottle of Sierra Nevada Ale, she leaned back contemplating the next day. She had her meeting with the Valencias in the morning, and really no other reason to be in Sacramento. She planned to check in with Detectives Banks and Chang to see what new developments they had as she didn't trust their commitment to including her in the conversation loop for this case. She'd take her laptop and put together the plan that she had delayed doing tonight. Hopefully her team would have provided her with feedback and she could sit in a coffee house with Wi-Fi getting some work done. If there was no reason for her to remain in town she'd leave right after lunch. After changing into her night clothes, she fell asleep minutes after her head hit the pillow.

CHAPTER 7

*T*he next morning, Jill took off for her 8a.m. meeting with the Valencias. She was looking forward to eating whatever Anna was cooking for breakfast that morning. She loved breakfast, and she especially loved breakfast cooked by an expert chef. While Nathan fit in that category he was not a morning person and she couldn't remember if he had ever cooked her a gourmet breakfast. He had on occasion made a wonderful omelet for dinner, but she couldn't remember him cooking pancakes, waffles, or crepes for her. After ringing the doorbell, she was again sitting in Anna's kitchen with great aromas all around her. All three Valencias were attired in what she would call business casual and clearly they were all morning people.

Jill looked over at Michael reading the *Sacramento Bee*, hoping that the story of the three deaths had not been reported on yet. She asked him, "Michael, did you spot any stories on our ambulance killers?"

"No I didn't and I hope I don't. Our family has no desire to comment to any journalist. I also worry about what it would do to the community here if people became afraid of all emergency personnel. Heck, if I worked in dad's old department and I knew the circumstances of the three deaths, I would hop on a plane to the East Coast until the police found the killers."

Christina added, "If the story ends up in the newspaper, I'm afraid the mortality rate will increase in the city as people become afraid to use ambulances. I looked up the data after you left last night and there are a hundred and fifty calls a day for medical emergencies. It will cause chaos if people can no longer trust the ambulances that arrive to take care of them."

"I would expect that the police have thought of that," Jill acknowledged. "The risk appears to be for the employees from Manuel's division. They need to take precautions, and should have been informed this morning or even last night to take those precautions, but they would also be a logical source of a leak to the media in this instance."

"I would hope that the leadership of the Capitol including the Governor is aware of these deaths and if that is the case you have to think that all of those brilliant minds will have thought of a way to keep people quiet," Anna predicted. "I would tell the employees that by speaking to the media they are painting a bull's-eye on themselves making it that much easier for the killer to find them. Surely that would incentivize people to stay quiet, but then again, there is a fool in every group."

"For many reasons, the police need to solve this case quickly," Jill observed. "My question for you is how far do you want me to go in this investigation? I could wrap it up today assuming the multiple law-enforcement agencies are doing a better or equal job to what I can do."

Anna tried to contain a snort, but it slipped out as she said, "Are you crazy? I want you on the case until the two men are arrested and charged with Manuel's death. First, you discovered that Manuel's death was a homicide. I am convinced if you hadn't performed the autopsy, we would have buried him assuming his heart gave out. If that wasn't an amazing first act, then your second act was discovering two additional connected deaths. I think you made those discoveries with about four hours on the job. I would keep you under contract just to see what your encore will look like. So, hell, no, I don't want you to wrap up the case today!"

Jill was a little embarrassed with the fulsome praise she had received from Anna.

Then Anna added a final statement as if there were any doubts about her support of Jill, "You are the only person who thought to say something to our family, were worried about our safety, and for that I want to see you through to the end of this case. Any questions?"

Jill just smiled, touched, knowing that even though the woman was grieving deeply for her husband, she had the energy to worry about her adult children and herself, and to make Jill feel like she walked on water in the investigative world.

"No ma'am! Okay then let me tell you my overall plan for the next few days. I may be called to do the autopsy on victim three in Placer County. The Sheriff indicated he wanted me to perform an independent autopsy if he could get the husband to agree to an exhumation. I'll be off the clock for you at that time." Anna just nodded, agreeing with the seemingly wise decision by the Placer Sheriff. "I mention in my contract that I have a group of associates that provide part time services for my cases and so they'll be doing internet searches for me. I also have a friend in Germany that runs a high tech security and software company. He has the best facial recognition software in the world. One of my team members has a boyfriend who is a graphic artist and he'll work on the video of the attendants on their way to your husband's office. Once he has the best picture possible, my friend in Germany will run it through his system for identification. "

All three Valencias were looking at her totally engrossed in what she was saying. Christina broke the intense atmosphere with the comment, "I think I'll quit my day job and join your firm Jill. This sounds like intriguing work."

"I love the work. I have also collected friends along the way that have an odd collection of skills to aid in my investigations. I have the opportunity to bring justice and truth to families like yours without belonging to a bureaucracy. I can't remember if I mentioned, but my day job is the ownership and operation of Quixotic Winery. The lab on my property helps me in analysis for cases and in formulating organic pest control, and scientific measurement of sugar and other quantities in my Moscato wine."

"Ok that's it," exclaimed Christina. "I'm running off and joining your circus, Jill!"

Jill appreciated Christina lightening the mood in the room as they were all smiling at her fanciful description.

"Ah Christina, I have done my fair share of boring and eye-blinding searches of the internet so I'm afraid the circus is all in your fanciful imagination. I've been chased by an Albanian sniper in a helicopter, but those five minutes of terror are placed against seventy-two hours of mind-numbing work looking for a needle in a hay stack. My advice is to keep your day job."

Anna had looked worried about her daughter's change of occupation, but then she relaxed with Jill's advice and Jill moved the conversation on, "These killers are obviously angry with the Department of Revenue and I have to think they communicated with it prior to these murders. So I need you to think back to things Manuel said about different clients and let me know if anything sticks out. I'll be searching chat rooms and websites to see if I can find a connection to someone or some group. I'm also going to work on insurance companies. The killers knew about existing medical conditions in their targets and used it to their advantage. This requires a special skill which will help limit our pool of suspects. I hope to hear updates from the detectives and if I don't, I'll have to make a nuisance of myself to get information. I also want names of people that they have letters from that are malicious. I assume that Detective Chang is going to work on getting any video footage from the two restaurants if only to confirm there are just two men involved in this killing spree. I also have a list of notes from my meetings yesterday that I want to turn into an investigational plan pending input from my team members today. On the expense side, I'm going to want to bring at least one of my team members here from Wisconsin. I'd bring them all but I'm not sure that I need their skills yet.

"Michael, one of my team members is a CPA; we often find in these cases that it is good to follow the money trail," Jill asked thinking she might save her clients some money. "If I need some financial analysis, is that an area of expertise for you and do you know where to look on the internet to find financial information on folks?"

After a smirk at his sister Michael said, "See Christina, you may be the doctor in the family, but I get to have more fun than you by joining Jill's circus."

"Children, children, stop fighting now," Anna said with perhaps her first big genuine smile in days.

Michael with a smile of his own, perhaps pleased to find his mother smiling, looked at Jill and said, "Yes I can help. I'm also a CPA, in addition to being a tax attorney. I need to know both tax code and accounting to understand and advise corporations. While most of my advice is related to how to account for revenues and expenses, I have provided an analysis of Board of Directors member's financial assets to assure a Board that there are no conflicts of interest. Sometimes you have to get pretty deep in personal assets to make that ruling and do some sleuthing to assure yourself that a candidate revealed all assets. While I have rarely performed that analysis, I'm up to the task here."

"Good to know," Jill noted."I don't have any names to look at yet, I just wanted to know your skill set should I need it. How much longer are you going to be in California? If I need your help, can you do it remotely for me from New York? Do you have the time in your day to do so?"

"I'm scheduled to return at the end of this weekend. I can

extend that but," looking at his mother and sister, "I think all three of us were planning to return to work on Monday. When I return to New York, I'll have a backlog of work, but I believe that everyone will understand if I parcel some it out so that I can give you any analysis you need, Jill. Finding Dad's killer is more important than work."

Anna reached over to put her hand on Michael's arm in silent thanks, and he responded to the gesture by placing his other hand over his mother's in silent support. Jill had worked with some pretty wonderful clients over the years, and this family was top of the list, a nice cleansing feeling after the bad taste left in her mouth from some of her previous clients that ended up being involved in their family member's murder.

"Thanks Michael, I have nothing for you to do at the moment; I was just checking your willingness and abilities. I think that is all I have for the moment. Do you have any questions?"

They shook their heads 'no' and she began to gather up her notes, "Let's hold on meeting tomorrow morning - if I am deep into internet searching, I can do more good staying at home and working. Let me see how this day goes, yesterday's discoveries had me changing directions multiple times during the day."

"Jill, if you don't mind, we could come to you," Anna suggested, and then laughed as she saw the panicked look on Jill's face. "I won't expect you to lift a finger in your empty kitchen, we could schedule for mid-morning, away from meal times. The kids and I could then go visit the Giant Sequoia Grove at Yosemite; it's our favorite family place where I will always feel Manuel's presence."

With that last sentence, Jill knew she couldn't say 'no'. "That will work. I'll let you know tonight if I am back in Sacramento tomorrow or working from home."

A few minutes later Jill was out on the driveway skimming her email to help her decide next steps. As none of the law enforcement agencies had invited her to meetings so far, she decided to head to a Wi-Fi location and finish reading all her email related to the case. It was there she found an email from Lieutenant Moss's assistant asking Jill to contact his office. After checking in with his office, Jill found herself on her way to a building she had never visited before – the California Highway Patrol headquarters on the west side of Sacramento. Lieutenant Moss had taken over a conference room which became the command post charged with protecting the Department of Revenue employees.

Jill was pleasantly surprised to see what looked to her to be cooperation between various agencies. After introductions were performed, she noted that Detective Chang's supervisor was in the room as well as Deputy Williamson.

Jill sat down and said, "Gentlemen, what can I do for you?"

"We have been meeting and making plans this morning when it occurred to us that we would really benefit by talking to you," Lieutenant Moss explained."There is a strong medical component to these deaths and we have no expertise in that area. Are you still under contract with Mrs. Valencia?"

"Yes, I am. I suggested she might cancel my services this morning as I think there are several capable law enforcement agencies on the hunt for the killer. She disagreed with my suggestion and so I am actively on the hunt for the killer."

"Contractually, we would like to work out an arrangement with you to pay you for your time related to the deaths other than Mr. Valencia. Are you willing and able to do that?"

"Yes, I am. If I'm able to work with your agencies, it will accelerate our finding the killers. You have access to records that I don't and I have access to technology that your agency doesn't so I think it's a win-win for me to work with your group. If you have a contract available right now I can read it and sign it as long as I have no problem with the language in the contract. This does present an accounting problem for me in that I don't know how I will be able to separate the work done for this agency versus the work done for Mrs. Valencia. In addition I will need to share some of the work in this room with her as I owe her that."

"I understand your dilemma Dr. Quint and I respect you laying out your concerns at the start," Lieutenant Moss imparted. "Why don't we pay you for any work you do in this room or for this command post and any private meetings with Mrs. Valencia are handled by her contract. I understand she is an attorney and I would like her word that she will not discuss whatever information you choose to share with her beyond herself."

"Thank you, Lieutenant Moss, for understanding my position," Jill said thinking that she would enjoy working with the Lieutenant. "Two addendums to your request; Mrs. Valencia's adult children are staying with her at the moment and she has shared everything with the two of them. One of the children is an attorney and the other is a physician and I believe we can trust them to keep matters private; secondly I had discussed using her son, Michael, who in addition to being a tax attorney is also a CPA, if I required any financial analysis. Unless you have that resource immediately available to this group, I would recommend we use Michael in that manner. I'm sure he would readily agree to sign the contract as all the family wants is justice for Mr. Valencia.

"Also if you look into my background, you know that I've successfully worked with other law enforcement agencies. What you may not know is I have a team of experts from out-of-state that normally help me on a case like this. As each of their skill sets comes up perhaps we can discuss at that point whether you have an internal expert or whether you want to pay my experts to get the work done."

"That sounds like the plan and we will cross each bridge as we come to it."

Jill took a minute to read over the contract and sign it. She also took a moment to email Anna Valencia about the new arrangement. She received a quick reply that Anna was on-board although she joked that Jill had gone to long lengths to avoid having her in her kitchen the next day. Jill smiled with the thought that Anna Valencia was such a kind woman.

Lieutenant Moss, with the contractual relationships dealt with, moved on to discussion of where they were with the case, "Dr. Quint, we were able to gather most of the employees last night for an emergency briefing on this case. We have bused the employees to a casino in Reno until we catch this killer."

Jill queried, "Just the employees? I had the Valencias increase their security as I didn't know if the killer had a list of targets strictly composed of employees or if they intended to move beyond the employees to family members, and please call me Jill."

"We did not think that the family members were targets, but to be on the safe side we offered to move children and spouses with the employees. Some of them took us up on the offer and so we have the entire family in Reno, others had no immediate family in the region and thus were not worried and a third group had spouses that couldn't afford to take time off work and so they've stayed behind in this region."

"You said, 'most of the employees'. Were you unable to make contact with some of the employees?" Jill asked, a little puzzled, a little concerned.

"We have three employees that are not in Reno with the larger group. Two of the employees are on vacation and they have agreed to stay a few extra days and check with us before returning to Sacramento. One employee, we have been unable to contact and we are concerned. He returned from vacation two nights ago and failed to show up for work yesterday and we've been unable to reach him on all known numbers."

"Did you search his home?" Jill probed.

"I have officers on their way there now," said the lieutenant with the sound of his voice conveying hope that they would find the gentleman alive.

"What about Mr. Steward? Do you think he could be a target?"

"We're not sure. He decided to visit family in Southern California for the time being."

"So what leads are you following at the moment?" Jill asked, ready to move on to the actual investigation.

"We spent a good part of the last twelve hours securing the safety of the employees," and Jill heard the exhaustion in Lieutenant Moss's voice. "We have a running list on the right side of the whiteboard of what we need to follow-up on. We were adding to that list when you arrived."

"Can we back up a moment and discuss suspects?" Jill requested. "I think if we have motives and suspects that it will drive certain tasks."

"Okay," replied Lieutenant Moss in a tone that said he was already regretting inviting Jill to the table. "We think the killers are people who are unhappy with the service provided by the Audit Division. So I think we can narrow it down to someone who pays California taxes."

"Individuals, or corporations?" Jill asked.

"Individuals as these two guys don't seem to be acting on behalf of a corporation, although it's always possible. It also must be someone who was audited as they are the only clients handled by the Audit Division. If you are unhappy about anything regarding your taxes and contact the Department, your complaint will go to our Taxpayers' Rights Division."

"So then knowing these limits, the suspect pool is at least one-thousand people after you remove females from that pool?" Jill calculated."How many letters has the audit division received in the last two years? This feels like a very methodical killing, well-planned and well-rehearsed, and the ambulance and defibrillator took time to buy and modify. Do you have a list of taxpayers who communicated by letter, phone, or email with the audit division over the last two years?"

"We don't, but we have an intern in the department as we speak creating a spreadsheet of those communications," replied the Lieutenant. "The problem for that intern is the phone calls. We record all calls and save the tapes for a year only. It means listening to countless hours of tape to get taxpayer names and then having to find a taxpayer's contact information which is more difficult if we don't have a social security number on the tape and are looking at a common name like John Smith or Jose Garcia. Compiling this list will take some time."

"I can imagine that the process you describe is laborious. I would focus on the first two victims' correspondence," Jill mused. "Since Manuel Valencia was the head of the unit that suggests to me these killers communicated with others in the audit division, and then when they were not satisfied with the answer, they raised the appeal to Mr. Valencia. It would be worth asking his assistant Amanda if he handled complaints personally or if they only reached his desk upon appeal."

The lieutenant nodded his agreement with Jill's arithmetic.

"Let's go to a different angle. These two killers had personal medical information about each victim, information not readily available, information sitting in insurance repositories, and information that takes technical skill to hack in and steal. What company insured the three victims?"

"What do you mean the killers had personal medical information?" asked a person whose name Jill could not remember; however, she seemed to recall during introductions that this person represented personnel for the Department of Revenue.

"What we know from witnesses from two of the murder sites is that the killers knew of their victim's heart conditions and used that information to gain compliance and submission by their victims. Not only did they have to gain access to personal medical information, they needed to understand the relevance of those medical conditions. In the third case, they must've known about the victim's strawberry allergy, perhaps used aerosolized strawberry extract to cause an allergic reaction, and then they were conveniently having a meal nearby which allowed them again to gain compliance from the third victim. So I think we need to look to either the insurance company or the physician's office as being a source of stolen medical information. As nearly all of this information is computerized, my guess is that the killers hacked into their insurance records and used that to their advantage. This skill set narrows the pool of killers. I suppose they could have outsourced hacking to some Russian or North Korean computer hacker but I think we should look at suspects with significant computer code experience."

"I'll go back and check our files to see which insurance company each employee selected," said Jill's unnamed personnel expert. "If they all had different insurance companies, then maybe we need to look at physicians. If I look at this from the killer's point of view, how would I find out which insurance company or physician I had to hack into to find this information? Where else might these employees have listed medical conditions? It is not required for our employer-sponsored health or life insurance. Did they have medical-alert bracelets?"

"Those are some really good questions because you're correct that you would have been looking for a needle in a haystack to figure out the physician information for each victim," Jill observed. "Let me step outside to call Anna Valencia and find out if Mr. Valencia had a medical-alert bracelet."

Moments later Jill found herself in the corridor, placing a call to Anna.

"Hello, Jill, what do you need?" asked Anna. "Did you want to reschedule my visit to your kitchen?"

"Gosh no," Jill laughed. "A question came up about how the killers got personal medical information on each of their victims. I wondered if you could tell me where Manuel noted that he had a pacemaker. Did he wear a medical-alert bracelet?"

"He had one, but he had not worn it for years," Anna disclosed. "Let me give some thought into where else Manuel listed his pacemaker. I don't believe his gym had that information, but I'll check. He did some 5K races occasionally, but I think the only information he had to acknowledge was there was a risk of death with running. I'll talk it over with the kids and send a text to you if we think of anything."

"Thanks, Anna. By the way I mentioned that we might need to use Michael's services to this group, but I don't know if it will come to that as they should have their own financial resources certainly within the Department of Revenue."

"I'll let him know, thanks, Jill," and they ended their call.

Jill returned to the conference room and indicated that Manuel Valencia had a medical-alert bracelet although he had not worn it for years.

"We could check those companies, but the problem is there is more than one medical-alert company and we would have to search them all. We'll check in with the other two victims' families to see if they had medical-alert bracelets."

"Dr. Quint, word has come through my office that the husband of the third victim has agreed to exhumation. Are you available to perform the autopsy tomorrow?" asked the representative from the Placer County Sheriff's Department.

"Yes, just give me an hour's notice of when you'll have the remains delivered to your coroner's office and I can be there. I usually carry an autopsy case in the trunk of my car."

She saw several people in the room shift as though they had chills running up their spine and felt the need to explain, "Folks, I don't drive around looking at car accidents to see if there is someone I can autopsy. As a consultant, I never know when I am going to get called for an autopsy and it is always with a short turnaround time, so I just need to be prepared. I also reduce mistakes by forgetting to do something during the autopsy; my kit keeps me organized. I also check the case in at the airport if I have to fly somewhere to consult. "

"Okay," responded Lieutenant Moss. "Let's return to motive and suspects. Can we do anything with the video surveillance from the Capitol and has anyone obtained any additional video from the two restaurant locations?"

Two other people spoke up in succession, representing police agencies whose names Jill had lost track of, "There wasn't video of the suspects inside the restaurant, but the exterior of the restaurant captured them on film," and "ditto for my restaurant only we captured the two of them exiting the driveway/parking lot in a Ford pick-up with fake plates."

Jill waited a moment to see if anyone else was going to comment then added, "I have an expert in video imaging and a second expert that manufactures software connected to worldwide databases in facial recognition. If you'll give me the best copy you can create, I'll send it off to my experts."

Lieutenant Moss looked at Jill suspiciously and finally asked, "Are these legal sources?"

"Yes to the video guy and I think yes to the facial recognition guy as the FBI, I believe, purchased access to his system, but I can't say for sure as I don't know the law in areas of privacy. It's a company based in Stuttgart, Germany."

Lieutenant Moss stared at her a moment longer before finally closing with, "You're full of surprises, Dr. Quint."

"I think this about wraps our conversation for now as everyone has work to do to find these killers. I would propose we meet again tomorrow at 8am."

Jill passed out her card to the people that were new to her in the room. She really wanted the video feed to see if Jack and Henrik could do anything with helping to solve who these killers were. It sounded like if they had to chase them down through complaint letters that it would take some time to sift through them all.

Just as she was about to exit the room, Lieutenant Moss saw that he had an incoming call from Detective Banks and he looked over at Jill and said, "would you mind holding on a minute, Dr. Quint?" and without waiting for her reply he said into his phone "This is Moss. What do you have, Banks?"

As Jill listened to Moss's side of the conversation, she deduced that Banks was saying they had entered the employee's residence and found him or her deceased. Moss soon ended the call, having written something on a piece of paper.

"Dr. Quint, would you like to join me at the Rossi residence? You can follow me in your car. We would appreciate your assessment of the crime scene."

"Sure I can follow you," Jill agreed and then added since he had taken on a grim edge, "I'm sorry about the loss of your employees."

"I've never lost an employee to violence of any sort, let alone related to an accounting job, four people with families, who served the state well. We need to find these killers. I think I have the other employees protected; however what if the killers move outside of the Department of Revenue, or start going after family members like Mrs. Valencia? The possibilities are endless. Where are you parked?"

Jill described the lot she had parked in as the facility was large —a total of 224 acres with many parking lots available to employees and visitors. The lieutenant would meet her at her car and then they would proceed to the crime scene. Fifteen minutes later, Jill was parking behind Lieutenant Moss's car in front of a suburban home, a typical ranch style likely built in the 1950s, and with other vehicles parked on the driveway and street. Jill saw the Sacramento Medical Examiner and a crime scene van. Jill grabbed her autopsy kit from the trunk, not because she expected to do anything inside the home, but rather because she didn't know if she would need a mask or other protective gear in the home. If that was the case, she liked using her own. She rolled the kit behind her toward the house.

"Before you ask, I am not planning to be the coroner at this scene, rather if asked questions, or if I am in need of protective gear, it's all in the kit."

"Dr. Quint, you misinterpreted my look. I was admiring whatever decision drove you to keeping it in your trunk on a permanent basis. From what I understand of the scene, we don't need any special protective gear."

"Thank you Lieutenant, that is good to know."

While putting on routine protective gear to prevent their own DNA from contaminating the scene, they spoke with Detective Banks.

"I know nothing about the victim inside," Jill noted. "What can you tell me about the employee - male or female, age, name, cause of death?"

"It's a male employee, in his forties, and at first glance I don't know what the cause of death is. There is no blood anywhere."

Jill followed the detective into a bedroom where they found the victim lying on top of his bed, crime scene attendants as well as the coroner in attendance. Jill glanced at the body and guessed the man had been deceased for at least three days.

The coroner looked up at her and she saw that it was John Garcia behind the mask.

"Hello, John, what have you determined the cause of death to be?"

"Hi, Jill, I've only been here five minutes ahead of you and I don't have one yet, and before you ask there are no burn rings on this gentleman, no pacemaker, and the medicine cabinet contains no medications to treat any heart condition. You want to come take a look?"

The man was fully clothed with his shirt pulled up. There were no signs of violence anywhere on the body. Jill put on her magnifying lenses and asked John if he had noted any injection sites.

"I hadn't thought that far yet. You can help me do a preliminary search here and I'll do a more extensive search when we get the body back to the morgue."

In silence they both slowly examined what skin was exposed on the front side of the body. The victim was olive-skinned and the darker pigment could make it harder to see some bruising. They finished finding nothing.

"Let's turn him over briefly and then we'll get him on the gurney for transport to the morgue," John said and they did just that and the cause of death was still not obvious when they got a look at his backside.

"Nothing remarkable there either," noted John again. "We'll have to wait to determine the cause of death until we complete the full autopsy. There are no clues that I have found in this house so far to even determine if this was death by natural causes or by homicide."

Lieutenant Moss came into the bedroom and said "Crime scene technicians have found a tiny webcam on, inside the living room. They're going to take that into custody and see if anything unusual is on it."

"That's good because in our preliminary on-the-scene examination, we do not have a cause of death for the victim," replied the coroner. "Jill, if you're interested in observing this autopsy, plan on arriving at my office in an hour as it's going to move to the head of the line of pending cases."

Jill was unsure of where she should go next. She had not had time to put together her plan for investigating this case as she had been overwhelmed by new information this morning. She also wanted to be available to send any video to Jack and then on to Henrik for facial recognition. On the other hand, this looked like an intriguing autopsy as it was rare that the coroner couldn't make a guess as to the cause of death at a crime scene. She thought a little bit more about her priorities and skills and decided she would best serve her client by assisting the coroner in determining the cause of death. He had not asked for her assistance rather he had offered her the opportunity to be an observer, but she could still contribute towards the resolution of the case. Besides she was downright curious about what the actual cause of death was as it was so rare that you couldn't guess at the scene. Had police randomly found the victim, she was sure that they would have thought natural causes as there were no marks on the body or any disturbance of the house. Weird.

"Okay I'll meet you there and thanks for the invite to observe," Jill added the last words for emphasis as she wanted him to know that she did indeed consider herself a guest.

Jill checked in with the Lieutenant and gained no new information about the crime scene. There was nothing more for her to do at this victim's house and so she said goodbye to him with the promise that she would be at his meeting tomorrow morning. The coroner's office was about twenty minutes away which gave her forty minutes to sit with her thoughts on next steps. She really needed to work out of her home office and so once she was done observing the autopsy she would head for home, stop by Nathan's and pick Trixie up, and let him know of her plans for this evening and the next morning. She had the eight o'clock meeting with the Highway Patrol task force and then an autopsy for Placer County in the early afternoon. She would make plans to dine at Nathan's house tomorrow but she saw herself driving into Sacramento to attend the task force for at least the next week.

It was too hot to sit in her car or even outside and get some work done, so in the end she drove to the coroner's office, checked in with the receptionist on the time of the autopsy, settled into the comfortable chairs in the air-conditioned lobby, and composed a brief note to Anna Valencia, and a longer note to her teammates with her impressions about the case and her thoughts of how she might use them long distance. At this point, she didn't see a need for them to leave Wisconsin and travel to California simply to do internet searches. With ten minutes left, she decided she would do her first search about people who hate the Department of Revenue. She visited two chat rooms and found loads of hatred for the department. She was glad to take a break from the hateful dialogue and have the receptionist call John Garcia to let him know she was there to observe the autopsy.

Minutes later she wore protective clothing over her street

clothes and observed as John and an attendant removed the clothing from the victim. The attendant left the room with the victim's belongings so they could be bagged and tagged as potential evidence or examined by the crime scene staff.

The coroner began his search of the victim's skin and once they turned him over he found a spot between the shoulder blades that looked like the mark of a Taser gun. They hadn't seen that at the victim's residence as the clothing had been in the way.

"It looks to me like it is a stun mark not a kill mark as I don't see any burn there," John noted. "I'll have to see what the organs look like inside, but at least we have our first physical evidence that this may not be a natural death, although we still don't know what actually killed him."

Finished examining the skin, John asked for Jill's assistance in turning the body back over and proceeded with his examination of the internal organs beginning with a Y incision in the chest. Jill listened to John dictate, "The heart was filled with dark red liquid blood. White froth was revealed in the lumens of the trachea and both bronchi."

"So those are the signs of someone who has died from asphyxia and it must be a gas or chemical agent as there are no signs of mechanical suffocation. He has no broken blood vessels or bruises to indicate any kind of struggle. Even if you were stunned with a Taser, I think you would still fight a little, but we have nothing here. Mind if I take dual samples of the blood, heart and lungs? I have my own toxicology lab at my home and I may be able to process some specimens faster than you."

"Wow, Jill, you have your own lab? What a dream job! Do you need an assistant? Wait, I forgot, I'm not ready to retire and I love my job here. Yes of course you can take duplicate samples. Give me your specimen tubes from your kit and I will fill both sets of tubes at the same time."

"John, since we may be dealing with a gas, I would love to get an air sample from inside the lungs. I would think any gas has by now dissipated, but you never know if you don't look. When do you think he died?"

"Based on what the crime scene folks collected, he was alive as recently as forty-eight hours ago, but given his temperature and the condition of his body I think the time of death was thirty-two to thirty-six hours ago as putrefaction is just about to start with this body. Is that the conclusion you came to as well?"

"Yes I agree with you and it would be so much harder to determine what killed our victim here if it was a day later that they found him. I'm anxious to see what testing yields as the causative agent. It's pretty diabolical. The mistake the killers made was the Taser injury. That's enough to make any coroner take a second look at their autopsy findings."

"Okay, Jill, here are the samples you requested. Do you want to stay for the remainder of the autopsy or were you planning to run off to your home lab and satisfy your curiosity as to what killed our victim?"

"John, you know me so well because yes I do want to run the samples home. Given the victim's blue fingernail beds, I'd really like to know what the agent was that killed him. I know it's not carbon dioxide or cyanide or chlorine. It might be a gas that I've never come across like helium or argon. If I get any results today, how should I reach you? I know my findings can't be used by you as I don't operate a state approved lab, but they will give you the evidence to put pressure on your own lab to get results back if you're interested in that."

"Absolutely, I'd like to know. Once I finish with this autopsy and its paperwork I'll be back in my office, which I have to leave on time this evening as my wife and I are entertaining company. I'll be looking for an email from you with the results whether I am here or at home."

"Sounds good. Thanks for inviting me to observe and I hope I have some amazing news for you soon."

Jill left the autopsy suite, disposing of her protective outerwear, and rolled her autopsy kit out to her car where she prepared to leave Sacramento for home. A quick glance at the emails that had arrived while she was in the coroner's autopsy room verified that she had no urgent reason to stay in the city rather than heading home. Fifty minutes later, she arrived at Nathan's house and studio to pick up Trixie and chat with Nathan for a few moments. Since she was itching to start processing specimens in her lab, she was thrilled that Nathan had an appointment with a client a few minutes after she arrived to pick up her dog.

Jill was pleased to turn in the gate to her home, always a welcome sight of peacefulness and serenity. Trixie was excited but held in place by her harness in the seat. Jill knew the moment she parked the car and let Trixie out of her harness, she would take off at full speed for a large oak tree that always harbored squirrels.

She changed into casual clothes, grabbed a diet Coke, retrieved the autopsy kit from the car trunk and rolled it into her lab. Despite the hundred degree day, her autopsy kit contained a battery-operated refrigerator so that her specimens did not further decompose while in transport to her lab. Two hours later, she had her answer as to what killed Mr. Rossi, victim number four.

CHAPTER 8

*N*itrogen gas.

She had completed a cursory search on nitrogen gas deaths which seemed to fall in three categories: diving accidents, suicides, and accidents in an area using liquid nitrogen. It was the suggested gas for the Death Chamber as people fall asleep before death takes them and there is not a feeling of suffocation as diatomic nitrogen molecules replaced diatomic oxygen molecules binding to hemoglobin in the blood system. All things considered about death, it was a reasonable way to die.

The air sample from the victim's lungs was heavier on nitrogen than one would expect. Blood samples also displayed a lack of oxygen. She dropped an email to John Garcia asking him to pass the information on to law enforcement as a preliminary cause of death. Nitrogen gas was easy to obtain as it was used in diving, in laboratories in the liquid form for refrigeration, and also in the manufacture of some beers in lieu of carbon dioxide. Thus obtaining a gas cylinder would be relatively easy.

Jill tried to visualize the scenario. The victim opens the door to the killers, and he invites them in and gets the shock to the back; or they push their way in, and shock his back. They then carry him to his bedroom, lay him down on his bed, put a mask of nitrogen gas over his face watch him drift off to sleep then die. They might have worn oxygen masks themselves to avoid inhaling the nitrogen and also falling asleep. Once decomposition set in, it would have been harder to detect high levels of nitrogen. Another twelve to twenty hours before he was discovered and natural decomposition might have provided the perfect cover for murder.

She finished her testing and moved on to putting together some overall thoughts about the case. She pulled up the emails from her team members as they always provided ideas on how to research the case and developed an outline of how to find this killer. Each clue they had about the murderers became a path to follow on how to track them.

What she really needed was the video surveillance matched to the facial recognition software as the easiest and fastest way to identify these killers. She had the video feed provided by Detective Chang but that was a small piece of all the feeds available. She dropped an email to Lieutenant Moss reminding him that she would like to view the video feed his office had already collected. Then she called George Fellows at the city maintenance yard. She had momentarily forgotten that Detective Chang had suggested this person as the man who had the video footage of all street cameras in the city. She didn't know how she would be able to limit her need for a wide range of footage, the many streets in and around the Capitol, so maybe she could drive to the site of the computer managing the camera footage and follow the trail on the screen. Before she did that she sent the video feed she already had to Jack to see if he could do anything with the image - make it good enough that they could use it for facial recognition.

George had been alerted by Detective Chang that Jill might call. They set up an appointment for the next day for her to take a look at the footage of the street cams around the Capitol. She also planned to get the address of where the other two victims were killed to see if there were street cams close to those restaurants.

Jill did a summation email for Anna Valencia. Anna was fine communicating through email as she was happy to see that there appeared to be sufficient resources applied to this murder investigation and she felt confident that someone would soon figure out who the killers were.

Next Jill composed an email for Henrik. She described her situation here and the fact that one of the law enforcement agencies had facial recognition software. If that software failed to provide her with the answer, she was asking for his approval in advance to use his technology. She mentioned her conversation with Lieutenant Moss and the question as to whether it was legal in the United States. The last sentence might ruffle Henrik's feathers as he worked very hard to do everything the right way. He would get the last laugh when one of these law enforcement agencies purchased the software as it was so superior.

Afternoon was fading into evening and it occurred to Jill that she had not been out running for the past three days. She changed into her running clothes, braided her hair, and grabbed the dog's leash and the two of them set off on a run. Trixie was having the time of her life, bred to be a carriage dog, somewhat frustrated with Jill's slowness. Jill on the other hand liked to exercise in the morning and so a run was much harder on her mentally in the late afternoon. She had always found that running cleared her head and so she was able to think about the case and more specifically about the killers. She had to laugh to herself that no sports magazine would ever print a story that 'deciphering who was a murderer' was a motivation to run.

An hour later, she had finished her run and taken a shower to wash away the sweat. She had a frozen pizza that was her go-to meal when she was deep in a case and not interested in doing more than hitting the microwave buttons to prepare dinner. She would eat that a little later, but at the moment she wanted to study the online community chat rooms where people who hated the Department of Revenue conversed. She had been shocked earlier over the rage she had found with this group. She was convinced that the motive for these murders resided in the heart of someone who really hated the state tax organization. These two killers had murdered four people so far and if they ever discovered where the employees had been moved, they would all be in danger.

She managed one more glance at her email to see what information was being shared. She found that one of the agencies had sent the video from inside the restaurant. The video was not focused on where the victim sat; rather, the cameras were aimed at all entrances and all cash registers. The two men involved in each restaurant were the same as the two men recorded walking down the halls of the Capitol before killing Manuel Valencia. She sent the video off to Jack to see what he could do with the facial images of the two men.

Jill tried to guess at their age, height, and weight. It was clear that they were sharing the uniforms of a paramedic and emergency services technician as one of the killers was a paramedic on the first video but not on the second. There was no picture of the ambulance captured in any of this footage. She wondered if they had even used it for some of the murders. They certainly hadn't needed to.

There was also the issue of the medical condition knowledge. Where had these killers found private medical information on the victims? The killers had very specific information that allowed them to spin a story that was believable by each of the victims. Had some insurance company been hacked? Was it medical alert? Jill tried to think of who might have this information and then she sent off an email to Jo to see if she might have some suggestions.

She created her own murder board and instead of adding suspects she added traits of the suspects: intelligent, able to acquire personal health information from somewhere that likely required computer hacking skills, some medical knowledge, funding since they had purchased a defibrillator among other equipment, one Caucasian, one African-American, both 30 to 45 years of age, patient as they had been able to stalk their targets, and a desire to disrupt and destroy the Department of Revenue perhaps with the purpose of stopping state taxation. It really helped seeing all those traits up on the board. She would take a picture of it and share with the group tomorrow to see what any of them could add.

It was time to take a break and fix dinner. She dialed Nathan while the frozen pizza was heating.

"How's it going? Did you find your killers yet?"Nathan asked.

"You really are the most supportive partner a girl could have with that opening question. Alas, no I haven't found them yet. I was doing my murder board listing the traits/skills the killers need to possess and it is a strange combination of skills. Maybe instead of looking for all skills in one person, the two of them have synergistic skills with a combined mentality of hating the state tax folks."

"When I think of the array of killers you have chased since we've been together, personally, I have found all of them to have weird skills, and in fact each of us humans probably has an array of weird skills."

"That's true. You have skill at cooking and I don't. I guess we'd call the two of us in the kitchen synergistic - you cook, I eat. I'm heating up a frozen pizza at the moment and then I'm going to dive into some chat rooms or communities where people clearly have a hate for the taxing authority of the state. I looked into it briefly earlier in the day and it's a very toxic group of people so I'm fortifying myself with pepperoni pizza and wine before spending a couple hours seeing if I can sense any killers lurking anywhere in there."

"Sounds like a nasty group of people. What's your schedule for tomorrow?"

"I have the 8a.m. meeting at Highway Patrol headquarters with the task force and then I have an autopsy for Placer County sometime tomorrow. In between the two scheduled events, I'll be dropping in to the city of Sacramento maintenance headquarters to view what they might've caught on camera of the departing ambulance. I wish I had Jack here for that as he's so much faster at viewing what I think is boring film footage. Oh well. Most of my cases seem to be about looking for a needle in a haystack and there's always some boring component of doing that. What's your schedule like and how did your meeting go with the client today?"

"I don't have any meetings scheduled tomorrow so I'll mostly be catching up with work. Let me know by mid-afternoon whether or not you'll be coming over for dinner tomorrow night, okay? I'll likely run to the store for supplies. The client I met with today was very amusing and I hope our working relationship continues in that vein. He is new to the wine industry and understands how important the label is to attract attention and buyers of his wine. He is growing the Viognier grape over on the central coast. That's a tough grape for a novice winemaker. I don't know what his background is, but it isn't in viticulture. I advised him of a few people he could talk to and get help and advice on the grape. The conversation with him reminded me of a dry sponge soaking in water. He knows enough to worry about this grape, so he gave me a budget for the label and then he told me to just do it; there was no need for him to provide input as I knew more about the topic than he did. I wish all my clients put their total faith in my designs."

"He does sound like an interesting client. Are you afraid your label will end up on a bottle of wine that tastes awful?"

"Actually he is self-teaching himself everything there is to know about growing grapes. I imagine him out in his vineyard with the textbook in hand. Probably talks to the grapes, strokes the vines, and hand waters the entire crop trying to make up for the lack of knowledge. He's got the work ethic to make this vineyard work. The real question is whether he has the taste buds to understand what he's producing. I'm thinking about mentoring him and setting up some wine tastings to help him understand what he doesn't want to grow. He has no ego which makes him easy to get along with."

"Sounds like the perfect client. Hey, my buzzer just went off for my pizza. I'll chat with you later and hope to make our dinner date tomorrow. Love you," Jill said and they ended their call.

Nathan at times, through his conversation, could provide brain cleansing for lack of a better descriptor. She felt better after talking to him and if she could get him on the subject of wine which usually wasn't too difficult then her brain seemed to relax and focus on winemaking rather than murder. Maybe it was just talking to someone she loved that was so soothing to her soul and yet had the ability to clear away the cobwebs in her head.

Taking the pizza out of the oven, Jill poured herself a glass of wine and took a slice of pizza and the wine over to her computer. She may as well eat while visiting the creepy chat room. Maybe the crazy people would drive away her appetite. A quick glance at her email showed three emails of interest to her. Jack had worked some magic with the video feed sending her two solid pictures of the suspects. She sat there staring at them trying to find their secrets in a flat picture. She also studied them looking for facial modifications like glasses, false teeth, or theatrical putty or cosmetics that would change their appearance. She couldn't tell from the picture if they had done anything to disguise their features. In the end she dropped an email to Detective Chang and Lieutenant Moss suggesting they run it through their facial recognition software. She was curious if they would find anything by the meeting the next morning.

She moved on to an email from Marie who was letting her know she could take time off and visit California to help on the case beginning tomorrow if she needed help. Jill looked at the time and decided it was not too late to call Marie.

"Hey Marie, it's Jill. How's it going there?"

"Can you hear that noise in the background?"

Jill listened for a moment and then replied, "Is that thunder I hear?"

"Yes one of those beautiful and violent summer storms. I appreciate that Mother Nature has given me the show during my waking hours instead of the middle of the night. What's up?"

"I was just reading your email and thought I'd talk the case through with you. Do you have a moment?"

"Yeah go ahead but you may have to repeat some things so I can hear over the noise of a thunderclap."

"So I've been keeping you guys apprised of this case. Since it is strictly one division within the Department of Revenue, I really think the killers were audited at some point by this division. I've spent some time in some chat rooms devoted to hating this taxing authority, and to say the group is unhappy is like you saying that thunder isn't making any sound. Are you able to spend some time doing your usual search of social media to see who is lurking out there? I have pictures of the guys and I think they're between the ages of thirty-five to forty-five so they are of the social media generation."

"Yeah I can do that. So you don't want me to come to California? It's a good time for me to take time off of work."

"I don't have to have you here to do the work for me, but it would be nice to have you here to bounce ideas off of and I always learn something from you as you go about your searches. I have to drive into Sacramento daily as I got myself on a police task force related to these murders. I don't know how long they will continue to let me be in the room since I'm a civilian but hopefully it will last until we find these killers. But what I'm trying to say is you would be alone at my house for several hours each day. Is that a problem for you?"

"Let me see… You're asking me if I have a problem staying in a Californian vineyard with unlimited wine at my fingertips and a dog that I can take for a run. Furthermore, with Nathan around, I get some wonderfully cooked meals. Hmmm, let me think about that. Okay I'm done. I'll make flight arrangements probably out of Milwaukee to save the client money and then I'll let you know my flight plans."

"Awesome, sounds like a plan, I can't wait to see you tomorrow! Have a great evening enjoying the thunder; you know you won't find any of that here."

After ending the call Jill thought about Marie's plane ticket. On the one hand she didn't really need Marie here in-person to do the work, but Jill knew she always benefited from having at least one of her team members nearby. She would see how the case went and make the decision later whether to charge the client for Marie's travel. If not charged to the account, she would pick it up herself.

She dropped a quick note to Nathan that there would be two guests for dinner tomorrow.

The final email was from Peter Kelling, of personnel. At least now going forward she would remember his name. His email said 'I checked the insurance for all four employees and we're dealing with two different companies. The state has several contracts and employees choose one of three health insurance companies. I've asked the two companies involved to check their records for signs of illegal access for the four employees. I won't get an answer back soon on this. The two different insurance companies have closed networks so there are at least two different physicians involved with these four employees, but I don't have that information in our records.'

Maybe she would bounce this question off of David Gomez, a teacher she had met during a previous case when she' solved the murder of his partner. David had superior hacking skills and perhaps if she talked it over with him she might understand how someone would go about getting the personal medical information that the killers have.

Done with the emails, it was time to return to the awful 'I hate the state tax authorities' chat rooms. If she really thought about it, she needed to look at conversations from two to three months ago when the killers were still in the planning stages or perhaps were meeting for the first time. After an hour of searching for something related to these murders, or for people to talk about how they wanted to see one department dead, she was coming up empty-handed. There seemed to be a lot of talking, and fantasy of what they would do, but fortunately little action. She gave it up and went to bed hoping that the pictures would work for facial recognition.

CHAPTER 9

*I*t was early the next morning and Jill was putting on trousers, a short sleeve shirt, and a sweater to complete the ensemble. She was wearing clogs knowing that she would have to do an autopsy sometime that day and clogs protected her feet and were comfortable to stand in for a few hours. She had breakfast at home before leaving as the state would not be filling her tummy upon arrival like Anna Valencia had done the past two mornings. She had a big travel mug of coffee and was ready to go. She fed Trixie and left her plenty of water and the dog would have access to her house and her yard in her absence. She had checked her email when she first awoke and there was an email from Marie with her flight times. She would be arriving at the Sacramento airport at three. Jill hoped she would get the autopsy completed before Marie's scheduled arrival so she could pick her up and return to her house. Maybe they both could get a run in before changing and going over to Nathan's.

Right on time, Jill entered the conference room where, much to her surprise, there was a light breakfast and a huge container of coffee. She refilled her coffee mug and offered a "good morning" to everyone around her and then the meeting started.

"Dr. Quint, I heard from the coroner that you identified the agent that killed our fourth victim as nitrogen gas," began Lieutenant Moss. "Would you give everyone in the room an idea of how the gas was used to kill the employee?"

"The purchase of nitrogen gas by a civilian is relatively easy as it is used for both scuba diving and the production of beer," Jill explained. "When one hundred percent nitrogen is inhaled, it displaces oxygen from reaching all of the body's organs. A victim feels dizzy, then falls asleep, and dies within ten to fifteen minutes. It's cheap and a painless way to be killed. We believe the victim was disabled by stun gun and then it would've been easy to place a nitrogen gas mask over the victim. If it had taken us an additional day to discover the victim, we likely would not have this information as nitrogen is a component of decomposition and elevated levels would not be as concerning."

"Thank you Dr. Quint. Does anyone have any questions? No? Then moving on, Dr. Quint sent us a nice photograph last evening to run through our facial identity system. The FBI recently updated their system and searches now take approximately ten minutes to run. Unfortunately, it only has about fifty-five million photographs and the US population is about three hundred and twenty million, or about one in six people will be in the database. Sadly, our two killers came back negative. Detective Chang, do you use a different system or did you get the same result as I did?"

"Yes Lieutenant. I got the same result – no matches," replied the detective.

"Dr. Quint, you mentioned you have another source for facial recognition software. Are you in a position to use that software?"

"I gave my contact a warning that I might be asking him for help. Would you like me to run those two photos through his system?"

"Yes, I would," was the terse response from the Lieutenant. Jill gave him a more in-depth look and decided he was likely short on sleep and stressed by the deaths of the employees it was his duty to protect.

"I'll just drop him an email right now," Jill replied. "It's a little past five in the evening in Stuttgart, so I don't know what kind of turnaround time I'll have on this request."

"Obviously let us know if your contact is able to identify these two men. Let's move on and discuss a few more updates. All of the employees have had a quiet day and night in Reno. We don't know who was on the killers' list of targets and having removed the immediate target we don't know if other divisions or leaders in the Department of Revenue are on the list. The department has descended into chaos without staff to answer phones regarding taxpayer questions. Those left behind worry about their own safety as the gossip has reached them about what happened to the Audit Division staff. The department has seen upwards of fifty percent sick call rates with calls from the union about what's going on. It's not my headache to handle more just a description of the fallout of trying to keep people safe."

Jill thought 'this is getting ugly; people are terrified because no one has a handle on what's going on and the hysteria is only going to spread; however like the Lieutenant, it wasn't her problem to solve'.

Just as they moved on to discussing a search of salvage yards for the ambulance, Jill got an email from Henrik. He had some amusing comments that she would respond to later, and he had a match but it wasn't the match to any traditional license, military, or law enforcement systems.

Jill looked up and said, "Lieutenant Moss, my contact in Germany located our two suspects on Facebook. Like you and Detective Chang, my contact is able to match the picture to traditional government systems including law enforcement, the prison system, the military, and driver's licenses among the major systems. His system then goes beyond to images on the internet. He did find a match on a Facebook page. I looked up that page and there hasn't been any activity for the past five months. It's a page devoted to a sovereign citizen group, whatever that is."

The lieutenant looked at another officer who had been taking notes for the task force and asked him to bring the picture on screen with the computer/projector set up in the room. It took a few minutes for the computer to warm up and find the internet. The officer typed in the sovereign citizen group and the Facebook page came up on the screen. Sure enough, there were the two suspects featured on a picture that had been posted to the page a year ago. The names given to the two men were nicknames clearly by the photo tag beneath the picture. Everyone in the room sat silently stunned looking at the pictures of the two men.

"We really need some fingerprints from these two gentlemen. I find it very difficult to believe that you could go through life without leaving an imprint on some government identification system. I think our next steps are to contact the FBI and find out what they know about this group; surely they have had interaction with them at some point. We should also work with Facebook to track down who opened this account and who the members are. We'll need a warrant to get that information out of the company. Finally we need to find that ambulance in hopes that there will be either fingerprints or DNA left behind. Does anyone have something to add? No? Then let's go start chasing leads down. Dr. Quint if you would stay behind a moment?"

The room quickly began emptying, people at once energized that the suspects had been identified as real people, yet dissatisfied because they still didn't know who they were, puzzling over the ability to be invisible to all government opportunities to be captured on film. How did one go through life without some form of identification?

Once the room emptied, Jill waited for the lieutenant to speak.

"I'm impressed with your German contact. If you don't mind, I'd like his contact information. If we can secure a contract with him, we will do so. If something in his software violates US privacy standards, I'll make sure I don't investigate that. The Facebook connection makes the killers real and provides us with some helpful information although I wish we had names for these two men. More impressive has been their ability to stay off the grid through an entire lifetime."

"Perhaps they didn't stay off the grid."

"If they have some form of identification, we sure can't find them. Nor can the mega-computer from Germany. That tells me that they somehow managed to avoid having the usual government identities."

"How about if these guys had the ability to change what was on the record for databases in which they were listed? For example, if I were them, I would keep my driver's license but substitute the picture listed in the Department of Motor Vehicles' computer. With the exception of law enforcement, who looks at a picture to see if it matches the picture in their database? Or if you wore a disguise anytime your picture had to be taken, how does the person taking your picture know that you're wearing a disguise?"

"Those are good points. I haven't heard of someone getting into the DMV system and changing data, but I'm not close to that issue. I also have not heard of anyone showing up in costume for their picture, but again, I suppose that could happen. "

"I believe my contact in Germany does security testing for firms so you might have him check your system to see if the State of California is protected when you contact him about his facial recognition software."

"How did you meet him again? I can't remember if you told me."

"I can't remember if I spoke with you or someone else either," said Jill with a smile. "I was on vacation in Belgium, and a woman at the table next to me had a severe nut allergy. I interceded and she made it to the hospital alive. Then the killer slipped into her room and finished her off. I worked with the Belgium Police Force to solve the case, and towards the end I came into contact with the victim's husband. He has been forever grateful that I found his wife's killer. Since that case, he has helped me on a few others. He has a highly protected server farm on his property that he lets European law enforcement train on. Helping me also works for his business as people have been so impressed with his products that he often gets paid business out of free service up front. So he is very much a legitimate businessman and just a very nice human being."

Jill left out a few details on that case; she felt her phone vibrate and saw the text from the Placer County Sheriff and quickly responded.

"Thanks, Dr. Quint, you are the first civilian who has been very helpful in my twenty plus years with the Highway Patrol and this is the most critical case of my career."

"I wish you would drop my title and just call me Jill. I think because I come at a case from a different angle that I am able to help. You're not the first law enforcement person to be surprised by my resourcefulness. Usually you would also have my team to be impressed with as well, but so far I haven't used them much. I do have a team member arriving today who is an expert at finding stuff on people from social media sites. Her day job is candidate evaluation as a human resources expert. She is much more thorough and successful at helping to identify people and their relationships than I am. She'll go to work on this Facebook clue as soon as she arrives."

"Sorry Dr. Quint, but I work in an area that requires you to never drop a title of someone, so you'll be Dr. Quint throughout this case. If your expert finds anything overnight, would you bring her with you to tomorrow's meeting? I find it very instructive to understand how people go about navigating clues."

"Will do. I need to head over to the Placer County Coroner's office. It appears from the text I just received that victim three's body has been exhumed and will be arriving shortly at the Coroner's office."

They parted ways and Jill began the drive to the city of Auburn where the coroner's office was located. It was a good twenty minute drive uphill towards the Sierra Mountains. She loved this drive along highway 80 as it represented some of the first views of the magnificent mountains that lay ahead. Unfortunately, she would be turning off the highway before some of the best views on earth. Maybe while Marie was here, they could take a little mini vacation to the Lake Tahoe region or Yosemite; she would have to see how the case unfolded and what their workload was.

Jill checked her watch and noted that she had about three hours before she was due at the Sacramento airport to pick up Marie. That should be plenty of time to do a thorough job on this autopsy. After she picked up Marie, they would head home to begin some serious work on this case. She also dropped a note to Anna Valencia to see if she was available for a phone update while she was driving to Auburn.

CHAPTER 10

*E*ntering the Placer County Justice Center, she was met by Deputy Williamson, and taken back to a conference room. He shared a simple contract for her services and it was signed by both parties. He then escorted her to the autopsy area where victim number three was waiting along with the coroner within the first examination room.

Jill held out her hand and said, "Hello, I'm Dr. Jill Quint and I'm pleased to meet you."

"Hello Dr. Quint, I am Trudy Wilson, the Coroner for Placer County. I understand this case might be connected to others in the area, and you believe that this should be changed to a homicide from the natural causes ruling on the mode of death."

Great, Jill thought, this person wasn't happy to see her.

"Actually, I believe John Garcia the coroner for Sacramento contacted you regarding similar physical findings and circumstances around the provision of CPR. The similarities, I understood, caused both you and Deputy Williamson to have suspicion that this might be related to the Sacramento case. Suspicion to such a degree that the family was contacted for exhumation which is never an easy conversation. I'm here as an independent consultant to conduct an autopsy. While I am aware of the physical findings, those marks on the victim's chest are not enough evidence to conclude that the victim suffered from electrocution, only a full autopsy will do that. Shall we proceed? I assume you'll be observing?"

"Yes I'll be observing," was the curt response from Trudy.

"Let's get started then," replied Jill and pointing to the case she added, "this is my autopsy case which has all the supplies I'll need to do an autopsy as I sometimes end up performing one at a mortuary which doesn't have the requisite equipment. I'd rather use your equipment, but I'll use my own face shield and gloves. If you point me to the dressing room, I'll change into scrubs and then put the other protective gear on."

A few minutes later they were ready to go. In silence, the two women stripped the victim of the clothes she had been buried in. Jill could see the signs of the previous autopsy. It was always creepy to her at the point while doing an exhumation where she had the body naked, but the face retained the makeup from the mortician. It felt like she was examining a big doll as the face did not seem real to her, but rather exaggerated under all that makeup and frozen in mid-expression. Sometimes it felt like the faces were grimacing, like the deceased was having pain over a second examination. If Jill had been by herself she would have slapped her own face - an attempt to knock out her crazy feelings about the deceased, but with witnesses in the room, she could only try to move on.

"After the autopsy on victim number two, John Garcia and I agreed that it would be good to put together an educational PowerPoint for coroners on the latest technology in both field-based and hospital-based resuscitation.

"I'm sure John will notify you as soon as it gets certified for CEUs. In addition to the red marks on the chest, the first victim had signs of burns in the lungs. Again the technology in place in the last decade no longer causes that kind of damage. So what would have been the side effects of resuscitation a decade ago are now signs of homicide. That and other non-autopsy evidence connects this victim to two other victims all with the Audit Division of the Department of Revenue. The same paramedics were involved; there was no 9-1-1 call and no communication with a local hospital. What are the chances of an ambulance traveling across two counties to handle emergencies? We think the killer purchased an old defibrillator and modified the joules on it to cause electrocution. It fooled nearly everyone.

"The first two victims were killed and buried with little fanfare," Jill continued."But then the killers got bolder with their third victim, and they performed their fake resuscitation in the Capitol Building. The daughter of the third victim is a physician and she interviewed her father's assistant and was unhappy with what she heard and that is when I became involved. He was a healthy, fit man who had a pacemaker for thirty years. He told them he didn't need their services and yet the killers talked him into it and soon he lost his life.

"Your victim had successfully eaten in the same restaurant for three years while her husband was getting dialysis across the street. She had a severe strawberry allergy and I believe that was the diagnosis you arrived at as the cause of death. She had an allergic reaction that sent her into cardiac arrest for which she needed the paramedic services. But the treatment they provided was not according to policy. First you contact a hospital, then likely you inject the victim with epinephrine. You use the paddles for patients in ventricular tachycardia and someone suffering an allergic reaction may have a rapid heartbeat, but it's not likely V-tach and using paddles on someone is on the paramedic protocol for this city for treating allergic reactions in the field."

Jill was hoping the explanations she was providing would help the coroner understand why the victim had been exhumed. There were all kinds of red flags about the circumstances of her death. However the room was still silent and she guessed she hadn't convinced the woman at all. Oh well, she had dealt with many a coroner or medical examiner that resented her presence and Trudy appeared to be another one of those.

They continued on with the autopsy and Jill ended up dictating nearly the same findings as those for Manuel Valencia. This body had the remnants of an allergic reaction to also account for, but in the end she ruled it a homicide based on the findings related to an electrocution. The Placer County Sheriff was now in an awkward position as he had findings from two different autopsies. He needed his coroner to agree and be willing to change the death certificate.

Deputy Williamson waited for Trudy to say something and when she didn't, he asked, "Trudy, do you agree with this finding and do you have enough information to change your death certificate?"

There was a pause, and then Trudy uttered a single word, "Yes." Then she went to a phone in the room and called the mortuary that would handle the reburial to come get the victim. After she hung up she brought up something in the computer and made a few keystrokes.

Then she turned around and indicated to the Deputy, "I've changed the death certificate. If you have no further questions, I'll go change and move on to other work. Dr. Quint, it was a learning experience," and then she exited the room.

Jill hoped she would never have a case again in this woman's jurisdiction. In the end they had gotten what they needed, but the atmosphere was chillier than the morgue's cooler.

Jill looked over at the deputy and asked, "I guess you need to go speak with the husband. Do you have everything you need here?"

Deputy Williamson let out a sigh and then said, "Yes I do. I really appreciate how easy it was to work with you. Thanks and the department will process your payment for services. If I can provide a reference for you for another law enforcement agency, don't hesitate to ask."

"See you in the morning at the task force," Jill said as she headed off to change her clothes. She hoped that Trudy had already cleared out of the room and when she opened the door she was in luck as the room was empty. She quickly changed and headed out of the room and then out of the building.

Checking her watch, she noted she had a good hour to get to the airport. Since it was so hot outside, she decided she would just park at the airport and wait inside for Marie's plane to land. It was coming from her connection in Minneapolis and looked to be a few minutes ahead of schedule. The airport had free Wi-Fi and so she just planted herself inside the terminal and checked her emails, then she went back to the Facebook page that contained the two killers. She made a thirty dollar bet with herself that Marie would have more information on the guys within two hours once she had concentrated time on the computer. If she lost the bet, the money went to charity and Marie would stay home in the morning, but hopefully she would find something and Jill would get to show off Marie's talents.

Marie was nearly upon her before she looked up, noticed her, and stood up to exchange a hug.

"Hey girlfriend! Welcome to California. It's close to one-hundred degrees of dry heat outside. Do you have checked baggage?"

"No checked baggage. I'm free to go immediately enjoy the oven outside!"

Jill repacked her tote and together they exited the airport walking to Jill's car.

"I had forgotten what this kind of heat feels like. Wow! Are we in an Easy Bake Oven?"

Jill laughed at the comparison. "Look at the bright side my grapes love this kind of weather and they're making lots of sugar at the moment."

"You sound like a farmer," Marie noted.

"Yeah well I guess I am one," agreed Jill with pride in her voice. "I worry about pests, study the growing season to decide when to harvest, celebrate sun and heat for their effect on the grapes, and hire help to pick the crop. That about sums up my life as a farmer."

"So what happened with your case while I was in the air?"

"Henrik helped and I completed an autopsy and if you can find any new information on our suspects, you're invited to a meeting tomorrow."

Marie laughed at the crib notes Jill had laid out and asked, "What meeting?"

"So in this case we have two suspects on video that committed the Capitol Building murder and they're seen on video entering two different restaurants which were the sites of the other two murders. Henrik came through again as his software worked to identify the two suspects. However, he, like law enforcement, could find no identification of the two other than their picture on Facebook. So as my social media queen, I have high hopes you will find more information on the two guys. If you do, a lieutenant in the Highway Patrol has issued you an invite to his task force on these two killers."

"Wow! You've issued quite the challenge," said Marie as though she was relishing the competition. "I don't think I've ever examined anyone with only a Facebook presence. Maybe they hacked into the state systems and replaced their pictures."

"Great minds think alike as that is what I told the lieutenant when we came across this information this morning. I get that as an adult you could try to avoid having your identity out there anywhere but to avoid it from the teenage years onward seems unlikely unless you had your picture changed in various systems."

"We're heading back to your house right now, right?"

"Yes, we will be there in about forty-five minutes," said Jill after looking at the clock and judging the remainder of the drive.

"I think I'd like to take Trixie for a run or at least a walk in this heat. Is that okay for the dog or will the asphalt burn her paws?"

"I'm fortunate with Trixie as some Dalmatians are sensitive to the sun, but she has spots in all the right areas so her nose, eyes and ears are protected. Typically when she and I go for a run, I have her off leash, I run on the pavement and she runs in the dirt of the fields as she can occasionally catch the scent of some animal by doing that. So as long as she stays on the dirt, I'm not worried about the pads of her paws."

"Great. Is Nathan cooking dinner for us tonight?" asked Marie, knowing about Nathan's cooking skill and Jill's lack thereof.

"Yes he's cooking for us. So we'll get home, go for a run, shower, and get a couple hours of computer work in before we drive over to his house. Is that time enough for you to perform a miracle?"

"I'm looking forward to the challenge. I've never had a candidate without a background before. I'm interested to see if I can find some information amongst some of my usual sources. I think you mentioned he belongs to some weird group. I'll probably take a deep dive into that group and see what I come up with."

"Sounds like a plan."

They continued their drive towards Jill's vineyard, enclosed in the cool air conditioning of the smooth riding car, catching up on each other's lives and mutual friends, and then spending some time deciding whether to visit the Lake Tahoe region and all of its beautiful places to hike in the summertime, or visit Yosemite for its world renowned views. In the end, they knew they'd need to play each day by ear; and so decided to stock the car with casual hiking gear, and bottled water so that they could, with no advance planning, drive to one of these scenic mountains. It was a shock after the drive to feel the heat at Jill's house as they unloaded Jill's briefcase and Marie's suitcase.

Marie said, "I feel an attack of sloth bear coming on. Would you be ready to go for that run in ten minutes before my attack of laziness completely overwhelms me?"

Jill laughed, "I need sixty seconds to change, and Trixie is always ready to go, so I'll spend the additional nine minutes checking my email."

As planned, they were both ready to go in ten minutes. Jill asked Marie if she had ever exercised in such heat before and she couldn't remember that she had. After stretching a little, they set off on a jog with Jill telling Marie to go ahead of her as she ran at a pace that was two minutes faster per mile than Jill's. Jill had found over the years that it didn't work to have Marie slow down as she usually ended up running faster than she was comfortable, and then had to walk portions of a run. The dog was confused, unsure of who to keep pace with and decided in the end to keep pace with Marie, but run back every few minutes or so to make sure that Jill was coming. Even the dog seemed to be saying to her, 'run faster'.

An hour later they had completed the run, showered, and were re-hydrating with a sports drink. Jill tended to stick to water, but in the high heat it paid to drink something with some sodium and potassium to replace what was lost through sweat. Sitting in Jill's living room, each with a laptop on their lap, Jill was showing Marie the picture that Henrik had found as their only lead to the identity of the two men and then Marie was off and running, bouncing around websites in search of clues about the two killers. With Marie doing her own thing, Jill stared at her murder board for a while thinking about the order of the murders.

Did the killers have a list they were following? Were the first two murders practice, before they boldly took on the Capitol and its police force? She hadn't seen a report yet on the complaints that were handled by the Audit Division. Nor had she figured out how they got medical information about each victim. Had they targeted people in the division with medical conditions? If the killer had wanted to kill Jill, she had no medical conditions, she had no allergies, and she had no vulnerabilities that these killers could entice her cooperation with a fictional story. Then she thought about the fourth victim and she could not recall him having any medical conditions. His autopsy had not shown any underlying disease and their Taser and nitrogen gas approach had worked on an otherwise healthy male. She also needed the division to explain how these four people were connected on the job. She decided to email Mr. Steward to see if he had any thoughts about how the four people fit together on the job other than working in the same division.

She also sent an email off to Lieutenant Moss. They had discussed citizen complaints before in his meeting, yet she hadn't seen any data presented and maybe he could light a fire on whoever had the data. Next she worked on like-crimes. There were enough people with a hatred of government that there had to be some prior attempts on lives of people who worked for a state or federal tax agency.

Jill was drawn into reading about some of the previous attempts to kill or injure employees of the IRS. In 2010 an irate citizen committed suicide by flying his small plane into an IRS building killing the Revenue office group manager and injuring many more in Austin, Texas. The IRS had a category called Potentially Dangerous Taxpayer (PDT) assigned to taxpayers that had demonstrated a capacity for violence against employees of the IRS, a list which had one-hundred-seventeen citizens on it in 2012. Jill wondered if she could deduce how many folks on the IRS list also hated the State of California. IRS offices in Los Angeles and Fresno were attacked in the 1990s. Another man was indicted in North Carolina for threatening an IRS employee in 2009, and the stories continued. She found far fewer state taxing authority threats which made sense as citizens paid far higher taxes to the federal government rather than the state.

She paused to look up at Marie who appeared to be lost in the chase for clues. Putting her head back down she decided she would go back and look at some of the anti-government groups. The groups seemed more focused again on the Federal Government rather than state government.

There were a few groups that also wanted state governments dissolved. Most of the groups seemed to be located outside of California in areas of the U.S. that were rural. They owned large plots of land in regions where the land was cheap and law enforcement minimally present. If you wanted to be isolated from government, then you needed to be self-sustaining and have land to stockpile food, arms, and people.

She tried to focus on the few groups that were known to be in California. Due to the proposition nature of California's election ballot system, the state seemed to have laws that sovereign citizen ideology would run afoul of - another reason for these citizens not to reside in California. The vast majority of groups that were known to cause problems seemed to fall into two categories - passive and active. The passive citizens simply didn't pay taxes and tried to avoid being caught. The active groups refused to pay taxes and actively went to court to sue Federal employees in an attempt to get a lien on their real or personal property in payment for failure to carry out their duties. The lawsuits filed were so absurd, that judges and other officials were flummoxed about what to do when faced with such a suit. Some officials had even had their credit damaged as a result of the false claims of the lien; you couldn't just ignore the filed paperwork. The Treasury Inspector General for Tax Administration was established under the IRS in 1998 and its Office of Investigation monitored sovereign citizen movement actions which are considered domestic terrorism. Guns are secondary in such organizations as their main focus is an anti-tax ideology.

These two killers were members of the sovereign citizen movement. Their behavior was aligned with the mentality of these groups, and true to their behavior, no guns were used in the deaths so far. Such organizations had sponsored a few attempts on public officials. Who was the group and where had the group's funding come from? No matter how big or small the political movement, they generally needed some source of funding to keep the communication and passion going.

She looked up as Marie sat up, stretched, and cracked her knuckles, a smile of satisfaction on her face. Jill looked over at her in silent inquiry.

CHAPTER 11

"*I* guess I am going to your meeting in the morning, I found additional information on our unknown persons."

"Yeah! Who are they?"

"I don't think this new information will help with naming these individuals, rather it provides more information on their behavior - what they think and where they hang out on-line. They use different names with different websites, but the picture is the same and the tone of the writing appears to be the same. I'll show you where I have been and what I am following. I haven't run down all the leads yet so perhaps I'll have even more by morning, but I am making progress."

Jill peered over Marie's shoulder as she discussed the journey she had been on chasing leads. She had started by following everyone on the original website. After individually following each person who had any activity on the site where the two men appeared, she had found additional appearances on additional sites. Still no identity and in fact the two men used different user-names on each site. As the suspects seemed very competent at hiding their identity, rather than looking for a real name, Marie was on the hunt through all these internet sites of where they might physically be; see if anyone ever mentioned where one or both men were at a particular time. She had no success yet, but Marie remained hopeful that the men would slip up at some point.

"I'll continue with this methodology and see what I come up with by the end of today," Marie asserted.

"I'm going to drop an email to the Lieutenant to let him know of your progress and your attendance at tomorrow's meeting. You might get another job offer from one of these agencies," Jill added cheekily.

"Yeah, right. I like the weather here, but I love my job, friends, and family back in Wisconsin, and I couldn't afford a house here."

"I know what you mean. Even though I've been in California for a while, I'm still amazed at the cost of housing here. Oh well, it will be amusing to watch them try and make you an offer. Do you need my help?"

"No, it will be faster for me to chase them down rather than take the time to explain my process to you and I'll admit that a part of this is intuitive."

"No problem, I'll go back to reviewing the sovereign citizen movement. We'll leave for Nathan's house in about an hour. As usual, he is making some sort of fabulous dinner and pairing it with a great wine."

"Jill, my friend, do you know how lucky you are to have Nathan? He is good-looking, fit, a great cook, and an all-around nice guy."

"I know I'm lucky. I pinch myself some days. He is also very forgiving when I pick up a new case and cancel dinner plans with him at the last moment, and he likes my dog. What more could a girl ask for in a guy?"

"Don't rub it in! I had better get back to my research as I would like to have all kinds of leads to show to your Lieutenant in the morning."

Jill nodded and the room fell silent as they were both engrossed in separate pursuits to find the killer. Sometime later, Jill called it quits and they left for Nathan's house. Marie had never been there, and so Nathan gave her a quick tour of his studio and home. Marie was fascinated by his 3D printer and had some suggestions for Nathan's experiments with beer glasses. She also met Arthur and was entertained by the behaviors of the cat and dog.

Nathan was such a good chef that he could cater the meal to each woman. Jill liked her food bland, while Marie liked it spicy. He had made scallops in a cream sauce, jasmine rice and, asparagus with butter and parmesan cheese. For dessert, he offered the ladies a choice of fresh berries in a liqueur or an ice cream bar. Jill had the berries, while Marie started with chocolate ice cream and added fresh fruit, whip cream, and a sprinkle of nuts.

"It's a good thing I am not around your cooking more often as I would weigh twenty pounds more. That was a great dinner. Thank you. I'll just go to bed now that I am so sated," Marie joked.

"Actually you would keep the weight off because there is always my cooking," Jill offered.

"What do you mean 'your' cooking'? Your definition of cooking is ordering and then heating a pepperoni pizza," Nathan scoffed.

"That may be true, but have you ever left my home hungry?" Jill asked.

"No, but I only get two meals from you - an omelet in the morning or a pizza if it is lunch or dinner."

"Children, children! Stop fighting over food!" Marie admonished with a grin.

They both had the grace to look chagrined as Marie continued, "Seriously, Nathan, I heard from Jill about your dojo. Can we walk over there and have you both demo your crazy kung fu moves?"

"Sure we could do that, but as a Master in hapkido, I feel obliged to provide a short lesson in terms and places of martial arts. Kung fu's meaning is any skill achieved through hard work and practice, not necessarily a martial art. So I might say that Marie is kung fu in social media investigations. My martial art - hapkido, is of Korean origin and Jill's T'ai Chi, is a Chinese martial art. As for a dojo, that is a Japanese term for a place where one practices the path of a martial art. In Korean, the term is dojang. Jill practices in a wu guan or the Chinese word for a gym where martial arts takes place."

"Nathan, thanks for the explanation of terms," replied Marie. "I can't wait to return to work and say that I am kung fu at social media. My co-workers will wonder what weird air I have sniffed in California."

"We are here to entertain," replied a smiling Jill. "I feel that I am too early in the practice of T'ai Chi to demonstrate anything for you, I'll leave Nathan to show you his spectacular moves; it's pretty cool. We missed seeing his bi-directional kick in Brussels, so I had him demonstrate it once we returned home. It's pretty cool and how many years of hard work did it take you to perfect that move?"

"I actually don't remember, but let's go over to my dojang and maybe I can convince you to become interested in a martial art," replied Nathan leading them over to another building on his property.

When they arrived at the building, Nathan explained his indoor and outdoor area. Inside the dojang, he had a punching bag and a couple of padded upright objects, that Marie suspected were used to imitate a man, but perhaps softer to kick or punch. He explained what was in the room and how he used it, then provided a narrative of what his workout looked like.

"I would offer to do the kick that Jill has asked for, but unless it is a life or death situation, I don't attempt a bi-directional kick until after at least thirty minutes of warm-up. I can show you a tape from the last competition I entered which was about five years ago. I am getting too old and too busy to stay in competition form anymore."

"Don't believe for a moment that Nathan is not in the best form, heck he took down the man in Belgium that tried to kidnap Jo, and he saved us from that killer in Colorado."

"When the adrenaline is coursing through my system because one of my friends is threatened, I can do all kinds of crazy moves," Nathan admitted modestly. "That's different from being at the very top of my game like I was for competitions. Besides my age bracket doesn't have many competitors. In recent years there have been zero or less than two entrants for my age. It's no fun getting a first or second ribbon just because you showed up."

"Okay let's watch the video," replied Marie.

Soon they were watching a competition between two men dressed in white track suits, using a variety of kicks, punches, and attempts at wrestling someone to the map. The two women grimaced whenever Nathan's opponent got in a hit to his body. At the end of the short tape, there was silence.

After a long moment Marie added, "That looked really painful. I bet you had bruises the next day. Did you lose any teeth?"

"No, fortunately I didn't. You take kicks to the head as much as to the face. I didn't have any concussions, but I saw others who did. That was another reason to leave the competition behind me - I wanted to save my brain."

"Good decision as I would think that it was only a matter of time before you did take the wrong kick to the head," Jill agreed.

After returning to Nathan's living room to gather their belongings, and a quick kiss exchanged between Jill and Nathan, they were soon on their way back to Jill's house. The plan was to get in another hour or two of research before proceeding to bed. Jill expected Marie to head first to her bed as she was on a time zone two hours ahead of California, but maybe Marie adapted quickly.

Jill was exact in her prediction when two hours later they both headed for bed. They had less than eight hours to sleep before waking up, getting dressed, and making the one hour drive into Sacramento's Highway Patrol office.

Marie was a little uneasy with a room filled with California law enforcement individuals. Unlike Jill, who had been with the group from the beginning, Marie had no sense of the interactions between agencies or the people in the room. Still, she knew she was likely the only person in the room with new information. Lieutenant Moss asked her to introduce herself with a few words about her background.

"Hi, I am Marie Simon, a resident of the great state of Wisconsin. Over the past five years I've worked as a part-time consultant on a variety of cases for Dr. Quint. My day job is that of a talent evaluator for a multinational corporation. I spend a fair amount of time every day on social media evaluating candidate behavior to determine fit with our company," Marie said describing her role and noticing frowns in the room. "While some of you may believe that candidates have a right to their privacy, what I find is there for the world to see, and the last thing we want to do is hire someone whose values are not consistent with our own. As you have all probably found out in your own hiring process, someone can have the right skills on paper, but the wrong interpersonal skills to be successful with colleagues or with the job. Thanks to our talent evaluations we have turnover that is seventy-five percent lower than any other firm in a comparable industry in the state. Those are real results that can save both yourselves and candidates from a bad experience.

"Moving on to the matter at hand which is the identity of the two suspect's pictures Jill forwarded to me, let me show you what I found," Marie said as she manipulated the internet on a big screen for all to watch.

Fifteen minutes later, everyone in the room had more of a feel about the murder suspects. They still didn't have names, but they thought they knew how they thought, who their friends were, and where they hung out. That would give them fresh material to focus the search on locating them. Marie had a few more leads to follow which she intended to do once the presentation was over. She would sit in the back of the room using the guest access to the building's Wi-Fi and research a few more leads. After that, her work was pretty much done as there were no additional suspects to investigate. Of course, she could take some of the names of some of the organizations that were on Jill's list of sovereign citizen groups and see what she turned up there. Marie tuned back in to the conversation and then decided that the meeting would go on for at least another hour so she would see what she could do with a sovereign group.

Jill meanwhile was speaking to the group about her results from the autopsy at Placer County yesterday. Mr. Valencia's death was definitely connected by evidence to the death of the third employee. The technique used on employee number four was different, but given his place of employment they had solid reasons to keep them connected to the case under discussion.

The conversation turned to letters of complaint that were sent to the department. Working with the Department of Revenue's staff paired with law enforcement, they had narrowed the suspect list down to about two-hundred citizens. As Jill had been doing a lot of research into the sovereign citizen movement and their behavior, she wasn't sure that they would necessarily write a letter of protest. Nationwide, they seemed to either try to ignore the taxing authority or on rare occasion to try to kill them. About a quarter of them made contact with the taxing office and for that reason she thought the list of suspects was likely far larger than the two-hundred developed by the Department of Revenue.

The Highway Patrol had located the ambulance used in the first three murders in an auto auction yard. They had been able to enlarge the video feed of the incident at the Capitol to find the vehicle identification number and were thus able to match it at the auction yard. They dusted for fingerprints, but the ambulance had been sanitized and no fingerprints were found. A few hairs had been collected, but all the crime scene staff could do was hold on to it for a match at a later date.

A piece of good news is that there appeared to be no more suspicious deaths overnight nor any threatening activity in the hotel where the Department of Revenue's audit division employees were stashed. Jill hated to be a wet blanket, but she suggested that Sacramento County and the surrounding ten counties be alerted to the fact that any state workers that had died in the past month or before the two suspects were captured be referred to this task force to verify the mode of death. After a little discussion the group agreed and Lieutenant Moss put it on his to-do list.

After a few additional reports, the meeting ended. While Marie had found more information on the two suspects, she didn't as yet have names for them. She had perhaps another two hours of work and then she thought she would've exhausted all avenues of investigation. Jill likewise was focused on the sovereign citizen movement and thought she likely had a few more clues to research.

The two women walked out to the parking lot with Jill looking at her watch. "We are perhaps an hour away from Yosemite National Park. We don't have time to see the entire Park or even in its major highlights. We essentially have two choices; we can hike the Nevada and Vernal Falls. It's a straight uphill climb and then a straight downhill walk that is hard on your knees and takes about six hours to complete. It's a spectacular climb next to the falls with a wonderful view at the top. If you're not in the mood for a hard hike, we can take the second option to drive and view the highlights of the Park which would include the giant sequoias, the view from glacier point, and a visit to the Valley floor to see more waterfalls and wild flowers."

"You know me; I love the chance for exercise wherever I go.

Let's take the first option of a hard climb to the top. Perhaps we'll have some wise thoughts surface from our brains in the quiet solitude of nature," Marie suggested.

"Yosemite is a very popular National Park and we will cross the paths of other visitors along the way. In the beginning, about the first half mile, there will be such a throng of people that you would think you were at a mall, and by the time we reach the first waterfall and begin the ascent to the second waterfall, it will feel like a national park again."

"Sounds like we're in for a hard hike! Is Nathan planning on cooking for us tonight?" Marie asked with a grin. "I'm sure we will work up an appetite."

"Actually I'll ask if he wants to join us on the hike. Like me, Yosemite is his favorite Park. That way he'll have also worked up an appetite for a big meal. It will be the best of both worlds if he can join us."

On the way to the park, she called Nathan, and learned that he had a couple of appointments with clients today and would be unable to join them. He did invite them over to his house for dinner, planning on a high carbohydrate meal for them to refuel after their busy day.

Within the hour, Jill was paying the entrance fee at the park gates. Just inside they found a restroom to change from their business casual clothes into hiking clothes. Jill had brought two small backpacks for them to carry water and some snacks that she threw together in case they had the opportunity to hike that day. It would be a hot day and she was sure they would need plenty of water. Fortunately they could refill their bottles at the top waterfall where the water came from snow melt which somehow Jill thought was cleaner water. They made a decision not to discuss the case until at least the second half of the hike. It would be poor etiquette to discuss the details of several murders while hiking with families in a renowned National Park. Jill knew that she could give it two hours and then they would have freedom to discuss the case out loud.

They mostly walked in silence as Jill being the shorter legged of the two women had to walk a little faster than her comfort range to keep up with the taller Marie who was impressed with the number of people on the trail and the number of foreign languages she heard spoken out loud. Jill had already had that same experience on many previous hikes and thought it a shame that more Americans had yet to have the opportunity to appreciate the beauty of Yosemite.

Pointing to the large waterfall that they were ascending around, Marie said, "What a fantastic place! I wish we had time to explore those other highlights you mentioned. It would be great if we could solve the case tonight which would leave me two days to come back here and see more of the Park."

Jill had a big smile on her face as she said to her friend, "I am so glad that you're enjoying this National Park. One of my favorite places to visit is Glacier Point." Jill pointed up at some cliffs and added, "That's it up there and I always think of the first explorers who saw this region and had the good grace to make it everybody's land. It was inhabited by Native Americans, but early efforts at logging could have done great damage to the giant sequoias that have been here for a thousand years. In the late 1850s tourists began visiting Yosemite including the famous naturalist John Muir and he made a big push with President Lincoln to set aside the land for the public. I like to think of the conversation between the first explorers going something like this, 'Hey Pete come over here and look at this view!' Today we see some of the same views as those early explorers and thankfully someone preserved the land so that a hundred and fifty years later we could still enjoy the beauty of Mother Nature here."

"Jill, if you keep this up I'm going to think that you're a poet at heart. I don't think I've ever heard you talk about grandeur of the earth before. It makes me even more impressed with Yosemite to hear how it has captured your heart over the years."

"On that sappy note perhaps we can move on to murder. Actually I brought pen and paper with me in case we think of some brilliant idea that hasn't crossed our minds before now. How else can we look for two suspects?"

"Let's start with what we have already. We have the two killers arriving in an ambulance, traveling to the Capitol building, and departing after they've killed Mr. Valencia. We have the ambulance used in this murder, but so far it has not provided us with any new information. By the way did anyone ask the auto auction place for any camera shots of these two men? I wonder if they have tried a disguise for any of their crimes versus what they look like at other times."

Jill pulled out her pen and paper and stopped to take a few notes, paper on her thigh to write. Marie was coming up with some good ideas.

"If they are wearing a disguise somewhere in all of the video that has been collected on them, it would further help us to chase these guys down through additional avenues," Marie mused. "Can you get copies of the various videos with the two men and see if they're all the same facial features?"

"I would have thought the police already did that but there is some disconnect between agencies so perhaps not," Jill interjected. "I was supposed to go to the city maintenance yard and watch street cameras, but I had to cancel the appointment. Maybe I'll try that tomorrow."

"If we do find another picture that Henrik can link to, that would be great so it's worth asking the question. I also think we need to explore the cyber side of the equation though. These guys had some personal medical information and they knew enough about the conditions to talk their way into the opportunity to kill each victim. There might have been a few insurance companies hacked into. Let me check some of my sources that discuss hacking; it's also one of the places I use to evaluate candidates. I want to know if they have tried to steal information. If they have, I cross them off as a candidate because if they have attempted to steal information from someone else, then they will attempt to steal from their employer, too.

"Henrik sure has been helpful to solving cases," Marie noted. "We and our clients were lucky to be kidnapped by him. Have you calculated your case solve rate since he has been around to help?"

"He has done two things for me, accelerate the speed of which we solve cases and case solve rates. Prior to his assistance, I would guess that perhaps twenty-five percent of my cases were never solved. Maybe I'll go back and see if Henrik can shed any light on any of my cold cases. I'll have to go back over my old cases and see if there was someone we couldn't identify, that he could make a difference with.

"Okay, I'll add that to our list," Jill said as she wrote down some notes. They paused to let a French speaking family pass them on the hike. Jill hoped the family wasn't that fluent in English such that they would be able to understand any part of their conversation that drifted upwards towards the hikers.

Jill was sweating profusely, the back of her shirt soaked, her headband working hard to keep the rivulets from running into her eyes. She paused to sip more water and was grateful that she had attempted to remove the make-up she applied that morning for the meeting. Having foundation mix with sweat made for a light brown stain on one's clothing and potential blotches in skin color. Marie was also sweating, although not with the gusto that Jill was showing. They drank some more water, paused to admire the scenery, then continued the climb to Nevada Falls at just under six-thousand feet of altitude.

Both women continued thinking about the case and what further clues they could follow. Jill thought that law enforcement was on top of the case and wondered what they weren't sharing because of inter-agency rivalries.

"Law enforcement seems committed and intelligent about this case," Marie stated. "Moving employees over a hundred miles away to another state and providing them with protection is a huge commitment. The lack of sharing of information between the agencies is more likely to be accidental rather than purposeful.

"In thinking about other areas that we could explore, perhaps we could look into the membership of your sovereign citizen movement and follow up on the individual names to see if they match our two suspects."

"That's an interesting idea," Jill agreed. "Preliminarily, based on the pictures I've seen, the two suspects do not look like they're blood relations. So they had to have met somewhere and chatted somewhere before planning these murders. That somewhere, most likely, is on the internet as I think these guys have computer skills to collect a lot of relevant information about victims before they murder them."

"It is good to be walking uphill and thinking about the case at the same time," Marie noted. "My brain is only focusing on two things – not tripping and clues to the case. When we get back tonight, I'll be refreshed on what to search for as we brainstormed quite a few new clues while on this trail. Perhaps Yosemite could rename the trail, the idea trail, rather than the mist trail. This uphill walk has cleared all of the mist out of my brain."

The two women continued uphill for another hour before reaching the spectacular summit of the Nevada Falls. Like from any other vantage points in the park, an observer could see where ice glaciers cut through granite rock to form the Yosemite Valley. Even though this was a low water time of year for Yosemite as the snow had long melted a few months ago, the roar of the falls was breathtaking and hypnotic. They dipped their feet into the cool water, ate their snacks, and drank more water so that they needed to refill their bottles. They both hated to leave such a place of beauty, but there was a silent urgency to get to the bottom of the hill, return to Jill's house, and carry out some more research. Jill knew from past experience to grab a piece of branch that she could use as a walking stick on the way downhill. The constant breaking with the use of the quadriceps muscle and the knee joint would have her in pain by the bottom of the trail. In past jaunts up this trail she had at times walked backwards downhill just to alternate the load on her legs. She would be interested to see if Marie had the same aches and pains by the end of the walk.

An hour and a half later they were back at the car park at Happy Isles parking lot stretching before getting in the car for the hour journey home. It was only four in the afternoon, and so they would be home by five, showered shortly thereafter, and back on their computers chasing the clues they had developed during their hike.

CHAPTER 12

*W*ith her long blonde hair drying in the still hot air of early evening during a central valley California summer, Jill went over her notes that she took on the trail. She sent some emails to her contacts at the various law enforcement agencies asking for a copy of video footage relating to each employee murder. She wanted to make sure that she did not have an additional facial recognition search for their faces. As Henrik had found copies of the original faces on Facebook, unless these guys were very crafty, it was unlikely that they wore the same disguise when out in public amongst their peers which had to be where the photographs were taken and it appeared that it was their unmodified faces that had been caught on camera. Her contacts all promised her copies that night. It was nice to see that even though this was beyond business hours, people on the task force were monitoring their emails on this topic.

Next Jill went back to the sovereign citizens groups. In some ways this was like looking for a needle in a haystack. There were several groups in each state; each had some kind of presence on the internet. Jill could waste a lot of time searching down everyone in every group. Perhaps Marie would have a suggestion of how to reduce the numbers of group members to research further.

"Hey Marie, I have simply too many people to run down. One estimate believes that there are half a million people who purport to follow sovereign citizen ideology. Furthermore, this one article said that in recent time, most new recruits to the sovereign citizen movement are people who have found themselves in a desperate situation, often due to the economy or foreclosures, and are searching for a quick fix. Others are intrigued by the notion of easy money and living a lawless life, free from unpleasant consequences. So with all that in mind, do you have any ideas on how I can limit the group that I am researching? With half a million potential suspects, I need to quickly pare this group down to a manageable number."

"Tell me more about the sovereign citizen mentality and maybe I can think of a way to reduce the numbers of people to look at."

"Sovereign citizens today grew out of the movement in the 1950s and 1960s that hated the government and blamed them for individual financial collapse. They were also a white supremacist group but in more recent years the greatest growth has been in the African-American population surprisingly. The targets of violence are often police and judges as they enforce the laws that they don't believe in. Their weapon of choice is paper. In many states they'll file liens against judges or police officers for absurd amounts; according to one article one of the suits asked for $1.4 trillion in damages, as retaliation for trying to enforce laws the judges are appointed to enforce. They usually have fake IDs; don't pay taxes, have fake vehicle registration and sometimes fake license plates. The television show, '60 Minutes' even did an episode on them after they shot and killed two police officers in the South. If you ever see someone driving around with a license plate from the Kingdom of Heaven, it's likely a sovereign citizen at the wheel. They believe in the right to keep and bear arms and politicians should be shot for creating more laws that don't make sense. One of the leaders of the movement has said that the ownership of guns and the threat of violence are required to protect the movement's rights. Oh and since this is all about the constitution, they don't believe that states exist - they call them the 'United States territory of' and you name the state."

"These people sound scarier than that Albanian sniper that was after you, Jill. How are they organized as a group?"

"That's just it - one of their fundamental values is no organization. There is a guy that writes a lot and even has a radio news hour once a week on the American Independence Channel. He seems to be the spokesman for the movement but not a leader as they don't have a leader. It is really quite ugly to read about."

"That much hate does sound hard to read about. Maybe this strategy won't work because we can't narrow down the candidate pool. How about if we focus on how the murders were committed. How would these guys know that Manuel Valencia was in his office and victim #4 was in his home? Did we check phone records for perhaps a call five or ten minutes before each kill? Or did we look at the tape to see if they walked in wearing a different uniform to check the availability of the victims?"

"Those are great questions! I had not thought of any of those issues before, but hopefully our law enforcement friends did. Let me send them an email and then we'll head over to Nathan's house for dinner."

CHAPTER 13

*A*llen Frost and Jerome Taylor were sitting in Jerome's apartment. They were both in their late 30s, Allen was Caucasian and Jerome was African-American. They had met while exchanging comments on the Fadask website devoted to the theories of the sovereign citizen group. When they lost their jobs in the recession of 2008, they had lost their homes and their wives. It was so unfair. Why did banks have the right to take a house from you that you had paid money for and lived in for five years, all because you fell behind on a few mortgage payments? It was the government's fault for allowing banks to charge law-abiding citizens high interest rates and even to raise those rates. Those very banks caused the overall price of land to escalate because more people were given loans and then more could bid housing prices up.

Now they both had discharged their debt. They had filed papers in court declaring the banks to be unconstitutional and as a result they were free of debt. The fact that neither man had approval from the courts for their absurd lawsuits was not relevant. Perhaps this is why the FBI had called the sovereign citizen movement "paper terrorists" as they used paper to clog up the court system. Cops who asked for identification from Jerome were shown papers indicating he was a sovereign citizen and needed no driver's license. Likewise when Allen was notified by city officials that he needed a $20 license for his cat, he filed five different lawsuits challenging the constitutionality of the city and their right to charge pet licenses. In the end they decided not to pursue enforcement knowing that the city would spend far more in legal costs than they would gain in license fees and on top of that he would fight collection for several more years and every time the license came up for renewal. The city consulted with experts about the sovereign citizen movement who advised it was better to fight these citizens over large payments like property or income tax than to engage legally with them for all fees.

The two men were both employed in the consumer goods industry. Allen worked for a national package delivery company using a software program to move goods around the country, while Jerome was a warehouse worker for a large retailer. It was hard to find jobs when you didn't believe in driver's licenses. They had taken a month off to execute their plan to eliminate the bastards at the State Revenue Office. Allen had first proposed it one night after months of frustration in dealing with the State tax people and Jerome had agreed. Jerome had been itching to take on a project that expressed his passion for the sovereign citizen movement. It had taken many more meetings before they had their plan. They had layers in the plan. First they decided who had harmed them the most in the office. They developed a list of six targets. They briefly discussed whether they wanted the employee that worked at the office or if they wanted to include their family as well.

After looking at a couple of the six targets, they decided to strictly focus on the employees, leaving the families alone. Some of the employees had families out of the region or out of state and it simply took too long and too much planning to reach all of the extended family members.

"I don't understand why we can't find our final two targets," Jerome puzzled. "When we did all of the surveillance two months ago, we had several places where we were supposed to find them. Maybe they are on vacation at this moment and we just need them to return."

"Maybe," Allen agreed. "We only have a few days of vacation ourselves from work and then we'll have to develop a new plan since I have to go back to work. I don't want to lose my job and I can't take another week off of work."

"Yeah man, me too. I've got to go back to work as well. Should we risk delivering a package to them to find out the scoop? Co-workers are so willing to tell each other's business."

"I suppose someone could be on to our scheme," Allen supposed.

"I don't think so," Jerome assured. "We would have heard it in the news. Besides we have ended the lives of the tax miscreants in a variety of law enforcement jurisdictions so they won't be able to connect the deaths. Especially as we took out the leader of these illegal tax enforcers; with the employees in two different locations, it will take management forever to connect the dots, as we have made all the deaths look like they were from natural causes."

"That's true. Even our fourth kill is well hidden. The idiots will never detect the nitrogen gas. Remember according to our research, they would have to find the body within twenty-four to thirty-six hours and in the United States Territory of California, Rossi's absence from work wouldn't generate any police interest to find him. Isn't that the grand irony! Residents of the territory pay all that tax money and the police won't even help them search for someone that could be in trouble."

"We looked twice for the final two targets at the movie theater," Jerome lamented. "I get that they might have skipped one week or two due to a vacation, but we missed them two weeks in a row now and we only have this week-end left to kill the two bitches. I thought they were like clockwork, seeing a new movie every Friday around seven in the evening. How about if you make a delivery to their office and see if you can pick up any gossip? That worked well in our plans for Mr. Valencia. They are so well paid; they probably took a long vacation."

Allen nodded his agreement and said, "I could do that. That really helped us pinpoint that Mr. Valencia would be in his office. I was amused that I delivered the package in a different uniform ten minutes before we came back as ambulance attendants to kill Valencia. Better still let's say we are picking up a package from their office location and say I got a call for pickup at this location. That way I don't have to leave any evidence behind; not that they're looking for us anyways."

Jerome smiled at that thought and added, "We could always go over to Rossi's house and see if his dead body is still rotting away."

They sat in silence thinking about the suggestion. Then Allen shifted on the sofa and said, "No, it doesn't tell us anything if the body is there or not. Just because the body is not there only means that it was discovered and removed and not that there were suspicions about the death and we don't want to be spotted."

"True, then I guess we are back to your suggestion of picking up a package from our final two targets. What are our other options?"

"We could be fake process servers and require their signature on a document," Allen suggested.

"Do we need a uniform for that?"

"I don't know," Allen said. "I haven't ever been served. Let me ask that question on the internet and see what kind of pictures we get. I know that sometimes the sheriff serves people with documents, but they may not be in full uniform when they do that."

After a few strokes of the computer keys Allen had his answer, "it says that most process servers wear business casual clothes and this one website discusses the use of disguises when process serving. The private investigator profession frowns on using disguises unless you've tried on several occasions to serve someone who is evasive. So we could use a disguise wearing a business casual suit, and try to deliver a summons to both of our final two targets. I like that idea."

They spent a few hours scripting out being a process server. Allen did the research on what they needed to do and Jerome created a legal looking summons document that they would try to serve. As it was getting close to the end of the day and they knew the targeted office was open for business between nine in the morning and five in the afternoon, they planned to process serve early the next day. After pulling straws, it was decided that Jerome would be the designated actor in their little scheme and he practiced his role to perfection.

The one thing they hadn't been able to locate was where the employees worked. All website and mail addresses were either post office boxes or the Capitol building. That didn't necessarily mean that that was where their office was located. So they had scripted an encounter with a Capitol employee if they needed to be told that the employee didn't work in that building. The two men approached the Capitol and after a fist pump, Jerome went inside the building in search of their final two murder targets.

Walking up to security just inside the entrance, he said, "I need to serve a summons on employee Julie Fong. Can you direct me to her office?"

"Sir, we send all summonses to personnel. They sign for them and give them to the employee. Would you like directions to personnel?"

"I'm new to process serving and I was told I have to place it in the hands of the person who it is intended for. So at this time I'll wait and see if there is another way to deliver the summons and if not I'll be back this afternoon and you can direct me to personnel at that time," Jerome said quite pleased with his ability to reason that excuse on the fly. Five minutes later he was back outside in the car with Allen.

"Apparently they don't allow employees to be served just

anywhere. So we're supposed to deliver it to personnel and they would deliver it to Fong."

"Did you do that?" Allen asked alarmed.

"Of course not! I told him I was new to the summons job and with luck I'd find some other way to serve the employee. If I can't find that, I said I'd be back in the afternoon to be directed to personnel. I was trying to keep any suspicions quiet."

"Bottom line is we still don't have any intelligence on our final two targets. If they're not at the movie theater tomorrow, then I suppose we could try again the next weekend, but I have to go back to work on Monday," Allen noted. "We need a new plan. I just don't feel confident that Fong is going to be at the theater tomorrow. Any ideas?"

They drove in silence back to Jerome's apartment. They were nearly there when Jerome said, "I suppose we could watch her house for the next twenty-four hours? If she is on vacation that doesn't tell us anything because we won't see any activity. Our final two targets are good friends and they socialize a fair amount outside of work. Perhaps the two of them took a month-long vacation somewhere?"

"I agree with you, I don't think there's any point in surveillance of her home. If they are on a month-long vacation I just want to verify it. With that crazy telephone system that they have, I'm fairly sure we can't just pick up the phone, call the Department of Revenue and ask to speak to her, but it's worth trying if we don't have any different ideas for what to do to find our targets. This was so simple when we planned this a month or two ago, and now we are stuck because we can't find our final two targets."

Over the next hour or so they searched the telephone book and the internet, looking for a number that would connect them to the Department of Revenue Audit division. After numerous searches and telephone calls around the department's robotic answering machine, they were both ready to throw the telephone at the wall in frustration. In the end, they left their phone number for Ms. Fong to return their call. The telephone number belonged to an unregistered cell phone just in case anyone was watching, but the bottom line was that their final two targets had vanished.

They thought all was lost until they watched the news later that evening. A reporter was going over a story that had been leaked to her by a relative of an employee that worked at the Department of Revenue. In this world of Facebook, Twitter, and email it was very hard to keep a secret among thirty employees and their friends and family. Seventy-two hours after they had been hidden in a Reno hotel, their story was being played out by the news. It was not just a small story that ran across the bottom of the screen but the newscasters were describing it as a breaking story and the national networks were soon reporting on it. Knowing their location and that they had been moved and consolidated made Allen and Jerome dream big. Should they act according to plan and kill the final two targets, or given this opportunity, did they strategize on how to kill the entire department at once? If they followed through with that big dream then it would fix the system for other sovereign citizen movement members. They could really become heroes within their movement and pave the way for other brothers to live comfortably and without threat by the illegal tax activities of any territory of the United States of America. The two men wished they had a third or fourth member of the movement to consult with. They were aware that sometimes groups like the FBI tried to infiltrate the movement; and so they were not sure who to trust and decided the best thing was to make the decision between the two of them. The fact that the employees had all been moved and consolidated was an exciting piece of information for Allen and Jerome, but either they were so confident in their disguise that they would never be worried or it had escaped their notice that this action by the state indicated that they were on the lookout for Allen and Jerome, and they knew they had mass murderers on their hands.

CHAPTER 14

*L*ike Allen Frost and Jerome Taylor, Jill and Marie had spent the previous evening searching the internet for information. They had a wonderful dinner at Nathan's house, and had both been itching to look up some new clues generated by their discussion while hiking in Yosemite. They were now on their way to the meeting with Lieutenant Moss and the task force devoted to finding these killers. Shortly after they arrived to the meeting, the group received bad news.

Detective Banks and Capitol personnel were pulled from the meeting to make new arrangements for the families to be secure.

"How did the news make its way to the public?" asked the lieutenant.

Before he exited the conference room, Detective Banks replied, "Sir, a teenager from one of the families, tired of not being able to see her boyfriend called the press in hopes of being released from what she called *her imprisonment.* She has been released from imprisonment all right; she's on her way to an aunt and uncle's farm in Iowa minus her cell phone."

That vision received a few chuckles from the room imagining the teenager's behavior. The chuckles were short-lived with the group realizing how much work would go into securing a new location to ensure the employees' safety. The lieutenant nodded his goodbyes as a couple of task force members left the room.

There were a few updates presented before the lieutenant got to Jill and Marie. There was still no answer as to how the two killers gathered the private medical information on each of their victims from other participants on the task force. Marie had the others in the room following her trail through social media to find more information about the two killers. It brought them no closer to their identity, but it added to the picture of them. Jill then added her intelligence gathered in the search for more information about sovereign citizen members. She ended with a link to the '60 Minutes' episode from four years ago. Jill asked if anyone had taken a look at more of the security videos from the Capitol building. She posed the question as to how the killers knew that Mr. Valencia was in his office at his desk rather than away at a meeting or perhaps even off that day. In the absence of Detective Banks, Lieutenant Moss had no answer to Jill's question. Jill added the question to their list to review and track the killers' movements.

Jill and Marie planned to look at the tape of the Capitol building after this meeting in hopes of finding the killers surveying the Capitol and the two restaurants before killing those three victims.

"I don't envy that personnel director," Maria mused. "To have the responsibility of keeping those families safe and on top of that the parents of the teenager are probably hated by the group because wherever they're moved, it's not likely going to be as nice as the resort hotel they were staying at in Reno. I would also think that once the general population knows about these two killers, necessary calls to 9-1-1 emergency operators are going to greatly decline as people are afraid to trust ambulances. Think of the work piling up in the Audit Division with all of these people not at their desks. I wonder whose depositing tax payment checks? Of course they are probably not sent to the Audit Division."

"I think there will be some form of chaos once people understand the details of these two killers. I'm not sure how much was said in the media about how the deaths occurred. Hopefully the fake ambulance story hasn't been broadcasted by anyone. Worse still, I'm afraid this will ignite some sovereign citizens into exacting their own retribution against the department. And it's not just the city of Sacramento that needs to worry; these two killers can easily reach the adjacent cities where there are over two million people."

"That's a lot of people who could panic," Marie agreed. "Of course depending on how much information the media has about who the target is, people will either get in their cars and head out of this region or say I don't work for the Department of Revenue so I'm not at any risk."

"I don't think people are necessarily rational about something like this. When I was in medical school, there was a serial killer on the loose. He would crawl into women's bedroom windows and first rape, then murder them. I took far more precautions than I ever had before and since. I was quite creeped out by the thought of a mass murderer running loose so I would bet that we would see a traffic jam leaving town. Why take a chance; what if you look like one of the victims?"

"You know, Jill, our cases are getting stranger and stranger. Are there more crazies in the world, or is that the nature of being called in as a consultant?"

"I think it's the media attention we've gotten from past cases," reasoned Jill. "If people Google us there's a whole body of work of cases that we've solved. I also think that we're dealing with the smartest and most psychologically sick killers. These deaths are not acts of passion, gang initiation rites, or simply random murders. Our killers have planned weeks to months in advance of who they're going to kill and why. They're very targeted in whom they kill which is good for us because it helps identify them and it reduces the general deaths that could be allocated to them."

"We've drifted into a strange conversation. Tell me where we're heading and what we're going to do when we get there."

"We need to check two sources for video clips of our killers. There are other cameras in and around the Capitol building and those cameras are administered by the lieutenant's division. There is a second set of cameras in and around city streets that the city operates. I want to see if our killers are surveying their kill sites before they do the deed. I would guess that they had been to each site - the Capitol and the restaurants, several times before they killed their victims to make sure their plan would work fluidly. They now know that we believe them to be serial killers or at least they know that several of their victims have been labeled homicides, so that may make them harder to find," Jill said as they entered the city maintenance yard building where the traffic cameras videos were stored. George Fellows showed them how to view footage and then left.

"I wish we had Jack here for this search as he is so much faster at looking for a person of interest in a large amount of otherwise tedious footage," Marie bemoaned after beginning the boring task of looking through lots of video.

"You bring up a good point," Jill agreed. "I wonder if Jack has software that we could use that would run through this looking for certain characteristics? Perhaps we could tell the computer to search for a picture of that ambulance and the two Facebook pictures of the men and see if it can find it. We would have to be careful there because we also want to look for other disguises the two might have used. I'll text Jack and Henrik to see if either has such a program."

The two women continued viewing the video footage, blurry eyed as though watching a game like rugby or cricket where there were people moving back and forth on a field chasing some kind of a ball, not understanding the rules or the whole point of the sport. Jill looked up and was surprised to see that they had looked for an hour already and had found nothing and they had hours of film to go. She took a moment to look at her email on her phone and discovered responses from both Jack and Henrik.

After reading each email, Jill looked over at Marie and said, "my best idea in the past couple days was sending that email to Henrik. Essentially both Jack and Henrik said the same thing—facial recognition software would help us look for objects like an ambulance. Henrik went a step farther and had a technician send me a zipped copy of his software for us to use. I feel like we should all go visit him and thank him for assisting us with these cases. I know we're planning a vacation to the United Kingdom in the fall, but I'm so grateful for his assistance that I might take a long weekend with Nathan and visit Henrik just to thank him in person."

"Like I said earlier, he's done a lot for our case solving and I think your idea of visiting him with Nathan is excellent. So I assume you're going to download this zip file to your laptop and load the software there. How do we then use it on the video footage in front of us?"

"I haven't a clue and this might warrant a phone call to Jack to see if he can walk us through moving the footage through my laptop. I will not place Henrik's software on this government computer."

"Why don't I call Jack, while you set up the software," Marie suggested. "It's in English isn't it, rather than German? That's probably a stupid question as Henrik is an international busi-nessman and would know that we needed an English-language version."

Jill nodded her approval to the question and smiled at Marie's asking and answering her own question. It was a large software program and Henrik had given her access through the cloud to his enormous server capacity. Marie was listening to instructions from Jack and taking notes while Jill was opening up the software for the first time trying to figure out how it worked. She thought it functioned like tax software wherein background computations and rules were hidden by a friendly front facing questionnaire. Marie ended her conversation just about the same time that Jill was ready to go with the software.

Marie sat back in her chair in front of the video screen and looked over at Jill and said, "When I compare our investigations today to what we were doing five years ago, it feels so much more sophisticated and technological. When you first started consulting, I think you asked for the help of Angela, Jo, or me on about one of four cases. Now you need our assistance with nearly every case. Part of it is a division of labor, but over the past five years each of us has refined our own investigative skills used not in our daily jobs but in our hunt for killers. Weird. Imagine describing those skills on a resume. I'm not sure a prospective employer would believe that I have or need such skills."

"Are you planning on changing jobs or going to work for another investigator?"

"No, it's more a statement about the weird work we do during these investigations. I'm happy with my day job and I'm happy working for you as an investigator and my vacation bank account is very happy that you call as often as you do for assistance on your cases."

"You're getting quite philosophical there," Jill murmured. "This feels like a two glasses of wine conversation and it's only ten-thirty in the morning here. Of course, if we were on-site in Henrik's computer lab, it would be six-thirty in the evening, which is a fine time for wine and any discussion about the vagaries of life. However, as the lead investigator here, I feel compelled to crack the whip and drive us back to the point at hand. What are Jack's instructions?"

"Since we don't want to install the software on the government computer, he said we're going to have to transfer quantities of video footage onto a flash drive to be read on your laptop. He gave me the names of a few software programs that will consolidate the video files since they can be quite large, to transfer to the flash drive."

Marie did a quick search of the video computer looking at its directory of programs. She found a program she was looking for and they were able to consolidate two weeks of footage onto the flash drive for use on Jill's computer.

"Now comes the most important part, what parameters are we searching for?" questioned Jill. "Let's start with a picture of the ambulance used by the two men that committed Manuel Valencia's murder. Fortunately, I have a picture of that saved in my file of information on this case."

Over the next hour or so, Jill and Marie were able to locate the ambulance in about thirty different film clips from around the city. Each film clip they would zoom in and verify that it was the same ambulance. Fortunately, there were distinctive scratches and dents in both the front and back so they didn't even need to zoom in enough to read the vehicle identification number in the windshield or license plate on the rear. They learned many things from these photos including the route the ambulance traveled, the seeming comfort with each other of the two occupants of the vehicle, and the practice they made with the vehicle prior to the actual day of the murder. They also noted no instances where their suspects had on different disguises.

"On how many different days did we see the ambulance?" asked Jill.

"Three different days."

"They always had the same uniforms, looked the same, had the same driver, and followed the same route to and from the Capitol building. Did I miss anything in describing the similarities of all these pictures?"

"I think they changed the license plate for each ambulance day. I wonder if it was the correct license plate? Don't they have different plates for commercial vehicles?"

After a short search Jill said, "It sounds like in California ambulances just have commercial license plates nothing special. Ambulance drivers have to have a special license but I don't know why our killers would seek one out—it goes against their philosophy."

"Do you think if we look at more video feed for more streets that we might find where the ambulance was parked? It's a tall and wide vehicle so it's unlikely to fit in your standard garage."

"It's worth a try. We could be faster if we understood the grid system in Sacramento," agreed Jill. "Let me see if Detective Chang has an officer assigned to that area that might direct us to the right streets to view. Of course, not all of the streets have cameras and we're more likely to run out of cameras before we run out of streets that the ambulance drove on."

After a short conversation with the detective, she expected the arrival of a traffic cop to assist them with their search. The two women took a break, stretching and walking, waiting for the officer to arrive. They were both afraid to change their search parameters as they didn't want to go over the same video footage again. Fortunately the officer arrived in the time frame promised.

Dressed in the gear of a motorcycle cop, tall and probably normal weight once you removed all of the protective gear, the redhead woman in her 30s introduced herself as Officer Heather Tennyson.

"Hello, I am Jill Quint and this is Marie Simon. Did detective Chang explain who we are, what the case is that we're working on, and what help we need? "

"Detective Chang just indicated that you needed help from someone who knew the streets in and around the Capitol. That's my beat and since the temperature is high again today, I'm glad to be off my motorcycle and inside an air-conditioned building."

"This is the case of the four employees of the Department of Revenue murdered over the past couple of weeks," Jill could see instant understanding by Heather. "The boldest of those murders occurred at the Capitol. We're trying to track the fake ambulance. Marie and I have isolated several views of the ambulance as the suspects performed several practice runs. What we don't know and what might be useful is where the ambulance went after those practice sessions as well as after each kill. We know it eventually ended up in an auto auction lot. We have a good picture of the suspects from the Capitol cameras, but we don't know if it is a disguise and again we don't know where they stored the ambulance. We have a program that can search for things like ambulances, but with all these separate video files, we need to narrow down our streets and we thought your knowledge of the streets might help us search faster."

"Yes, I can help with that and since I have applied to take the detective's exam, this will be a great experience. In fact if you don't mind, I'll contact my commanding officer to see if I can volunteer my off-duty time beginning tonight to help in any way with this case."

"Heather, we would love to have your help on or off the clock," replied Jill. "We have a fair amount of traffic work to do as in addition to this Capitol killing we also have two women murdered in restaurants well outside of your beat area. It's a lot of video work and we're not very fast with it."

"That's ok; I'm familiar with the system as I have used it to reconstruct car accidents. Show me your object recognition system and walk me through the dates and times of the incidents and their practice session and I'll find more pictures for you."

"The software is on my laptop and it cannot be copied or transferred. I'll open it up for you. I'll work other clues with Marie while you do your search."

Soon there was mostly quiet in the room as everyone would have bursts of key clicking followed by silence as the typist read what was on the screen. An hour later, Heather sat back and said, "Got it, followed the trail that the ambulance took and even the location where it was parked."

"That's brilliant," replied Jill with a grin and a high five. "Marie and I worked about a quarter of your speed and we didn't put together the details like you have. If you have the location of the ambulance, we need to tell someone about that so they can go search - perhaps Detective Chang and Lieutenant Moss. Can you put together a written summary of what you've observed? I have no desire to look at any more of that video footage and I'll trust whatever you come up with. How about the restaurants? Did you find any video footage related to the two men driving away from those locations?"

As Heather was answering Jill's questions, Jill was dialing the detective and the lieutenant. She was highly fortunate to get the both of them together on a single phone call and she described Heather's findings with regard to where the ambulance was stored. They both took the address down clearly with the intention of investigating the building immediately. They knew they wouldn't find the ambulance there as they had seen it in the auto auction, but there might be fingerprints or other DNA evidence that would be useful in identifying the men. Done with the phone call she turned back to Heather who stated, "As you know, one of the restaurants was outside of the Sacramento jurisdiction so I can take a guess based on where the ambulance was stored, what the route that was taken through Sacramento, but I can't see them drive away from the restaurant in El Dorado County and enter the city of Sacramento."

"I'm not sure they took the ambulance to the two restaurant locations; so it's slightly more probable to find them in their own car which might provide the clue we need to identify these two men. Can you use the facial recognition of the men crossing back into Sacramento to find them in any of the cameras?"

"Let me try to find some video," replied Heather.

Jill was feeling a tinge of excitement because this was the first real new information they had on their two suspects in almost twenty-four hours. She took a moment and reviewed her inbox to see if there were any emails with new updates from the task force. After lengthy discussion, rather than moving the thirty or so employees and their families from the hotel in Reno, the Highway Patrol instead decided to beef up their resources and protect the employees in place.

The Capitol security had also been instructed to notify supervision if anyone appeared for an appointment or delivery or any business with any of the thirty employees from the Audit Division. One of the guards had noted the individual who appeared with a summons for one of the names on the list. Jill asked Lieutenant Moss if they had pulled the video tapes from that encounter at security. Perhaps their suspects were searching for the employees but had not known yet that they were moved a hundred miles away. Jill volunteered to review the footage to see if they had a suspect match if the lieutenant could get it sent to her.

If indeed it was one of their suspects, had he been planning another kill in the Capitol or had he simply been trying to verify his or her location? These guys practiced their route and tactics for killing their victims. If one of them appeared at security, was this just practice for the real thing? If it was the two suspects then it would also tell the task force that there were more people on the kill list and the job was not complete yet.

Jill received a call and the caller ID said 'Detective Chang', "Hello, this is Jill."

"We are at the public storage unit building where Officer Tennyson saw the ambulance parked on video. We're getting a warrant to search the premises which should come through momentarily. If our suspects have stored anything in this unit and in particular a defibrillator, we might want you on the scene to identify the equipment. I expect the warrant to come through in about ten minutes."

"I'd be happy to help and I'll stay on standby until I receive a call from you."

They ended their conversation just as Heather identified several pieces of video footage that contained the two men in a private car. It was excellent news and an indication that if the detective needed her on scene she was free to take a laptop with her. She was highly protective of the software that Henrik had given her. She would not violate his trust.

Heather brought the videos up on screen and using a city map was able to show Jill and Marie some of the traffic patterns of the two suspects. She'd also run the car and its license through the DMV only to find the plate did not match the car. She had the name of the plate's owner as well as the car's registered owner as further details to follow up on. Heather had run a quick check on the vehicle to see if it had been reported stolen; there was no such report.

"One or both of our suspects are quite brilliant with the internet and data," Jill considered. "I think one of the reasons we can't find them is that they've been able to hack into all of the major government systems and wipe out any evidence of their identity. I wouldn't be surprised if the owner of the car completed a stolen car report and our two suspects somehow went in and erased it. Call me paranoid, but I've never come across two men before that we couldn't find somewhere in our systems."

"Is there anything else you would like me to find on our street camera system?" asked Heather.

"No, but you have been enormously helpful," replied Jill. "Can you give me your contact information so that I can reach you if we have more questions?"

"Sure and please call if you need another set of hands, I'd love to have the opportunity to work on this case."

Before Jill had an opportunity to respond, her email ring tone sounded for emails from Detective Chang. Opening the email, she said to Heather and Marie, "Detective Chang would like us to drive to the storage shed. He got the warrant and wants me to look at a defibrillator, and Heather, he wants your expertise on the security system at the storage company."

All three women quickly wrapped up their belongings and followed Heather's motorcycle to the storage unit.

"I've never had a police escort anywhere, it's pretty cool, "Jill commented.

"As long as it is not our funeral we're being escorted to, I'm cool with the escort," Marie grinned.

They soon arrived at the storage building thanks to Heather's escort. As they parked, the detective walked over to Jill, handed her gloves, and said "We're dusting the storage unit for finger-prints; I'll bring the defibrillator over to you."

The three women looked into the storage unit to see what was there and noted what looked to be the other medical supplies used in Mr. Valencia 's death—a stretcher, a paramedic toolbox, the defibrillator, oxygen cylinders, and a second toolbox which was empty.

After speaking to the other officers, Heather headed over to the office where the security footage was kept. Marie took Jill's laptop and joined Heather, guessing that they would need to use Henrik's software, knowing that Jill didn't want it out of her sight for a minute.

Another officer was already there speaking with the storage unit business employee. He pulled records on who rented the unit and how they had paid. Unfortunately it wasn't any help as the gentleman provided false identification and paid cash for a year that started two months ago. Soon Heather and Marie had run the video and noted all arrivals and departures of the two men. Inter-estingly they appeared to not be using disguises or were always in disguise as their features never changed in all of the views they had of them. Detective Chang and Jill arrived at the office to learn what Heather and Marie had seen on the video feed.

"The men have not been here for three days," Heather summa-rized. "That's not to say they aren't coming back, but based on their history, they've been here at least once a day, every day, for the past three weeks. We could easily set-up a camera that will notify us of their next visit should they come back, but this place has a feeling of neglect to me and intuitively we should not expect them to return."

Detective Chang nodded and Jill asked, "I wonder if any of those fingerprints that we found in the storage shed will identify the two killers. How soon will you have the results back?"

"The actual computer will run the prints in under thirty minutes," noted the detective. "It will take the crime scene unit time to drive back to their offices and process the prints. We should have the results back in probably ninety minutes. I want to get a list of previous owners of the storage space, so we can eliminate their fingerprints. I'm sure there are many different fingerprints in that space and sorting through who our actual killers are will not be easy and that is if they have left their fingerprints behind."

"Did you lift any fingerprints from the defibrillator machine?" Jill asked. "While there is likely to be fingerprints of the previous owner of that defibrillator, we know our killers operated the machine although from the pictures I've seen of the Capitol they had latex gloves on at the time. Because they were so well practiced as they were for these murders, it suggests that they practiced with this machine as part of that preparation prior to electrocuting the two employees in the restaurants."

CHAPTER 15

*A*llen and Jerome sat in the apartment planning their next steps. There were two more people on their murder list that they had not succeeded in killing yet. Thanks to the news, they now knew the employees were stashed away in Reno.

"Should we plan to eliminate them in Reno?" Jerome asked. "I'm sure we can be creative and successful. We hadn't failed until the damn territory hid the employees. I'm sure we can create a plan that will take care of these final two. Since the dead people have been discovered to be homicides, we don't need to put as much energy into hiding our actions."

"How would you go about it? What's our plan to kill them? We thought we were going to kill them in the dark movie theater, but that probably won't work in Reno" Allen noted. "It was going to be our easiest of the six kills - two-for-one at the same time. We need to complete the mission. Let's go back and remind ourselves while we set forth this plan."

With a nod from Jerome, Allen continued, "We are members of the sovereign citizen group. The state of California is an illegal entity not specified by the constitution. As such, it is wrong to tax any California citizen and this is why we have refused to pay taxes."

Allen stopped and paused, taking a deep breath, pacing himself like an evangelical proselytizer, he looked over at the other man staring deep into his eyes to assure himself that Jerome was with him every step of the way. What he saw there convinced him that Jerome would follow his leadership.

"Let's review the actions we took prior to killing. We explained to our targets many times and to each of them separately that we would not be paying taxes assessed by an unconstitutional state," Allen looked for Jerome's agreement and then continued using his hands for emphasis. "We notified them of our rights in person, in writing, and over the phone. We filed papers to sue them in court for their illegal actions. There comes a point, where a line in the sand has to be drawn and we are very, very close in this country with the terrorist cops, corrupt as hell courts and absolute godlessness of all the self-proclaimed honorable government actors. Our line in the sand was crossed when they filed paperwork to garnish our wages. Once we're done killing our targets, we can undo the damage inflicted on us and file the paperwork to stop the garnishment. They won't be able to reach us again, they'll be years recovering from all these deaths and maybe then California will see the light and abolish this division, maybe by then other sovereign citizens will convince them to end this unconstitutional state."

Jerome was really warming up to Allen's perspective and statements and added, "Maybe we'll need to move on and kill additional targets. We could do research and find out who actually filed the paperwork to take money from us. I think our targets made the decision, but others have been involved with taking our wages. Let's kill them all. Perhaps we can find a meeting where they are all present and blow them up or something. Let's take a moment to compose a list. I have to go back to work on Monday. Over the next few days we can finalize our list then kill on the weekends going forward. If we do find them in one location, I could take a single day off of work to complete that mission."

"That sounds like a plan," said Allen with renewed excitement. "I was depressed with the thought of our kill list coming to an end. It's not that I have a desire to kill good people rather it is becoming increasingly important to me that we bring an end to taxation by a fraudulent state and I think the only way we can get there is by killing everyone in that department. If the state can't take in revenues, and it won't be able to if we kill all of its leadership, then it won't be able to pay its employees and it will dissolve into chaos without the usual stolen dollars from taxpayers. I don't know why we didn't think of that months ago or why no one else in the sovereign movement thought of it either. We took out the most obvious of this illegal state's employees, but there are lots more that implement these false laws and fees. I looked up the department and there are seven other executives involved and three board members. That's ten more people we can add to the kill list and more importantly that is ten less people that can interfere with sovereign citizen rights. It's a good starting place."

The two men traveled through a range of emotions, moving from a sense of frustration at the start of their discussion relating to the failure to kill the final two people on their list, to excitement for their bright future with the potential to do great damage to the state tax agency with a few more well-placed murders. They would become heroes within the sovereign citizen movement.

"So how about my idea of killing them all at a single meeting," Jerome remarked. "I bet they have public meetings of the board and maybe we could get them all there?"

Allen was quiet, looking at meeting information on the internet, when slowly a smile came over his face and he said "The Tax Board meets quarterly and ninety percent of the people on our new kill list will be at that meeting scheduled for a week from now. If we don't have a plan in place by next week we will have to wait an entire quarter before we can try again using this approach. I would really like to be successful next week as I think it's much more crippling to have all these deaths so close together. In three months they could hire new people to assume the positions of the people we just killed. I would rather do it sooner rather than later."

"I agree and how do we want to go about killing everyone at that meeting? We need to do surveillance on the meeting location so that we can understand the obstacles to killing them all. Let's drive over to the building right now and look at that meeting room so we can start planning. We may want to share our plan with others in the sovereign citizen movement if we need additional manpower. I would prefer not to do that because I want the glory of these kills and I want to be remembered as one of the two men who had the courage to act on our principles. I want to be heralded for our forward thinking and tactical planning after we annihilate the California Department of Revenue!" Jerome stated.

They went out the apartment door and got into Allen's car to drive to the building where the Department of Revenue meetings were held.

CHAPTER 16

*J*erome looked over at Allen while he was driving and asked, "Do you have any experience with explosives? We'll need something big to kill an entire room of people."

"I did build bombs when I was in the military. It was a terrible experience and I got out as soon as I could and joined the movement shortly thereafter."

"You served in the military? I've never meet a sovereign citizen who served in the military. Why did you volunteer?"

"I enlisted out of high school because my family made me do it," Allen asserted. "I had heard of the movement even at that early age and would speak to some of our ideas with my family. They couldn't begin to understand and we ended up fighting a lot. As the end of high school approached, they tried everything to get me to change my way of thinking. They even had me see a psychiatrist. In the end they threatened that they could have me committed to a mental institution unless I enlisted willingly. I don't know if they could have really done that but it scared me enough to enlist and I stayed there for the minimal time of three years, I ended up being trained by them in computer science and explosives. I was really good at building, operating and defusing bomb timers."

"Wow, Allen, that's an awful story. Do you still stay in contact with your family?"

"No! The day I left for boot camp was the last day I saw my family or communicated with them. They sent me letters, but I paid extra postage to have them returned unopened. My parents and sister died in a car accident about a week before I left the army. A highway patrol car was chasing a suspect in a car. That car slammed into my family's car killing them all."

"I'm sorry. It's one more reason to hate this illegal state with its illegal cops that do nothing to protect the innocent, just another stupid example of our taxes going to waste. As sovereign citizens we shouldn't have to be bothered by cops from a state that is unconstitutional. Why can't everyone see that this is wrong?" exclaimed Jerome.

"Yes well, I doubt I would have stayed in touch since our ideologies were so far apart. Here's the irony of my life - my father was a politician in local then state government. From my observation, nearly all of the work he did was for his own reelection to a different office. I did not see any benefit to local or statewide citizens based upon his actions. Observing this in my teen years is what really drew me to the movement. I thought it was just a big waste of money and people created rules because it was work not because we needed it in a society. At the same time, I took a history class that studied the Constitution in depth. That was when I began to question whether California should be a territory or state. My understanding from that class and further study over the years confirmed that California should be a territory without state or local government."

"Allen, that is so brilliant, I wish I had discovered the movement in my youth. I wouldn't have remained so unfocused and so confused by the actions of the state. Instead in my spare time I would surf the internet looking for ideas, looking to form my own thoughts about the world at large, looking to find a connection to people of like theology. I spent some time pursuing various Christian groups thinking that might be where I would find my kind of people, but it never really worked for me. Finally when I stumbled upon the movement four years ago, I finally felt like I belonged, that I was connected to my fellow man, and that I had a purpose in life."

"We all arrive by different routes to the core of being a sovereign citizen," Allen summarized. "I'm glad I have you to partner with while we explore actions to take as sovereign citizens. I feel we will be friends for life after this experience."

Thirty minutes later they arrived at the building that housed the Department of Revenue open-to-the-public quarterly meetings. Because they wanted the opportunity to scan the building several times to work through their plan, they had applied facial disguises including wigs, cheek enhancements, and glasses. They applied pieces of scotch tape to their fingertip pads so as to make sure they left no prints in the building, but would be invisible to any security that might be there. Hopefully, there wouldn't be any security.

They located the building and it was very large with a parking lot that would rival any mall's lot. The structure was four stories tall with at least four interconnected buildings. They decided that Allen would enter the building and ask directions to the auditorium. He could say, if asked, that he was planning to attend the meeting next week of the Department of Revenue and possibly speak as a citizen but he was nervous and sometimes seeing a meeting room ahead of time eased his discomfort.

With the script in mind that they had worked out, Allen entered the building and approached security. The guard, whom Allen could tell was rolling his eyes in his mind, maintained his professional demeanor and he simply provided directions to the auditorium after Allen went through security, advising that there was a different public meeting going on and it shouldn't be too disruptive for him to peek inside and get a sense of the auditorium.

It was a good thing that Allen had gone on this first visit as he would have to give some thought about how to get explosives through the security scan. It shouldn't be too hard he thought. He entered the auditorium quietly as it was in use. Fortunately those inside ignored him and after he put his phone on silent, he was able to take several pictures to share with Jerome later.

Ten minutes later, he was out in the car, sliding into the driver's seat. The men stayed quiet until they were on the freeway.

"That was easy," Allen revealed. "I took pictures of both the security and the auditorium and I already have some ideas on what to do. After seeing another worthless taxpayer funded meeting in session while I sat in the room, I am so excited to implement your idea of killing everyone at this meeting next week. Even if we don't find our final two targets, I'll feel that our mission is complete if we kill this group next week."

"The government can't keep the employees in Reno forever, so eventually they'll return home or perhaps the government will put them into witness protection. If they return home, we can kill them then," Jerome proposed. "I do agree with you that our best achievement would be to kill everyone at the meeting. We would be noted in the annals of the sovereign citizen movement as being on a level that the Oklahoma City bombers were to the militia movement."

"Good point, Jerome. I'll have to read up on their approach. I just remember that their bombs leveled part of a government building and they killed a lot of kids in a pre-school. I want to avoid harming any child. There weren't any kids in the meeting today and there normally shouldn't be kids in one of these meetings unless it's with a member of the public attending the meeting."

"Sounds like a plan. I wonder how the authorities figured out that our four kills were murders, and not just by natural causes.

We've been watching the daily news the past month and we've not seen anything about the four deaths other than the obituaries in the paper. What changed that? Who and how did someone figure out that these were murders rather than normal deaths? We probably should spend some time looking at that question just to stay ten steps ahead of law enforcement."

CHAPTER 17

*J*ill and Marie planned to run each of the two killers' photographs through their facial recognition software. While they appeared to be the same photos taken from various cameras it never hurt to see if a different angle or a different resolution somehow gave the computer more information to do a match with. It was also approaching one in the afternoon and Jill was hungry. Doing a quick search on her iPhone, she located a Packer bar five miles away. There was a preseason football game scheduled to start in ten minutes featuring their favorite team, the Green Bay Packers. After a short drive, they soon walked into a dark bar called 'Strixe', attached to a bowling alley.

Once their eyes adjusted to the dark, they noted that there were more decorations related to the San Francisco 49ers and the Oakland Raiders than the Green Bay Packers, no surprise given the region of the country they were in. Walking up to the bar, the bartender wore a name tag that said 'Billy' and just below his name was the logo of the Packers. They instantly felt a sense of camaraderie with the stranger thanks to the logo on his apparel.

Behind him on one of the bar's many television sets was indeed the preseason game.

With a pained smile, Billy rocked over to where the two women sat. Jill instantly noted that his gait was likely due to pain in his hips and probably pacing on his feet behind the bar was not helping the situation.

"What would you like to drink?" Billy asked.

Since they were in the middle of an investigation Jill settled for a Diet Coke while Marie threw caution to the winds and ordered a Bloody Mary. When he returned with their drinks, Jill couldn't resist asking, "How did you become a fan of the Packers?" She liked to ask that question when she came across a Packers fan in an unusual geographical location. The answer was always interesting.

"I was born and raised in Wisconsin."

Jill pointed at Marie and said, "She's here visiting from Green Bay; what city are you from?"

"Eau Claire."

Marie smiled and asked, "Northwest of Green Bay. What do you think of the Packers at the start of the season?"

"I'm unhappy with the Defensive Coordinator, I always say I'm going to start a petition to have him removed," Billy provided with an unhappy look on his face.

"At least the defense is improving," Marie replied. "You have to agree with that - we moved up in the rankings from the previous year to last year."

"Did we win the Super Bowl?" Billy criticized.

"No." Marie murmured.

"Did we even play in the Super Bowl?" Billy further emphasized.

"No."

"Where did we end up in the offensive rankings?" Billy asked, going in for the kill on his conclusion.

"I'm not sure but we were in the top five, maybe top three."

"Exactly! We would've won the Super Bowl if we had had a better defense." Billy said as he walked away to serve another customer.

Jill and Marie smiled at each other; this bar was going to be the perfect place to watch the first quarter of the game. They could see around them various plates of food that seemed to be delivered from a restaurant adjacent to the bar and bowling alley. Betsy's Restaurant menu featured delicious burgers, sandwiches, and appetizers giving the two women plenty of choices to mull over. It would be a fun place to watch a game during the regular season and the women were disappointed that they would have to leave such a fun atmosphere and return to work. As far as they could see, it was Billy and the two of them that were Packer fans, no one else in the bar cared about the team that was owned by the modest-sized city in one of the coldest regions of the continental United States. It was over a hundred degrees outside, but inside the bar were three people who had sat in an outdoor football stadium for three and a half hours, in temperatures that would freeze your beer before you could finish drinking it, as only true fans of the game could experience while cheering on the Green Bay Packers. Jill and Marie reveled in the kinship feeling common to Packer fans, before moving on to discuss the case.

The bar had Wi-Fi in it and so they were using Henrik's software to again search for the images obtained from security and city-wide cameras of the two suspects. This time they had a bit more luck when they found a match for one of the suspects in an old military file from nearly two decades ago. They studied the two pictures for the similarities the software program saw. In the end, Jill just shook her head trusting that Henrik's software was infallible.

"I'm going to step outside and make a call to my two contacts on this case. I don't think it should wait until the end of the first quarter," Jill said cheekily. Fortunately with preseason football you couldn't miss much as it was mostly about players fighting for a position on the squad. She dialed their numbers and again had both on a conference call.

"Detective Chang and Lieutenant Moss, I'm going to forward you some new information on our suspects that I just gained from the facial recognition software," Jill said hitting the send button on her email account. "We have a match from one of the photos from the storage facility. Apparently one of our suspects served our country in the Army and it looks like he enlisted right out of high school. His name in the newspaper article is Thomas Allen Hull. I am curious as to why this didn't show up in our earlier searches - both yours and mine."

The picture was from a newspaper located in southern Oregon that announced engagements, anniversaries, graduations, and enlistments into the military.

"Do either of you have a contact with the military?" questioned Jill. "I believe that Henrik's facial recognition software includes the military as I would think that your software program does. I'll be interested to hear what the military says."

"As we have so many military bases in the state of California, the Highway Patrol has forged good relationships with all of them. The largest Army base in California is Fort Irwin in Southern California," noted Lieutenant Moss. "Let's see how quickly my counterpart in Southern California can find the information for us. At least we have the name. It may not be the name he goes by now, but perhaps we can track more information about him. We've speculated before at one of the suspects' abilities to hack into systems including many government systems apparently, but maybe he never knew that his hometown newspaper paid tribute to him when he left high school to join the military. It wouldn't have been on a computer rather he would've had to do a microfiche search which may or may not be indexed. Okay let me get to work on this gentleman. Still no identity for our second suspect, correct?"

"Correct, we have no identity for the African-American

suspect in our videos," Jill agreed. "We're going to do a full search now on Mr. Hull, but I think it would be helpful to have Army records. I'll feed both of you emails as we gain information about our suspect."

In the noisy bar environment which quieted somewhat at the end of peak lunch traffic, Jill and Marie were keeping one eye and one ear on the preseason football game and the other eye and ear on their internet search of Thomas Allen Hull. Running into one dead end after another, whoever Mr. Hull was, he had done an excellent job of wiping his identity off of most major population databases. Social media was a bust as well; so they made the decision to move on to the family acknowledged by the newspaper article of his enlistment. The more she read about the family, the more she somewhat understood his connection to the sovereign citizen group. His father held many public offices and had a record of approving nearly any spending bill. Further research reviewed the family's tragic death within a week of Mr. Hull ending his enlistment with the military. It didn't take a psychologist to help Jill arrive at the conclusion that he likely never had closure with his family. They really needed his military records to understand his skill sets and any personnel reviews that he received. He was honorably discharged so it was not likely he had trouble with the military but simply he didn't want to be there. Focusing on his family, Jill and Marie developed a list of family friends from public pictures of the father of which there were many. Using tax records they formed a list of neighbors around the Hull house. The car accident that killed the Hull family had occurred eighteen years ago and it was likely that memories would be dim by now, but they had to try as he was one of two men suspected of killing four Department of Revenue employees.

Jill and Marie received word that there would be a special meeting of the task force in another three hours and looking up at the game, the first quarter had come to an end. Unless you were a coach or coordinator the rest of the preseason game would be a bore. It was time to move to another location. With the inspiration of a good idea, she sent an email to Lieutenant Moss asking if there was an empty conference room or office they could use for the next several hours. At least then they would have high speed internet, privacy and quiet to do their research. He responded that there was a room available so they headed his way.

Marie murmured, "I don't suppose we could nap along the way? The comfort food we had at the bar coupled with the Bloody Mary has me dying for an afternoon nap. Perhaps you can find a coffee house and I'll get a large coffee, probably iced, given this heat."

Jill smiled and nodded, "You could still get a hot coffee as the building is likely over air-conditioned."

Marie agreed, "Hot coffee it is then!"

A short time later, they were ensconced in an empty office, provided water, guest access to the building's Wi-Fi, directions to restrooms and vending machines, and then they were left alone to work in silence. An aide in the Highway Patrol office had shown them to the room so as yet they had no new information from the Army on Hull. They spent an hour putting together a profile of who might be able to provide them with more information about the Hull family. Then they began the telephone calls.

"Hello, this is Dr. Jill Quint, is this Mrs. Austin?" Jill asked when a female voice answered the phone.

"Yes it is. Do I know you?"

"I'm calling on behalf of the California Highway Patrol where I'm working as a consultant in a criminal case. Approximately eighteen years ago you were a neighbor of the Hull family. Is that correct?"

"Yes Nancy Hull and I were good friends. It was such a tragic loss when the whole family died in that automobile accident. It was a horrific accident in that the vehicle caught on fire and cremated everyone inside since the fire was so intense. Their remains were contained in a family urn as they couldn't separate the fragments and ashes. I lost my best friend that day. How could you possibly have a criminal case that involves a family that's been dead for that length of time?"

Jill suddenly realized she was in dangerous territory. She did not want to publicly accuse Thomas Allen Hull to a complete stranger. Thinking quickly she asked, "Actually while investigating our current case we had a question arise about Thomas Hall, their son who was not in the vehicle at the time of the accident. We have been unable to reach him to ask him any questions. So we are looking at friends and family of the Hull family to see if they might fill in some of the blanks for us or help us locate him. What do you remember about Thomas?"

"Wow you're really dipping back into my memory with that question. Thomas was enlisted in the Army at the time of the accident and I'm sure it was a great loss for him at the time."

"Did you speak with him at the family's funeral?"

"No, he didn't attend. Nancy's family handled the funeral and services and said they had received a phone call from Thomas that he would be unable to attend services. We all thought that was strange as no one had ever heard of the military not granting emergency leave for a situation like this. Furthermore Nancy had mentioned within the month before her death that Thomas was leaving the military within the next few weeks as his enlistment was up. He had not communicated with them since his enlistment so I would've said they had a strained relationship."

"What did you know of him personally? Did you have children that were his age and who might have socialized with him? How had he done at school? Can you think of any comments you heard or observations you made about the son?"

"Thomas was a very smart kid. He did well in school, played no athletic sports that I can remember and no my children did not associate with him. He was different. In some cases his ideas were a hundred and eighty degrees different than anyone else. If you asked him about something, and I once made a mistake of asking him if he had taken his driver's test, he gave me a response that was maybe ten or fifteen minutes long about why driver's licenses were unconstitutional. I remember this conversation twenty years later and I'll have to say that I still don't understand his reasoning. I think because of these ideas of his he seemed to have few friends. I know that Nancy worried deeply about what he was going to do with his life with his vision of the world. Somehow they put tremendous pressure on him to enlist in the military and that was the last I saw of him for twenty years."

"What do you think he would have done if he had not enlisted in the military? Had he ever expressed a desire for a particular career?"

"He was so difficult to talk to that I avoided any deep conversations with him as I would usually end up mad or frustrated. Once Al and Nancy focused on directing him toward the military, I never heard them talk about any different career for Thomas."

"What were Al and Nancy's occupations?"

"Al ran for a different political office every four to six years depending on the election cycle. At the time of his death, he was the mayor of Crump Falls, Oregon, but running for state Senator in the upcoming election. Al had set his ambitions on being the next governor of Oregon. Nancy was a schoolteacher at a local elementary school and the perfect political spouse for Al's ambitions."

"How about the daughter? What was her relationship like with her brother?"

"She was four years younger, a high school senior at the time of her death. Ellen worshipped her older brother as younger sisters do and I remember her being the best at video games - she beat every kid in the neighborhood. She would be as puzzled as the rest of us in trying to understand some of his views."

"Can you think of any close friends that Thomas had in high school?"

"No I can't picture him socializing with anyone before he left for the military."

"Can you give me any names of other people from your neighborhood or the social circle of the Hulls that I can talk to about Thomas?" Jill asked in her final question for the woman.

"I was Nancy's best friend, Al as a politician had many friends but I would say his closest confident was Tim Stevens. I would give you his number if I had it, but I don't."

"That's okay Mrs. Austin; I have a number here for him as he was on my list to call. I really appreciate you taking the time to speak with me today," and they ended the call.

Jill looked over at Marie and said, "Thomas Allen Hull is an interesting character. It sounds like he followed the theories of a sovereign citizen movement beginning in his teenage years. Following an organization like that is a pretty deep commitment for such a young age. Interesting conversation but essentially there is no new information as to where he lives. In theory he should still be in Oregon but we've seen him near the Capitol of California on two different video feeds."

"Until you had this case, I had never heard of the sovereign citizen movement," Marie mused. "Now I can read all about them on Facebook and Twitter and Homeland Security is calling them one of the largest and most dangerous domestic terrorists groups. Their only saving grace is that most members are very independent so they're not organized and they don't act as a group. They often have pairs of citizens that cause problems, but not a large group. Do you know that there is one sovereign citizen who filed court papers stating that the Queen of England at the time the Constitution was created agreed that America would only be taxed on paper and tea and that was his defense for not paying the IRS? The judge that heard the case responded to the citizen that at the time the Constitution was written, England was led by a King not a Queen."

"Seriously, that really happened?" Jill laughed.

Marie just nodded her head as they had a laugh about the court case. Jill moved on to call Tim Stevens to see what information he had regarding Thomas Hull.

Jill tried the same approach as she had with Mrs. Austin repeating the introduction and explanation for the call, "I understand from Mrs. Austin that you were a good friend of Al Hull. I'm interested in learning more about their son Thomas. Can you give me your assessment of Mr. Hull's son?"

"I know that Al and Nancy struggled with Thomas. He began following some strange group around the age of fourteen or fifteen. The more time he spent by himself, the more energy he would put into explaining the beliefs of the group. Over time he grew to hate his father's job and indeed all politicians. I can remember him saying that all local and state government employees were being paid by stealing money from hard-working residents of the territory of Oregon. It was a really strange speech and Al never brought him to any political fund raising event for fear that he would share his odd beliefs. As time went on they were so distressed by Thomas's behavior that they took him to a psychiatrist. In the end, they hoped a stint in the military would fix his belief system."

"From what I read about groups like the one that Thomas followed, they generally do not support the military or military service. Do you know how they got Thomas to agree to enlist?"

"This is a confidential conversation? Who are you sharing the answers to your questions with?" Tim asked with a concerned tone to his voice.

"Mr. Stevens, as I stated at the beginning of the call I'm working as a consultant with the California Highway Patrol regarding a criminal investigation which I can't elaborate on at this time. Thomas Hull's name has come up during the investigation. Understanding his motives, his past behaviors, and really just about anything you remember about him may help us predict where we can locate him to have a conversation with him. There is a task force set up between the California Highway Patrol and the Sacramento Police Department and a variety of other interested law enforcement partners trying to solve a crime. Information that you are sharing with me will be shared within that group. We have no intention of having any of that information leave the conference room where the task force meets and certainly we would not be releasing it to the press," Jill said crossing her fingers on the last statement as she was not in a position to speak for the task force.

There was a long pause on the other end of the phone and Jill waited it out while Tim Stevens sorted through some kind of family secret that he debated releasing.

"Al and Nancy threatened Thomas that if he didn't sign up for the military voluntarily, they would instead have him committed to some kind of mental health hospital. I don't think they could have done that as Thomas wasn't sick rather he just had a different value system but the boy didn't know that the threat was hollow. I think he was resigned to doing the minimal service he could and never speaking to his family for the remainder of his life and with the sad fate of the automobile accident he got his wish. Al told me that their letters to Thomas were returned by him unopened and unwanted."

Those few words gave Jill a sense of the possible regret of the family for their actions toward their son, and how strange that he had picked those beliefs up at such an early age. Most followers of the sovereign citizen movement joined after a frustrating experience and negative outcome with a government agency. Thomas's negative experience was a relationship he had with his father the politician, a figurehead for government agency.

"That's a sad story, Mr. Stevens. Were you aware of any friends that Thomas had growing up or in high school? Were you aware of any career plans that he had before the military was his designated career?"

"Thomas was a hard teenager to bond with and I can't recall

ever seeing him hang out with a bunch of kids his age. He never shared his thoughts or feelings on anything other than the mantra from his group so I don't even know if he had a career in mind before the military became his career."

"Can you think of anything else to tell me about Thomas that explains his life or his skills? You know what division or trade he was directed towards in the military?"

"He was a very smart kid, but as Al and Nancy were unable to communicate with Thomas in the military, I have no idea what he did while he was in the Army."

The conversation had grown to a close, and so they ended the call. She wished she had Angela here to handle these calls as she was so good at interviewing people. She paused to look at the clock and decided it was time for them to leave for the conference room. Upon her arrival, she saw the reason for the meeting as there were new members that had been added to the task force.

"Special Agent Leticia Ortiz, are you joining this case? Was that the reason for this special meeting? Why is the FBI involved?" The agent just laughed at Jill's questions spewing forth one after another.

"Hello to you too Jill Quint! I should've figured you would be up to your elbows in this little problem here in Sacramento. Normally, Sacramento would have its own Special Agent, but the FBI is recruiting for the position and so I'm covering this office. Lieutenant Moss already briefed me, but I'd appreciate you taking a few minutes before the meeting starts to bring me up to speed."

Jill took a moment and introduced Marie to Special Agent Leticia Ortiz from the San Francisco Federal Bureau of Investigation regional office. Out of the corner of her eye she noted that the room was starting to fill up, so she gave Special Agent Ortiz a high-speed summary of the case. Just as she was finishing, the Lieutenant called the meeting to order.

Introductions were made and Jill and Marie noted new government agencies involved in the task force. Besides the FBI, the Army had sent a liaison with a paper copy of Thomas Hull's record of service in the military. There were also criminal profilers from Sacramento PD and the FBI. The Lieutenant discussed the findings at the storage facility and the identification of one of the killers. Jill followed with her description of the conversation with the two family friends while Marie spoke about the social media activities of their suspect as well as other sovereign citizen movement members. Then the Army representative dropped the bombshell.

Starting with the facts of start and end of service and locations he journeyed to with the military, Jill tuned back in when she heard him move on to the skills area.

"Mr. Hull completed basic training and was then assigned to first computer science skills, and then ammunitions as bomb timers were connected to those with computer skills."

Lieutenant Moss instantly was on high alert as well and so he started with the questions, "Can you be more specific about computer science training," deciding it was better to understand the first skill.

Army Representative Hanson said, "Twenty years ago, the Army used computers in a variety of settings, but predominantly for the operation of machinery - tanks, planes, ships, and bombs. We also used them for email communication at the highest levels. His skills list includes mainframes, data extraction, and general office computer set up. He was so talented at this that he was transferred to our ammunitions area. We have some of our best computer science recruits designing and activating timers for weapons for our military."

Ortiz asked, "Does he know how to build a timer for a bomb, or the bomb itself or both?"

"He knows how to do all of that and he was one of the most talented students ever to serve the Army."

"If he was so successful I am puzzled as to why he left so soon," Jill observed. "Are there any notes in his record to indicate whether the military tried to convince him to stay or thoughts about why he wanted to get away from something he was so successful at?"

"The military is generally not open to speculation about the motivations of our soldiers. I can tell you at the time that his enlistment was coming to an end there was a discussion about how to hold onto him, but it was felt that the military was not the best place for someone of his ideology."

"Can you translate that for me?" Moss asked. "We know that he's a long-term member of the sovereign citizen movement and in fact he was likely a member at the time of his enlistment. Did he discuss his ideas with his fellow soldiers? In the end was the military happy to see him go? He is presently our number one suspect in the commission of four murders and we don't know that he's finished. Furthermore he has a partner perhaps for the first time in his lonely life. He's also had information about each of his victims that suggests he was able to hack into either life insurance companies or doctor's offices to gain personal medical information that was used against each of the victims. Does anything in your report speak to that skill?"

"No, sir but there is evidence of his computer ability in the Army. When we got the call this afternoon for information on this former soldier, we searched all of our systems to gather information. His name and very existence had been wiped out of all Army computer systems. Fortunately, at the time of his enlistment, there were substantial paper records on microfiche, which is where this information came from. We have not had a forensic computer expert look at our systems to understand how and when he was removed from all Army records."

"Does your paper file contain a copy of his fingerprints?" Detective Chang asked.

"Yes and here is a copy for you," Hanson replied passing over a sheet with fingerprints on it.

"Let's move on to a discussion about our suspect's ammunitions training. According to the records you have, what skills does our suspect have in regards to building and detonating bombs? What kind of explosives did he work within the military? Can you describe his experience?" Moss inquired.

"Upon entry to the military, every civilian takes the armed forces vocational aptitude battery test. We use this test to help us place new recruits in a job that most matches their innate skills and thinking ability. Mr. Hull had an achievement score better than ninety percent of his classmates. The Army offered him the choice of five skill areas and he chose studies in ordnance. Basically, he knows how to build bombs that are used in training for the military or for deadly force. There is not much that he cannot figure out how to destroy with the ordnance."

There was silence in the room for a while as people mulled over what that could mean for the Department of Revenue and/or the region of Sacramento.

Special Agent Ortiz urged, "Let's get those fingerprints analyzed to see if he is connected to any crimes since he exited the military. We have potentially a very talented criminal mind at work here. He may have done nothing criminal in the intervening years or he may be connected to several unsolved crimes. As we don't know what aliases he is functioning under, if we can get some connection to DNA or fingerprints related to crime scenes, then we'll know a little more about him."

Several law enforcement agencies were scanning the prints to be sent to their crime labs. Jill took a moment to go through the various options of Henrik's software system. Since you could match objects like ambulances, she wondered how a set of fingerprints would do from a matching perspective. She just shrugged and thought she'd try it and see what happened. She got a copy of the prints from Hanson, used her iPhone to scan the picture in an email to herself, then using the laptop she opened her email and then the attachment and ran it through the object recognition software on her laptop. She figured it would take a while and so she glanced away from the screen and tuned back into the meeting. Several law enforcement agencies thought they would have results from the crime labs within about thirty minutes to determine if the prints were connected to any other crime scenes. Jill gave her laptop screen the merest of glances and was startled that there were matches awaiting her review.

CHAPTER 18

*J*ill opened the first of eight fingerprint matches. It was the fingerprints taken from the storage unit that very morning. She had to stop for a moment and marvel at the brilliance of the technology in her laptop. The fingerprints had been uploaded in Sacramento to some law enforcement server and yet within two hours they were swept into a software server in Stuttgart Germany and were now available for her use. Wow! She didn't understand the technology behind Henrik's software program, but she was blown away by its speed and efficiency. She quickly looked through some of the other matches and then spoke up to the group at large who had begun speculating about the role of their suspect's ammunitions expertise.

"Hey folks, I have eight fingerprint matches to the Army's fingerprints for Mr. Hull. Give me a moment to connect my laptop to your projector and we can all go through them," Jill said as she moved around the conference room looking for the cord that would connect her laptop to the projector.

She looked around the room and saw a variety of expressions on peoples' faces. There were looks of disbelief, there were looks of disbelief coupled with disapproval, there were several blank looks, and then she noted the smirks on both Marie's and agent Ortiz's face. She knew who her supporters were in the room.

"As some of you know, I have a facial and object recognition software program on my laptop on loan from a friend in Germany. Before you ask, the software is sold in the United States and is legal for use here. I provided the computer with the finger-prints that the Army has of Mr. Hull and it gave me eight matches including some of the fingerprints from the storage shed collected this morning, so that gives me a sense of accuracy."

Jill continued through the other seven matches most of which were related to the present crime spree. There were two addi-tional crimes they could connect to Mr. Hull. "Three years ago he had sent a letter to the IRS covered in a white powder. The letter had come back negative for hazardous materials, but it had been dusted for fingerprints and those fingerprints had been retained in the system and matched to the Army's copy of Mr. Hull's fingerprints. These prints were also on a document given to police during a routine traffic stop five years ago. The document proclaimed him a sovereign citizen thereby releasing him from the burden of having a driver's license."

"Until this recent crime spree where he is suspected of killing four people, he appears to have what I would call a mild criminal background in light of the capabilities we know him to have based on his Army training," Lieutenant Moss observed. "So we know he's been a sovereign citizen for some twenty years and during those twenty years he may have wanted to end the lives of what he considered to be fake employees managed by an illegal state. That's been his normal behavior for much of his life. However, several weeks to months ago he formed a bond with another sovereign citizen and he turned violent and I suspect there is no putting this genie back in the bottle. He may feel very self-satis-fied with the pain and damage he has caused the state government by his actions."

"I would have to add that his hacking abilities are extraordinary. He has managed to remove his identity from all major government and military systems," Jill asserted. "I suspect he has also used that knowledge to get into computer systems that contain medical information. Those same skills may have given him the knowledge of how to make changes to a defibrillator such that the electricity administered electrocuted its victims."

"I am new to this case, and two facts disturbed me here," Agent Ortiz stated. "We still don't have any identity on his partner despite the fact that we have a picture of him; and if someone was going to bomb the Department of Revenue, when and what would be the target?"

"Most people that use bombs, bomb an event or bomb a location, "announced the profiler with the Sacramento Police Department.

Detective Chang asked, "How many buildings in the city of Sacramento is the Department of Revenue located in? Do you have any other large buildings across the state that house employees?"

The expert from personnel said, "They are in two buildings in Sacramento – the Capitol and the town center which is on the south end of town. We also have a location in the San Francisco Bay Area and three in Southern California."

Another person in the room spoke up and Jill had forgotten who he represented. "Are bomb making substances available for anyone to purchase? Where would he get the supplies to build a bomb?"

Since Jill's computer was still hooked up to the projector she said, "I think I'll try to buy the supplies over the internet. I'm going to Google what is in a bomb and then I'm going to see if I can buy those substances. Why don't the rest of you continue with the discussion?"

Within five minutes, Jill and the rest of the conference room had their answers. Bomb making supplies were readily available on the internet and could be delivered in twenty-four hours. It was a scary reality to be so visible on the screen.

The personnel expert had silently been giving thought to major meetings in the department while the conversation continued. He had attended many of the leadership meetings and had begun writing down the major meetings that he could think of and then it struck him what meeting would be the target.

"Folks, if I was a crazy maniac killer and I wanted to go after one of the major meetings of the department where a lot of the leadership are present, I would go after the oversight board of the Department of Revenue. It meets quarterly and the next meeting is next week in the auditorium at the town center complex. The board members and all the senior leaders of the Department of Revenue are present for that meeting. By law, the meeting is open to the public and it actually invites public participation. So a stranger could get into the room relatively easy. There is security on the building, but it makes a very good target."

Lieutenant Moss responded, "Mr. Kelling, that's a very good guess and I would have to agree with you that that meeting makes a good target. We do have security on that building, but I think I'll operate on the assumption that there will be a plot to bring explosives to that meeting and act accordingly."

Jill added, "Lieutenant Moss, if I were Mr. Hull, I would visit the building to look at the setup. Do you have cameras on that building and at all entrances? If you do, it would behoove us to view the video looking for suspects. Detective Chang, Officer Tennyson offered to help and she certainly was a great aid in speeding up our viewing of the other city video footage. If you would loan us her right now I'm sure we could go to wherever the video feed is and not only look to see if he's been there, but probably set up a notification system for the next time the facial recognition software finds a match in a visitor's face. Also back to Agent Ortiz's comment, despite numerous searches we have been unable to identify Mr. Hull's accomplice. From the video, we know he's an African-American, medium height, somewhere between the ages of 30 and 40 but that's all we have on him so far. We've made significant progress in identifying Mr. Hull but it has not led us any closer to the identity of the second suspect. Does anyone have any suggestions for us?"

Ideas were tossed out for the next quarter of an hour and with each suggestion, Marie had an answer as to the results of the suggested search. One of the agents that accompanied agent Ortiz offered a suggestion that Marie found intriguing. She went to work on it as the conversation continued around her on how to protect the employees of the Department of Revenue. Detective Chang interrupted the conversation to inform Jill that Officer Tennyson was ready to meet them to view the video feed. Lieutenant Moss indicated that the feed was kept at the town center security office. As he was anxious to take a look at a potential bombing target, he brought the meeting to a close and offered to escort Jill and Marie to the large government complex.

On the drive over, Jill asked Marie, "So what are you searching for next, I saw your lightbulb go on in the meeting."

"I was going to ask Heather to take the two faces and see if either of them visited the Department of Revenue to discuss an issue they had with their taxes. If we could focus on a certain time, I felt we could go back and figure out what taxpayer name they filed under. We'll need some help from the department for them to give us names and I don't know much about the law, but this somehow feels like it would need a search warrant in order for us to obtain the information."

"Marie, those are some brilliant ideas! Once we arrive at this building we'll have a conversation with the Lieutenant to see if he can get the ball rolling tonight. If we could get dinner delivered to us somewhere we could put another four or five hours into searching for these two guys. I would guess he'd have the warrant in under thirty minutes, but then we need the right department representative to match who they interviewed versus who was on camera and finding the right person might take some time."

"Sounds like a plan! It's going to be a long night ahead with no dinner cooked by Nathan, just a sad day all the way around," said Marie with a pout.

"Is his cooking the only reason you came west?"

"No..... I came to drink your wine as well!"

When they pulled into the parking lot of the town center complex they heard that Heather would not arrive for another five minutes so Jill took the opportunity –to ask the lieutenant for his help in getting a search warrant, and providing the critical department contact so they could continue the search into the night. He had just finished making calls to line up resources for Jill and Marie when Heather arrived on her motorcycle. They briefed Heather on the progress of the case and their thoughts about a potential board meeting being bombed the following week. They also discussed their approach for identifying the second suspect. She jumped right in offering to help. Her short exposure to the two women had informed her that she would learn a lot working with them on solving this murder and it was concrete experience she could mention when she applied for the detective's exam.

The lieutenant arranged for a tour of the security check area as well as the auditorium. The four of them stayed quiet in front of the security guard but they looked into each other's eyes and knew their thoughts were on 'what a perfect target the auditorium made!' After the short tour they adjourned to the security office where the monitors for the building were housed. Heather began working her magic running the video feed through the facial recognition software and they almost immediately got a hit.

"That looks like Thomas Hull going through security," Marie noted. "I don't see the second suspect with him. Do you have a day and time for this visit? Do you have cameras that follow him out to the parking lot and watch him get in a vehicle?"

"The visit occurred about four hours ago. Cameras don't follow him beyond the security check point. I wonder where he went inside the building. We need to call that security guard at home and see if he remembers the conversation he had with your suspect," Heather paused and then apologized to the lieutenant. "Sorry Lieutenant Moss, sir, I didn't mean to suggest that you should follow my orders."

Jill really liked the lieutenant when he said to Heather, "Not a problem Officer as I agree with what you suggested. The Sacramento Police Department is lucky to have you among their ranks. Why don't you continue with the search while I track down the security guard?"

Heather continued to search, but they saw no further visits by their suspect or his accomplice. Heather then took a look to see if they could follow the suspect out to the parking lot. There was a camera on the exterior of the building that showed him walking outside the building. But the range of the camera failed to cover most of the parking lot. Heather looked around at the other video feeds and found nothing. She then went outside to look at cameras posted on the building across the street, she also looked at the street lights to see if they had cameras on them. They might have some options in that area, but she was more interested in moving on to the actual Department of Revenue visits by the public.

For a variety of reasons, the Department met its citizens individually to discuss their tax situation. Perhaps the conversation was about an audit, or maybe an incorrectly completed tax form, or maybe a taxpayer wanted to protest a penalty. Their plan was to go back two to six months and run all visitor faces from locations that met with the public through the facial recognition software looking for a match to their two suspects. Given the elaborate charade around three of the four murders, it took some planning and practice on the suspect's part to get it right. Some interaction with the office became the ignition switch where the suspects as sovereign citizens felt that the Department of Revenue had overstepped their authority. A deadly force response was required and Jill estimated that the plan and the partnership of the two men might have taken at least two months to form. Regardless, if they found nothing in their target time span they could always enlarge it on either side. The footage of a month took about fifteen minutes to run through the facial recognition program so it wasn't a terrible waste of time if they had to add additional months.

Fortunately they did not have to drive to the actual office location to view the film as the video footage storage was all centralized to their present location, it being the largest location housing Department of Revenue staff. Heather switched to the location which was geographically about three miles away and began to bring up the archived footage. They started with the most recent month first and found no matches to their two suspects and again had the same result for the next month. However at four months out the suspect who was not identified yet visited the branch office. The camera footage showed him entering and exiting the building with perhaps a ninety minute stay inside the building. His expression in both directions would be what Jill would describe as grim. They now had their time period for the lieutenant to use to gain a search warrant for that office. They watched the video a second time counting the number of people that entered the building after their suspect and there were about eighteen visitors that they would potentially have to sort through to find the name on the tax return of their suspect.

The three women were really excited with this finding. Jill high-fived Heather for her expertise with the video system and high-fived Marie for coming up with the idea. The lieutenant had returned to watch their search and was already on the phone to a judge seeking the search warrant which he was granted after a ten minute conversation. As tax returns contained no reference to race, the only reduction in the number of tax returns for them to review was gender. They could eliminate tax returns with female names on them. Marie, using social media and Heather, using the driver's license database, should give them the means to zero in on their suspect's tax return. In the interim, Jill was running additional months through the software to see if there were any further visits by either suspect. Within fifteen minutes, they had eliminated all but two. Now they just needed the IT person to arrive to tell them what was on the two returns that might be indicative of a sovereign citizen.

CHAPTER 19

*A*llen and Jerome arrived back at Jerome's apartment after they had surveyed the auditorium where the last meeting of the Department of Revenue Board would be held next week. It would be the Board's last meeting as it was their intent to kill everyone present at the meeting. But first they wanted to look at how they had erred and not made the deaths look like natural causes. It was best to study your failures so you did not repeat them going forward for the next mission.

"Allen, it's a good thing you have such brilliant computer skills," Jerome praised. "I feel like you can go anywhere and look at anyone's secrets in a computer system. Where do you think you should go first to figure out how they knew that the deaths were murders?"

"I was thinking about that on the drive back and I think I should go to the medical examiner's office first and see what is in the autopsy reports. I'm going to access the El Dorado office first as I think the smaller the office, the easier it is to gain access to it."

Within half an hour, Allen had managed to infiltrate the medical examiner's server where he noted that there were two autopsy reports.

"This is interesting; there are two autopsy reports on the server and they appear to be about a week apart. Let me pull up both reports and see what the difference is." Allen paused to read the document."Okay the first report states that the cause of death was an allergic reaction, the mode of death is natural causes, and it's signed by the medical examiner. The second report says the body was exhumed, the cause of death is electrocution and the mode is a homicide, and it's signed by Jill Quint, M.D. with a co-signature of the same medical examiner. Who is Jill Quint, M.D.?"

"Allen, why don't you pull up the other autopsy reports from the County of Sacramento and I'll research Jill Quint," Jerome offered.

Another forty-five minutes went by with Jerome compiling enough information on Jill Quint to almost create a dossier, while it took Allen some time to gain access to the medical examiner's office operated by the County of Sacramento. Once he did and read the three autopsy reports, he turned and looked at Jerome.

"We need to add this Dr. Quint to our murder list. She's the one who convinced both medical examiners that the mode of death was homicide. What did you find out about her, Jerome?"

"There's quite a lot about her but here's a summary. She was a forensic pathologist with the state crime lab five years ago when she quit and opened a consulting practice offering a second opinion on the cause of death. She's been involved with several high profile cases. She has a very bland website with contact information on it. She also has a vineyard about an hour south of here in the central valley and she actually did a press conference outside the gate to her property about a year ago. It appears that besides doing the autopsy that she provides investigative services as well. I found her home address and I looked it up on Google Earth. It's nice and isolated so we should be able to go after her there. She seems really smart and perhaps we might do a favor to our brothers and sisters in the sovereign citizen movement to eliminate her. Although I must say that Jill Quint had a case about a year ago in San Francisco; she took down an ex-politician that stole from the city coffers which is consistent with our belief system."

"Dr. Quint stills needs to die. Remember, her actions are likely what caused the state to hide its Department of Revenue employees from us which is preventing us from completing our original mission."

"The website says that she does investigative services; do you think she's helping the police find us?"

"I don't know and I would have to spend a lot of time searching through multiple agencies to figure out if she is assisting them. Let's just assume she is and plan the kill at night on her property. This time I don't care if the authorities figure out it's murder. We could head there tonight and do surveillance on her property for practice and then strike tomorrow night. How do you want to kill her?"

"I like the Taser to immobilize her and then we can either electrocute her or gas her with nitrogen. I don't like to use knives or guns. Our method of killing is quicker and gentler. If we have to hike into her vineyard it's easier to carry a small nitrogen gas cylinder than for us to return to the storage shed and get the defibrillator."

"Okay, surveillance tonight then we will take her out tomorrow night," Allen agreed. "Let's move on to planning for next week. I'll upload the pictures I took so you can view the area I'm talking about. Ideally we would just leave a backpack in this auditorium with the timer on it and be ten miles away at the time it detonates. But the likelihood of that happening is small."

"What is the interior like in the auditorium? Is it movie theater seating? Could we tape something to the underside of a chair in that room? But maybe I should back up first – how big a package are we talking about? Give me a sense of how much explosives and what size they are so I can understand what we need to leave behind in that auditorium."

"I'm going to have to build the bomb from scratch and I have to make sure I order the supplies today so they reach us by tomorrow or the next day at the latest. I haven't touched explosives in nearly twenty years so I'll want to go over them extensively before I build the perfect bomb for next week."

Jerome looked a little alarmed, "Is this safe? Do you remember enough about explosives to build a bomb for our mission?"

"Yeah I'm fine. You build a bomb once and you never forget it. What I was talking about was the actual individual materials to construct the bomb. In the military, we had different materials to work with than I'll probably be able to order over the internet," Allen said as he launched into a shopping spree for the components of a bomb.

"While you were shopping for your bomb components, I did a little research into what meeting will be held in that auditorium before the meeting we are planning on attending. It's the California Environmental Protection Agency hosting a meeting on the drought. That boring topic is a well-attended meeting according to last month's minutes where there were approximately one-hundred people in attendance, which is great for us as we can hide in a crowd like that. The two meetings are back-to-back in that auditorium which will make it very easy for us to leave behind a back pack with the timer to blow the room sky high ten minutes after it starts."

"That's good news as that makes it easier to plant the bomb. I think we have everything under control. I'm going to head home and catch a nap before we venture out tonight. How about if we meet back here at midnight? That will put us at Dr. Quint's house about one in the morning for surveillance tonight and traveling tomorrow night. Sound like a plan?" Allen received a nod from Jerome for his question and he left the apartment.

As Allen headed out to his car, he paused to think of the satisfaction he got every time they lined up a target to be killed. He was amazed that it had taken him nearly to his fortieth birthday before he figured out how much joy there was in killing employees of the state who perpetuated the illegal taxation system in place. He had followed the movement with passion for nearly twenty-five years, always feeling impotent in his struggle with government officials. He hadn't felt this happy in years. He was also grateful to have met Jerome who was proving to be a perfect partner for their schemes. He had some good suggestions, he wasn't squeamish, and they each had private space so they didn't get on each other's nerves. These were Allen's traits of a perfect friend. Yes, indeed, he felt relaxed and content for the first time in decades.

When he arrived home, he quickly fell into sleep awaking as his alarm let him know it was close to midnight. He dressed in all black clothing and had a black knit cap that he cut holes in so that his face would be covered. It was a quarter-moon that night so they would be able to stay well-hidden while they surveilled the good doctor's house and grounds.

Jerome was blessed with ebony skin and didn't need to cover his face. He was also dressed in black. They took Jerome's car as it was a dark burgundy, while Allen's car was silver. They grabbed binoculars, set their cellphone cameras to no-flash and were ready to go.

Parking a mile away and walking towards the doctor's property, they were amazed that no cars passed them on the road. They needed no sprints for cover should a vehicle come along. Before setting off, they had decided they would approach the house through the vineyard. The vines would give them cover and their steps on the dirt would be silent. The house was a two-story and the lights appeared to be out in every room and so it appeared that she was asleep. There was exterior lighting that illuminated the area around each building on her property. They walked around the entire house in stealth mode looking at each door knob to decide which one to pick. The skill of picking a lock belonged to Jerome and he carried a kit and took the opportunity to practice opening the door. When he was successful, they crept back to the vineyard and left the property at a faster speed than the methodical slow pace they had taken to approach the house. Soon they were back to the car and an hour and a half later each man was asleep in his own bed with dreams of a successful kill the next day.

CHAPTER 20

*J*ill was nicely snuggled into Nathan and sound asleep, when he woke her up.

"What's wrong?" Jill asked, waking up fast and clear headed.

"There is someone on your property; your phone was vibrating the alarm," Nathan whispered.

Using her cell phone she watched intruders approach the house on video. She gave a quick glance around her bedroom looking for weapons. Nathan had plenty of self-defense skills and she could likely get off a credible side kick to the intruder's crotch, but she wanted more. She tiptoed out of bed and grabbed a lamp taking off the shade and lightbulb. It would make a very nice weapon. Then she thought of Marie down the hall.

"Let me go wake Marie up and get her in this room with us," Passing the phone over to Nathan, she added, "watch where they're going."

Grabbing a robe, she hurried down the hall and woke Marie up with a whispered, "My alarm system is showing intruders on the property. Come back to my bedroom with Nathan and I so we can protect you."

Marie leapt out of bed and quickly entered the bedroom sitting on the large bed with Jill and Nathan. All three were glued to the screen. Trixie, who Nathan had called a worthless watchdog, slept through the entire conversation and all the movement.

Marie urged in a whisper, "I think those are our two killers that we have been searching for the past several days. They have the same walk as the other video. One guy is covered by a ski mask and that is probably Thomas Hull, and the other is our unknown suspect as he is an African American in complexion. Do you have any weapons in this room? Did you call the police?"

"First, I went and got you. Remember that Nathan is a black belt in hapkido, and each of us can wield a lamp - they're heavy so it will be like swinging a sledgehammer at them. I haven't called the police yet as I wanted to see what they were going to do - where they might leave prints. Beside they haven't killed anyone with a knife or gun, so we just need to stay away from the defibrillator paddles or a Taser gun. I think they're cowards and if we make noise they'll turn tail and run. I want them to leave behind some forensic evidence."

Marie whispered back, "You're a scary friend! I would have been on the phone to the cops as soon as they crossed the property line. But I get why you're waiting since we think they are going to kill all those people next week."

They continued to watch the men canvas Jill's property and then they approached the back door, directly under Jill's bedroom window. The unnamed accomplice took out a pick and was able to get in through the door. Marie headed to the corner to grab the lamp, the pair to the one that Jill hand in one hand. Nathan was focused on the screen as he seemed to be stretching his muscles preparing for the coming battle.

Then they watched the unknown suspect shut her door and the two men exited her property through the vineyard and then left the range of her cameras. Nathan then exhaled a long breath.

"Were they practicing? Are they planning to try and kill me tomorrow or at a later date?"

"I don't know, but I need a huge glass of wine and some hair color for the grey hairs that have sprouted in the last seven minutes," Marie whined.

Nathan reached over and hugged her and then laughed and said in a fake British accent, "Keep calm and carry on now and if that doesn't work then by all means swallow a large glass of wine. Come on, you should be used to these out-of-body scary experiences with Jill as a friend. Didn't you lead the group on a hike through the woods as a deranged doctor was chasing you on the golf course? How about the paralysis on the ski resort last fall? Do I need to go on and enumerate all of the weird experiences that you have had with Jill?"

"Hey this is the first time that I have been in bed sound asleep with the boogie men approaching my bedroom. I'm entitled to a little hysteria."

"Let me go get you that glass of wine, then I am going to call Lieutenant Moss and tell him what just occurred," Jill said. "I'm thinking we'll want to move out of this house and stay with Nathan until these two men are captured, but I really think this was a practice run for them and they'll be back a different night to kill me."

She exited the room leaving Nathan and Marie sitting on her bed. Marie looked at Nathan, "How does she stay calm through these situations?"

"I think she is very goal driven and there is a part of her head that is panicking but it's overwhelmed by the part of her brain that is analyzing how to solve the case. She watched the two men intently looking for where they were leaving fingerprints. She wants the two men captured more than she is worried about her safety, mine or yours. Sorry but we'll always take a back seat to that mind that wants justice for the victim and I am okay with that although I think I want a glass of wine too."

"I guess that is one of the things that I love about her as a friend, too," Marie commented just before Jill returned to the bedroom carrying three glasses and a bottle of wine. Marie stood up and gave her friend a hug before sitting down again and accepting the glass of wine that Nathan just poured.

Jill sensed that a private conversation had taken place between Nathan and Marie just before she returned to the bedroom, but as they both seemed at peace with each other she let it go and said, "I'm going to call the lieutenant now and if I miss anything in telling him about our visitors please speak up."

A groggy voice said, "Lieutenant Moss."

Jill winced and said, "Lieutenant, this is Jill Quint. Sorry to call you in the middle of the night but our two suspects just visited my property."

With that one sentence the lieutenant became wide-awake and his mind shifted into cop mode, "Tell me what happened? Are they still there? Is anyone hurt? Did you call your local police?"

"They're gone and no one is hurt and I didn't call my local police as I thought you might want to send a forensic team here to collect fingerprints," Jill said as she went on to describe the visit by the two suspects ending with, "I really think this was a practice session since that seems to be their pattern. I think they'll be back to kill me tomorrow or the next day. Their entire visit is on video thanks to my security system. I've had suspects try to kill me in the past so I have a fairly sophisticated security system that alerts me whenever someone enters my property."

"I think I remember you telling me you live in the Palisades Valley, but I'll need your exact address. I'll contact your local Sheriff to see if they have a fingerprinting officer on duty. If they don't have the resources, I'll send someone from the Highway Patrol and I'd like to come visit your property now as I think we'll need to set up a sting operation to catch our suspects. I trust your instinct that this was a practice session. They seem to strike within a week of their practice sessions if we look at their past pattern with the other murders."

"Needless to say, I'm moving elsewhere in town -I'm not staying in my own bed to be a sitting duck. Our unidentified suspect number two had a lock pick kit with him and he unlocked my door but then they relocked it. It was practice. With the adrenaline rush of the last fifteen minutes, I'm done sleeping for the night. I'll call my local Sheriff and talk to them about finger-prints. As there have been murder attempts on me in the past, I do know they offer that service. Unfortunately I think this will result in a renewed call for me to sell my property and leave the county."

"Didn't your local Sheriff's station get hammered with bullets from some black ops group that was after you last year?" Moss asked, recalling an incident vaguely related to the county he was about to visit.

"Yeah that was me and it was an FBI helicopter and a Cali-fornia Highway Patrol helicopter that came to the Sheriff's rescue so you'll find them very cooperative here. It takes under an hour to get here from Sacramento so I will expect to see you around two thirty," and they ended the call.

Next Jill put a call into her local Sheriff and explained the situ-ation. Her favorite deputy, Deputy Davis, was on duty tonight and would be there in fifteen minutes. Additionally a crime scene technician would be roused out of bed and sent to her property within the hour. All three of them decided to exchange their night clothes for jeans and sweatshirts as they likely would not be going back to bed. Fortunately she had some spotlights that would greatly improve the lighting once everyone arrived. Given the dew that normally formed overnight, it was advisable to dust for fingerprints now rather than waiting for the morning.

Jill also gave some thought to the performance of her security system. She had the option of triggering bright lights and loud alarms whenever someone crossed into her property. She had chosen silent alarms sent to her computer and cell phone more because deer occasionally triggered the alarms, but tonight it had worked in her favor to lull the suspects into showing their game plan. The only thing she would fix would be to add an audible alarm in her bedroom to make sure she always heard it when she was asleep.

Just about the time that Jill finished getting dressed and putting a pot of coffee on, Deputy Davis arrived. As always, Jill was comforted by the deputy's demeanor and presence. She was a tall African-American woman gifted with a sarcastic sense of humor and sharpshooter skills that had saved Jill's life on more than one occasion.

"You know my shift is not complete without a call from you, Dr. Quint. Who's been trying to kill you now?"

Jill thought, *damn I love this cop*, but said, "I heard you hadn't had the opportunity to shoot at anyone recently so I wanted to provide you with a chance."

After the exchange of a few more quips between the two women, they got down to business with Jill showing Deputy Davis the video feed of her midnight visitors. She then went on to explain the bigger case that she was involved in and then Lieutenant Moss arrived followed by the crime scene tech. With Jill tied up, Nathan took to her kitchen to see what ingredients he could find to feed everyone. He was hoping to bake cinnamon rolls as they didn't take a large variety of ingredients to make. Jill must have picked up a few ingredients in anticipation of Marie's arrival as her refrigerator looked a little fuller than usual.

Jill introduced Deputy Davis to Lieutenant Moss, "I'd like you to meet Deputy Davis. She has managed to be on shift every time I've had trouble on my property. She is also the best sharpshooter in this part of the state."

"From what I've read about Dr. Quint, the Sheriff's Department here must need a full-time deputy to deal with the activity on her property. Pleased to meet you, Deputy. Did Jill brief you on our current case?"

With a handshake at the introduction and a nod in answer to his question, the three of them moved on to discuss next steps. With Jill slowing down the video, they looked at each surface touched by the suspect's hands on her property. On the way in the two suspects wore black gloves, but they took them off when it came time to pick the lock on her door. With this in mind, the crime scene tech lifted multiple fingerprints off the door knob, door frame, and the wall around the door. Being that it was a door, it was a reservoir for fingerprints but with the aid of the security footage they could narrow the space that they were looking at. When they took their gloves off they had stuffed them in a pocket and forgot to put them back on during their return trip out of the vineyard. They left a fingerprint on one of the stakes used to hold a branch of grapes, when one of them tripped. It wasn't much, and untreated wood was notoriously bad at collecting prints, but it was better than nothing. An hour later the crime scene tech left; which left the five of them sitting around Jill's kitchen table with Nathan's cinnamon rolls and coffee to plan for the repeat visit by the suspects.

"Where were you planning to move Jill?" asked the lieutenant. "Are you staying in this town and under Deputy Davis's jurisdiction?"

"Yes I'll just stay with Nathan and his house is also in the Palisades Valley, but the opposite end of town from this house."

Looking at Nathan, Deputy Davis asked "What kind of security system do you have in your house? I've been so busy chasing criminals away from Jill's house that I've not had the opportunity to check anyone else's security in this town."

"That's a nice quip, Deputy Davis, and possibly true as you've never been to my home," replied Nathan with a smile. "To answer your question, I have extensive security on my house and studio. I have to for business purposes as I store many wineries' proprietary designs. Everything you saw tonight from Jill's system I also have, but unlike her, my system has audio alarms and lights."

"We'll put a guard on your house and probably station three people at Jill's house," Moss described. "We have some undercover officers that we can make up to look like you, Jill. We'll try not to burden your department, Deputy Davis, as this is a Sacramento problem that has followed Jill to the Palisades Valley."

Deputy Davis nodded but left it at that and so Jill couldn't resist saying, "Go ahead, Deputy Davis, and tell the lieutenant that in the previous times that you've protected me, the problem never originated in the Palisades Valley but always followed me home."

"If the shoe fits, you must be Cinderella," chuckled the Deputy. "I assume you'll notify the Sheriff of Palisades Valley on the totality of your operation. He'll likely want to support you in some way."

"I will and am open to suggestions on that support. I'd love for you to protect Jill and her friends since from the sound of it you been successful several times in the past," said the lieutenant with a genuine smile.

"On a different topic, Lieutenant, was your IT person able to identify our second suspect?" Jill asked. "I don't think I'll be able to get anymore sleep this morning and we could start working on searching for the suspect if we have a name or social security number."

"We got it down to two names," Moss replied. "I'll email the names and numbers to you now and maybe you'll have some good news for us by our 8 AM task force meeting."

"Sounds like a plan, Marie will only be on site another day and a half before she returns home to Wisconsin. She'll continue to do work for us from that location, however her day job will be her priority and we might have to wait till the evening for her to have time to do any research."

Soon everyone had departed and that left Jill, Marie, and Nathan alone in the early morning quiet. Nathan asked, "Are you sure they're not going to come back tonight? Isn't it rather risky leaving us here unprotected?"

"We have pretty good history with these two suspects to know that in each murder they executed so far they have done surveillance on their target, sometimes multiple surveillance trips, and so far they've scheduled their kills at least twenty-four hours after the last surveillance. So based on prior behavior, I do believe they won't be back tonight or rather I should say this morning. In fact I feel pretty confident that they won't be back."

"Okay then I think I'll go back to bed; I need to get some more shuteye. I assume you'll make enough noise when you're dressing to leave to wake me up at that time." With a nod from Jill, he headed upstairs to return to sleep. It was only when he returned to the room that he realized that Trixie had slept through the entire affair which was amazing given the number of strangers on the property. Oh well, it was like he told Jill, Trixie made a rotten security dog. With that last thought, he and the dog were both curled up in different spots of the same room, sound asleep.

Marie and Jill were pumped full of adrenaline and coffee as they settled into Jill's sofa with their laptops, reviewing the names that the lieutenant had emailed to Jill. The first was Jerry Lewis and the second was James Smith.

"They both sound like fake names although I know at one time James Smith was the most popular name in the U.S."

"I agree with you that they both sound fake. I'll take Jerry and you can have James."

Half an hour later, James was ruled out on age. There had been no picture of him to determine if he was African-American or Caucasian, but they had managed to determine that he was over the age of 65, so he was ruled out. Jill was having poor luck with Jerry and Marie joined on the search and that reaffirmed Marie's skill set as she had a picture of him within five minutes.

"I don't know why I bother to do searches with you around. I just wasted a half-hour of my life; I would have been more productive going outside and watching my grapes grow."

"Now Jill, don't whine when you're bested. It's unbecoming of you!" said Marie with a laugh and Jill had to toss a pillow at her.

"Okay, show me what you found on Jerry Lewis."

"He works for a large retail warehouse company. He's attended employee picnics which should give the police a business to search for him or at least his address. I can't tell from this picture which company he works for so I'm going to follow some of the other people in this picture to see if they indicate where they work and then we'll know."

Jill just sat back and watched Marie work her magic. It was rather like watching Jo digesting a large column of numbers and spitting out what it all meant, or Angela surgically excising critical information out of her interviewee. She was blessed not only with a great set of friends, but wow they had the best complimentary skills a private investigator could ask for.

Another fifteen minutes of searching and Marie had the answer. "He works for Zellers department store. They have about a thousand stores throughout the U.S. with a fulfillment center in Roseville -wherever that is."

"Can you email that to the lieutenant? I'm sure he'll want to see the trail you followed to pinpoint Zellers so I think it's easiest if you email him. He will likely need that information to obtain a search warrant for employee records. While you do that, I think I'll compose an email for Mrs. Valencia; I haven't updated her recently about the case and she deserves to know we're closing in on these two killers."

"It is almost four in the morning and I'm now starting to crash and burn. I'm too old to do all-nighters. Perhaps we could go back to sleep until six thirty and then take half an hour to get ready and then hit the road at seven to make the eight o'clock meeting with the task force."

"I think that's a superb idea. I'm starting to feel loopy from the lack of sleep and when that happens, my mouth runs away from my brain and I say stupid things," Jill said clicking the send button on the email message to Mrs. Valencia. "See you at six thirty."

When Jill crawled into bed, Nathan must've been in a deep sleep as he didn't even budge at the movement of the mattress that she caused by laying on it. She set her exterior property alarms on audible and the phone alarm for wake-up tune at six thirty. Moments later, she dropped off into a deep sleep.

CHAPTER 21

The task force meeting the next morning was bristling with new information - most of that coming from Jill and Marie. Jill provided an update on her nocturnal visitors and Marie demonstrated the path she took to determine that suspect number two worked in some capacity for the Zellers Corporation. The crime scene lab in the Palisades Valley had processed the fingerprints collected in the middle of the night. Some were identified as belonging to Jill or Nathan or prior criminals that had made attempts on Jill's life. There were two sets that remained unidentified. The fingerprints were clear but whomever they belonged to had never had cause to be fingerprinted and thus their information was not in the system.

The lieutenant went over the plan that would be staged in Jill's house every night for the next week waiting for the suspects to attack in the middle of the night. He also went over blueprints for the auditorium as well as the building at large. While he didn't think the bomb would be planted well in advance of the targeted meeting next week, he was still having a dog search and sniff for explosives, surveying the building in the evening after the employees were gone. State workers had become very sensitive about the case and the least little bit of adversity that came their way, caused hysteria. Three buildings had already been evacuated for nothing, because the employees had seen or felt something suspicious. Routine business was very disrupted and complaints were flowing into the department and the legislature over the non-responsiveness of the Department of Revenue.

Special Agent Ortiz was listening to the situation and looking for where her agency could lend assistance, but the Highway Patrol and the Sacramento Police Department seemed to have everything under control. She couldn't think of anything to add to make Jill and her crew or the employees of the Department of Revenue safer.

The lieutenant had someone else working on getting the search warrant for the Zellers Corporation. They had to tread carefully here as this was a private corporation that needed to make sure that any release of information was done under the direction of the search warrant. Marie had shown his officer how to follow the internet trail of the suspect as the Lieutenant predicted that the judge would want to see the evidence in this case.

The lieutenant moved around to Detective Chang and asked, "Were you or your staff able to locate any new information on our suspects?"

"We spent the night chasing a very complicated identification scheme developed by our suspects. Starting with the social security number on the tax return, we weaved through five identities before each one gets killed off. Each identity is used for two consecutive years and then never again. We have someone in our cybercrime section tracking what is going on. How could someone work for a large employer and yet change their social security number every two years? I don't believe that a major employer would allow changes like that with their employee's identification. There's no legitimate reason for an employee to change their Social Security number that frequently. We checked with the Social Security Administration and there are legitimate reasons to allow a person to change their Social Security number however they keep the new number linked with the old and certainly I have to believe that if someone had five requests two years apart to change his Social Security number that they would block it. That suggests to me that these are after-the-fact changes. I mean that someone is going into all the computer systems in the country and making these changes which would lead me to conclude that all major computer systems have been hacked into."

"In the FBI, we've had intelligence that there is a cyber-ghost on the internet who with the greatest of ease, is able to hack into multiple systems, and make changes most of the time, leaving no proof behind of their actions. This person is so ghostly that we're not sure if he or she is real or if it's a figment of our creative imaginations," Special Agent Ortiz shared. "Detective, I would like to connect your expert with the agent who has been chasing this phantom on our end."

Jill asked."Beyond her capabilities, who does he or she work for? Since our suspect's data has been changed that suggests to me that he was a target of your ghost's hacking rather than perhaps a random citizen."

After a pause, Ortiz responded, "We've been chasing him or her for three years and we believe he or she is linked to the sovereign citizen movement."

There was silence in the room for a few seconds while everyone digested Special Agent Ortiz's news. Then there was a volley of questions at once. Lieutenant Moss had to get control of the meeting. "It appears to me, Agent Ortiz, you've had a key piece of information that you have held back from this task force. Is my perception correct, Special Agent?" Moss's words were delivered with linguistic perfection and a soured look on his face as though yet again the FBI had let him down.

"Not really, Lieutenant, I was informed about the ghost shortly before the start of this meeting. Our cyber division is based in

Quantico, Virginia, so I'm not aware of much of the work they do. Like all Special Agents, I get regular communications from our HQ on criminal developments. We were informed about this cyber-ghost perhaps eighteen months ago. At the time, it was a for-your-information message about the probability that the ghost existed and the efforts to track it down. Frankly I had forgotten about it, but when I filed a report on the situation here, I received a call from Quantico's expert who is in the air on her way here to join this group. She has been tracking the ghost for several years and would like to look at the evidence here. She did say that she hoped you were not taking meeting minutes and saving them on an internet connected computer. If you have, the ghost may have accessed them and either deleted or changed what you have recorded."

As the agent was speaking, he searched the laptop in front of him for the minutes of the task force meeting. He pulled up the minutes from two previous meetings and was alarmed with what they said. The minutes referred to different participants as being idiots and the governor was described in even more derogatory terms. These were not the words that Moss had used to describe the meeting.

"Agent, thank you for that warning! The minutes have been modified and for the record many of you in this room have seem-ingly been called idiots by me. That is the farthest from the truth and I will be deleting these minutes and strictly keeping paper copies from here on out. I would appreciate if everyone on the task force as well would revert to paper until we catch this ghost."

"If we wanted proof of the ghost's existence, it sounds like we have it, based on what you've seen with the change of your minutes," Ortiz noted with satisfaction. "That was a mistake by this perpetrator."

"When does your expert's plane touchdown in Sacramento?"

"About another two hours," replied Special Agent Ortiz glancing at her watch.

Jill had been thinking about a cyber-ghost while they were speaking and it made her think of David Gomez from a previous case in Colorado and Henrik, her friend in Germany, who ran a software security company. She debated in her head whether to say something to the task force about potential resources, but then she decided it was best to have a private conversation with each of them to understand their capabilities in assisting the task force in finding the ghost.

Essentially, Marie and Jill had no work required today by either the task force or by Mrs. Valencia, although Jill had called her to update what was happening with finding her husband's killer. Marie was leaving the next day to return home to Wisconsin. She would see what Marie wanted to do for the remainder of the day after the meeting ended.

The conversation wrapped up and Jill and Marie stood up to leave. On their way out the door, Special Agent Ortiz stopped them.

"Jill, you had that look in your eye that says you have another option that you're going to pursue to help solve this case. What is it?"

"Am I that transparent?"

"This is not my first rodeo with you. So what were you thinking of doing?"

"Since the original case that you helped me with last year, I have had several more cases that have allowed me to develop a network of friends with particular skills. Both David Gomez and Henrik Klein have been very helpful in previous cases in figuring out what people are doing with computers. Henrik in particular runs a multinational computer security company. He's the one that has supplied me and several other agencies in the United States and around the world with computer recognition software that goes beyond just passports and drivers licenses and other official documents that people have. It also searches the internet and does facial recognition matches to pictures on Instagram,

Facebook, and whatever social media is used by a particular country or region of the world. Because of his security software background, Henrik has extensive experience with blocking hackers from getting into a system. I've seen a demo of it and I am massively impressed. I was planning on calling him to see what kind of input he might have to help us with this ghost. He has some pretty spectacular hackers on his payroll who could be our best bet at finding the ghost. However, that is a long shot and I might be completely off base so I thought that I would call him first and see what his thoughts would be about our case. If he thinks he can contribute something, then it would be good to connect him with your lady who's been hunting this cyber-ghost."

"Actually, Jill, that sounds like an excellent plan," replied Ortiz genuinely intrigued with Jill's contacts. "I would like to meet this friend of yours who has such incredible computer skills. If he or his company can assist in the apprehension of this cyber-ghost, we would probably want to have him on retainer for the foresee-able future in order to gain his help with other cyber-crimes. Why don't you give him a call and see if he is okay with me joining your phone call. If he is, then we'll schedule a conversation in say ten minutes. Sound like a plan?"

As far as Jill was concerned, this sense of willingness to work with people outside of the justice system was what made Special Agent Ortiz better at her job. She had worked with some people who assumed that America was the pinnacle of intelligence and that was the wrong attitude. As far as she was concerned, the soft-ware that Henrik had created and now sold was superior to anything that local law enforcement presently used.

"That sounds like a plan. Give me a moment and I'll see what he can do to assist with this case," Jill replied as she contacted Henrik. Given the time change, it was approaching the end of day in Germany, but at least it wasn't the middle of the night there. She thought she would get his voicemail as he was chief executive officer of a major German corporation. Frequently, her cases often left him with new business in different cities of the United States.

"Henrik, how are you doing?" Jill asked. She had learned to accept as European graciousness wherein you ask somebody how they were doing, how their family was, before you gave them your business reason for calling.

"I'm doing well and you and Nathan and your friends?"

"We're all doing well and in fact Nathan and I were chatting about coming to visit you in a month or two for perhaps four to five days. I wanted to thank you in person for all the help you have given me over the past year and maybe we'll visit a few wineries while we are there."

"That's brilliant, let me know when you are coming and I'll make all the arrangements for you. I'll take some time off work to be your host and lazily tour the German countryside."

"Henrik, you don't have to take time off work - we don't mean to burden you."

"Jill, I haven't taken any time off since you were here last fall. I can manage a few days off, and I would love to learn a little more about wine and winemaking from you two. I'm pleased and excited that you're coming."

Henrik sounded lonely and sad and she would have to make sure they visited him soon. She then went on to the reason she called him, "Henrik, I wondered if you would have an interest in helping with our present case?"

"Is my facial recognition software not working?" Henrik asked sounding alarmed.

"Henrik, you know that is a great product and the software program is working just fine! No, the Federal Bureau of Investigation is asking if you have the expertise to assist them in apprehending a cyber-ghost. Have you ever chased one of those before in one of your systems?"

"A cyber-ghost? That sounds intriguing. Tell me more about it and I'll let you know if I can help."

"Thanks, Henrik. Before I say any more, the FBI would like to chat with you now; is this a convenient time to talk?"

"Really, your FBI wants to talk with me, Henrik Klein, a German businessman? You must have an urgent problem on your hands. I am free for the next thirty minutes, so why don't you conference them in?"

A few seconds later, Agent Ortiz joined the call and explained what they were dealing with. She then asked him if finding the cyber-ghost was something with which he had some familiarity.

"Yes, I have had ghosts try to attack my software and when that didn't work, they went after my server farm. Neither succeeded. I employ staff to hunt for ghosts continuously in my system as that is one of the top business threats to a company like mine. Would you like some help? We can discuss our approach for searching and killing ghosts in software."

"I would as I believe the ghost in our system has facilitated the deaths of at least four people that we know of and we believe there is a plan to kill all attendees at a meeting next week. The FBI's top cyber-ghost hunter is scheduled to arrive at a local airport in an hour. Would you be able to join a conference call with your staff in about ninety minutes?"

Henrik agreed and arrangements were made for the call.

"We should invite Lieutenant Moss to this call," Jill asserted. "Like me, I doubt he understands the technical details of cyber-ghosts, but his agency has been a victim of the ghost and he'll certainly want to know how to get rid of him or her. Depending on what everyone hears on this call, Henrik's company may suddenly have some new business from the United States."

"Jill, I suspect that for the remainder of my career with the FBI that you will be the most interesting civilian devoted to justice that I will ever come across. It's not just that you're amazing with autopsies, or your friends that team up with you to discover clues, but along the way you acquire additional friends who fill key holes in your organization. I say 'friends' as it is clear that you admire these people personally and professionally and the respect is mutual. Yes, that is a good idea, let's include the lieutenant."

Jill looked a little embarrassed by Special Agent Ortiz's praise of her team and friends, so she just nodded and returned to the conference room hoping to find Lieutenant Moss and extend an invite to him.

CHAPTER 22

*J*erome and Allen were debriefing the night's surveillance exercise. It had gone well; they hadn't been discovered and Jerome had been able to pick the lock. Tonight they would go back and kill the doctor in her bed. Allen was bothered by the ease of it all. He had managed to avoid being caught by any authorities by staying two steps ahead. It would pay to do some research now just to make sure that the previous evening had been as easy as they thought.

Jerome opened his laptop and contacted the sovereign citizen movement network. The login was a pain. Each time a visitor had to answer five to ten security questions depending on the mood of the server that day. Then you had to change your password. It was only good for twenty-four hours. If you took a bathroom break while searching something, bam, you were logged out by the server. The system had more security than any other system he had used in his entire life. He had followed the movement for nearly a decade starting before it was so easy to communicate because of the internet. With the advent of the internet, computer experts joined the movement making it even easier to change names and assume new identities. Currently the movement had someone in it who behaved like the Wizard of Oz. He was behind a curtain no one could see, but he was turning the movement into the Emerald City. If you needed something searched or erased somewhere in the internet universe, you simply requested the work from a particular mailbox and it was done. So far this wizard had changed identities for Jerome numerous times, and hacked into company records updating his identification with his new identity, and most recently the wizard had gotten into the minutes of the Highway Patrol and made a fun mess of those. Sometimes it was better to change than to erase. When both he and Allen had gone to work at their respective employers, they had asked to be called by their nicknames that way as their names changed in the background of human resources, the front-end – the people they dealt with every day on the job didn't notice any name changes.

Each request that Jerome and Allen had sent the wizard was handled quickly, most of the time in under eight hours. They each had some creative skills to get into computers but they felt like amateurs when compared to the wizard. Allen had searched both the police and the Sheriff that supported the city of Palisades Valley and he had been unable to find a police report for a break-in at Jill's house the previous night. It should mean that their activities the previous night had not been discovered. Now he wanted the wizard to also take a look just to make sure he hadn't missed anything. In his past experience, things that seemed easy on the surface had a tendency to turn into a hot mess at the blink of an eye.

With that taken care of, they went back to planning the bombing of the meeting the following week. "Allen, did you remember to ask for that day off work? My supervisor approved it this morning," Jerome noted.

"I also got approval for next week. The supplies we need to build this bomb should begin arriving today. I have them being delivered to my mailbox that I rent at the Arden Fair strip mall.

I'm going to wear a disguise for that pick up and I would like to do a surveillance run of the property to check on the camera locations. I can use a ball cap to cover up most of my face if I keep my head down and away from any camera locations."

"That's a good plan. Let's go survey the parking lot now. We could park down the street and walk by the strip mall checking out the cameras as we go. That way our car won't be caught in any security camera footage. You have all the supplies going to the same rented mailbox?"

"No. I have three rented mailboxes and I divided the supplies up among the three locations so maybe we could do that surveillance run on all three locations this afternoon," Allen suggested as he heard a ping on his computer. It was an email from the wizard.

"The wizard found the police report in the trash file. Someone must've warned them to not post any information about the Department of Revenue deaths, but they had already posted it and had to put it in to the trash to hide it from me. They're getting devious and very alert to our plans. It says here that Jill Quint is moving out of her house and into that of her friend, Nathan Conroy, listed in the same city. We'll have to pay him a visit. I think we should avoid the practice visit and go for the kill tonight."

"We have never carried out any kills without a practice session first. Are you sure you want to do that? Why don't we at least drive out to the property this afternoon so we can see what we're getting into? We won't break into his house - it's more to get a layout of where we should park and walk tonight."

"You're right, Jerome, we can at least get the lay of the land, choose a parking spot and decide where to enter his property. Let me pull a picture up on Google Earth."

They studied the picture of a street view look of Nathan's house. It was a big one-story Spanish adobe building with beautiful landscaping and fountains in front. The two men got a sense of the land staring at the picture. Unlike Jill Quint's property, this guy had no vineyards. Instead he had several outbuildings of indeterminate use.

"Let's go and start our surveillance run to the mailbox locations, the auditorium, and then drive to the guy's house in Palisades Valley which is an hour from here. Jerome, what disguise do you want to wear today? I think we can stay with the same disguise in all locations."

"I think we should wear the bland look. Nondescript clothing so that if anyone was trying to describe our appearance they would have to say we look like a plumber or electrician or a delivery guy. While I have full beards and the baseball cap wigs I also have a hat that will make us look like we're bald underneath the ball cap. I also have some fake sleeves to wear that will make it look like your entire arm is tattooed. Let's take my car since we had yours yesterday at the auditorium and I'll put the fake plates on it. What else do we need?"

"A couple pair of sunglasses would be good as well as clear plastic frames for when we can't wear sunglasses. Let's add to that - binoculars, water, and our Taser. We never know when we could be threatened."

Jerome rubbed his hands together and said, "I am really enjoying being a member of the sovereign citizen movement. Planning these kills has brought me happiness for the first time in probably the last decade. Knowing that we're removing corrupt people who enforce the corrupt laws of any legal state is very satisfying. I only wish we could tell our story to fellow brothers of the movement, but you never know who you can trust. I really want to learn from you on how to build a bomb in case I need to do it in the future and you're not around. I mean I always hope you'll be around; you've been such a good friend. I haven't had such deep conversations with anyone until I met you. Have you met anyone else in the movement that you like and trust?"

"I've had a few meetings with other people in the movement,

but we haven't clicked. Most people are not as focused as I am on the movement and they bring other baggage like bigotry or religion. But those thoughts don't belong in the movement. We are very specific in our beliefs. We fight against all parts of the government that have been illegally formed from local government to state government. We are citizens of the original colonies that became the United States of America and everything that came after us was created by a conspiracy of the government. The only other person in the movement I trust besides you is the wizard. Whatever I've asked the wizard he has never let me down. The wizard has even helped me improve the computer skills I left the military with to a far higher level so that I can infiltrate many businesses. I would love to meet him someday."

The two men got in the car and started their journey of surveillance. First on the list was the first mailbox location. They parked four blocks away in a grocery store parking lot. They stayed on the outer sidewalk of the strip mall looking for cameras on the outside of any of the stores, particularly those focused on the parking lot. Neither man could spot anything to worry about. They then visited a fast food outlet inside the strip mall to get another look at the mall's activity and again they saw nothing to worry about. They repeated the process for the next two mailbox sites. The only concern came from the third mailbox company where clearly there were all kinds of cameras both on the exterior and the interior of the store. Allen would have to wear a completely different disguise when he visited the third store and now that they saw the camera placement he knew where to keep his eyes focused when he walked inside. Unfortunately, given the size of the packages that wouldn't fit in his mailbox, he would likely have to speak to whoever was running the mailbox company, but there was nothing they could do about that.

At the first mailbox company location, Allen picked up the first of five packages of supplies he required to build the bomb for next week. If any cop looked into the trunk of their car, he might be alarmed and wonder why two men were driving around with fifty pounds of black powder and fifty pounds of smokeless powder. The powders could be bought by anyone in gun and ammunition shops across the U.S.as gun owners used the powder to make their own shells and hobbyist cannonball and rocket makers also used the substances. It was the basic ingredient for a homemade bomb.

They moved on to another visit to the large government building where the auditorium was located. Allen had obtained enough pictures of the inside from his first visit. This time he wanted to look at the outside of the building as perhaps they could place the bomb on the side or the top of the building at night with the advantage of not having to get the explosive through security.

Studying the building, Allen said to Jerome, "I remember from my days in the military that the best bombs are placed under people. If the power of the explosion doesn't kill someone, sometimes landing on their head after being tossed through the air would do it. If we did the roof or the side, then we need the blast to kill those inside."

"How about doing both locations?" Jerome asked. "How would you get on the roof and where would you specifically need to place the explosives on the outside of the building?"

"That is a good question. I'm trying to think back to my training and my actual experience. We blew up abandoned buildings for practice, but it was always about placing the explosives inside a room. I can also remember throwing explosives at the side of the building when we were under fire in Iraq, and it stopped the enemy's gunfire, but I don't know if that was because of the smoke or because they were dead. My unit didn't stick around to find out. I'm also trying to think about what they taught us about the thickness of the walls and structure. As you can imagine, an American building is a much stronger construction than those in other parts of the world. If you have a flimsy structure to start with it takes a lot less powder to destroy it."

"Since I never served in the military I don't think I can provide you with even one sentence of advice on what to do here," Jerome said wishing he could help. "Is that something you could look up online? Perhaps read up on how they make buildings implode and that might help you understand what would happen with exteriorly placed explosives. Do you have any thoughts on how we would get up on the roof? Is this something you would need help with or would you do the placement yourself?"

"If I do a roof explosion, I'll pack the ordnance with a lot more gunpowder than I would if it was inside the auditorium. While you drive, I'm going to look up what the bombs that destroyed the building in Oklahoma City were made of - I am not looking for a bomb that size - it was huge, I think it flattened more than a city block. I just want a single room destroyed."

"Are we finished here?" Jerome asked.

"No, I am still exploring the idea of the roof or the side of the building. The side of the building should be pretty easy - drop a big package and run. I think we need to look at the uniform of the maintenance guys at this place and then get a maintenance cart like what they use and fill it with a bomb. If the cart sat there five or ten minutes and looked like the maintenance carts that they used here every day, no one would notice. Let's drive around the building and see if we can spot a maintenance cart on a delivery dock. We can also document all of the cameras. To reach the roof, we'll need to go up an interior stairwell. If we can figure out another way to destroy the auditorium from the exterior, I would like to avoid any more trips inside that building."

They drove around the campus of the large government building before making their way to a loading dock. After all, a building that size required supplies to make it run. They spied the loading dock and found a convenient parking place to observe the building's activity. They watched two companies—an office supply and a food company pull up to the dock, journey inside and then come back out pulling a cart with them. Allen and Jerome took photos of the carts. After spending nearly an hour on the campus, they gleaned all the information they could think of from the visit and it was time for the one-hour drive out to Mr. Nathan Conroy's house.

As they pulled away from the building, Allen said to Jerome, "It just makes me sick to see all those people running around without a care in the world while you and I are driven to the brink of poverty because we have to pay taxes to support those people. I would blow up the whole damn building if I could."

"Why don't you?" asked Jerome. "Can you just increase your order of gunpowder? Then we could act like gardeners and drop a large potting soil bag and a plant in a one gallon container every five feet along the exterior walls of this office complex. Then you could build a timer to detonate all the bags at once."

"I really like your idea, Jerome, but I don't want to take on more than we can handle. I haven't built a bomb in almost two decades. Let me have some success with destroying this auditorium and its occupants and then we'll move on to bigger targets. I like your idea of disguising a bomb in a bag of potting soil, and we'll probably use that idea for when we want to move on to a bigger target."

Allen looked over at Jerome while they were driving trying to assess how Jerome felt about being denied the opportunity for a glorious and damaging explosion but truly he wasn't confident of his skills with explosives and the last thing he wanted to do was blow himself up. He did not want the bombing of the auditorium to be his first and his last attempt to eliminate people representing the state of California. Finally when he repeated that thought aloud to Jerome and saw agreement then the tension in the car eased.

As with their trip the night before, the two men followed the state highway out of Sacramento and into the central valley where

Jill and Nathan had homes. Soon there was nothing but fields of agriculture and then they saw large acreages of grapevines, their sign that they were approaching the Palisades Valley. Following the traffic directions from their GPS, they were soon at Nathan Conroy's home. It was the other side of town from where they had been the previous night visiting Jill Quint's house. There was a sign out front that said Conroy Designs and that had not been visible on Google Earth. They drove past it a mile or two and parked, grateful to have cell phone reception in such a small town.

"'Conroy Designs, full service wine label and branding studio devoted to assisting winemakers with graphic materials that reflect the winemaker and his or her grapes,'" Allen said while reading Nathan's About Me page. "Wow, he has pictures of over one-hundred wine labels that he designed. I've even drank some of this wine. Oh well, there might be no more designs for him if he doesn't wake up alive tomorrow."

"What's our game plan?" Jerome asked. "Wait until midnight and drive out here. We could slip into the house and Taser all of the occupants, or just kill Jill?"

"The second option -let's just kill Jill. We have nothing against anyone else in the house. We can Taser them at the start so they are disabled and then we'll do a quick nitrogen gas kill of Jill and be out of the house in twenty minutes."

"They'll see us but then again they saw us last night when we visited Jill's property. We should still wear a disguise, but I think they'll know who we are. So we park on the street and climb over a side fence into Conroy's backyard, then I will pick the lock into the house, and we will head into the bedrooms with the Taser. Are we expecting just the two of them at this house?"

"Yes and since we don't know if they are sleeping together, let's plan on heading to the master bedroom first. If they're both there, then we quickly Taser both of them and put the gas to Jill's face. We may have to Taser the guy a second time just to give us a clear path out of the city. We don't want him calling the police before we even get off the property."

"Sounds like a plan," Jerome enthused. "I'll drive by Conroy's house once more and then we'll head back home. We'll have a long night tonight after the long one last night."

They headed back into the city with Allen making a list of what they needed for tonight's assignment – black clothing, the Taser, a nitrogen gas cylinder with mask, the lock pick kit, and gloves. Both men felt supremely confident that they would kill the insufferable Jill Quint M.D. that night.

CHAPTER 23

*J*ill had facilitated connecting Henrik's engineers with the FBI and Jill, Marie, Moss, and Ortiz were now bystanders to a geeky conversation that made absolutely no sense to any of them. They could tell the conversation was moving forward as it became a case of dueling computer keyboards with one person typing away furiously, then the other, buffeted by conversation spurts in between. By the end of ten minutes of conversation, Jill was working on other things. When they were done with business, the two women were going to rent a kayak and paddle the American River. It was filled with snow melt, so even though it was blazing hot in Sacramento, the river would be cool.

After forty-five minutes of conversation and lots of keyboard typing, it appeared that the telephone call was coming to an end. The four observers abandoned the other work they were doing and prepared to listen to the FBI's expert on cyber-ghosts.

"Thank you, Dr. Quint, for making this connection for me. I have essentially been working in isolation for the past three years mostly because my work is not understood by many people. However, the two people in Germany not only understood my work but could tell me how to accelerate it," said Madeline, the cyber-ghost hunter. "I had glimpses of this ghost over the past three years – a digital fingerprint here or there. It was occasionally enough information for me to figure out where the ghost was and shut them down and out of the system but that was all I could do and the ghost would pop up again once they found a new system to attack. I now have a piece of code that I can use to trap the ghost and I'll have him or her within twenty-four hours according to my new friends in Germany and I believe them as this is what I've been searching for the past couple years but had been unable to figure out what to do on my own. Give me ten minutes to insert this code then I'll walk you through what I'm doing while the computer is working in the background."

What could any of them say but 'okay' to a twenty-year-old wonder kid whose actions might save the lives of the Department of Revenue employees as well as future targets of the sovereign citizen movement? And so they patiently waited for her to finish inserting her piece of code. At least they had a vague idea of what that meant. As promised, a short time later she finished and turned around to speak to the group.

"I was recruited to work for the FBI while in high school or maybe I should say I was offered the opportunity to work for the FBI in lieu of going to prison for hacking into the Social Security Administration system and increasing my grandmother's pension payments. At the time, it was just my grandmother and I living together and we were having a hard time paying the rent, buying food, and keeping the electricity on. I always had a knack with computers and so I decided that I would simply increase my grandmother's monthly check to fix the problem. So I worked on the solution for about two months and figured out how to do it. I wasn't greedy, I didn't increase Granny's check by five thousand a month, no, I just added two hundred dollars a month as that would close the gap for us. So I did and we had the power on continuously for six months and neither of us never went to bed hungry.

"Unfortunately I was caught. Apparently the Social Security Administration routinely runs a report looking at changes to pension checks. While two hundred dollars didn't seem much at the time it set off the warning bells on this report because there were no life events that could explain the increase. So Granny got a letter saying there had been an error and that her check was being reduced back to the original amount and she would have to pay back the overage. As you can imagine, I was outraged over this. So I increased her check even more but added code that made it look like she was paying back the overage. When her account came up a second time, it was referred to the cyber-crime division of the FBI for investigation. We worked out a deal; for the past five years I've worked for the cyber-crimes division of the FBI and my paycheck has made Granny very comfortable. All of this is just background and an explanation of my credentials.

"For the first few years with the FBI my job was to look for and report hackers just like myself that were getting benefits from various federal programs by manipulating the IT systems of the federal government. At first I thought everyone would be like me just trying to get an extra two hundred to help keep the power on, but I've exposed a whole bunch of greedy lazy fools who were out and out stealing from the federal government. I hacked into the system and made a change to the program that directed the printing of my grandmother's monthly check. It's a very unso-phisticated way to get what you need. On the side, I started chasing this ghost as I could see it making changes in different systems, but money, on the surface, was not the outcome of these changes. Rather this individual changed identities, erased records in the military, issued fake licenses, issued birth and death certifi-cates and things like that. On one hand, it's not a priority if no money is being stolen, however what should be frightening is this person's ability to move around various government systems making changes at will. Once a day, I set aside some time to chase this person through cyberspace and bounce through twenty-five to fifty computers throughout the world before I end up in a dead-end location being gobbled up by this Pac-Man figure from the 1970s. The ghost was always one step ahead of me, and taunted and teased me into keeping up the battle. Your friends from Germany rock; they showed me how to write the code to cover the dead-end and continue the chase down another street."

Jill had been nodding at the explanation, understanding about one in ten words. Then they heard a beep from Madeline's laptop.

She reached over and hit a few keys and then a furious conversation with herself erupted as she typed away with a speed that Jill envied. Madeline looked over her shoulder and said, "The ghost has taken my bait and I'm doing the usual chase through cyberspace after her or him. In about two minutes time the ghost is going to freak when it sees that I've jumped the curb on the dead-end street. Let the games begin!"

The four spectators were staring at the screen expecting to see a computer game based on Madeline's description instead all they could see was computer code scrolling down the screen. As a group they all leaned back at nearly the same time realizing they didn't understand what was going on but hoped new clues would follow at the end of Madeline's furious activity.

"Ha, now it knows I'm in the chase. Where are you going to go next? Okay I got it!"

"Got what?" asked Moss looking at Madeline's hands as though they contained something he could arrest.

"I've got the IP address and therefore the geographical coordinates of where the ghost was during this flurry of activity. I'm just going to enter them into Google Earth and I'll know where the ghost was sitting at the time of the most recent hack."

"Can you tell what it was changing somewhere in the internet? Was this ghost visiting the FBI server, the California DMV?" asked Ortiz.

"Give me a minute on that," Madeline declared. "I think we better let the Dallas field office know that our ghost is hanging out at the public library on State Street or I should say was hanging out – it's not likely to be there now."

Special Agent Ortiz stepped away, presumably to contact the Dallas office. Moss just shook his head at the complexity of following a ghost through cyberspace. Marie and Jill looked expectantly at Madeline for an explanation on what the ghost had been tampering with just before shutting down.

"The ghost was in a large retailer in the personnel section creating the name of a new employee and deleting the name of another. Prior to that the ghost was in the Palisades Valley Sheriff network and prior to that they tried to punch through the FBI but didn't get anywhere. By the way, Lieutenant, the ghost made a run at your server and read some materials."

The lieutenant looked so taken aback by her pronouncement that he actually looked at his fly to make sure he zipped up before moving back to his seat and looking at his own laptop. The three women hid a smirk.

Madeline volunteered, "Lieutenant, if you would like I can track where the ghost went inside your server. This way you'll know which documents are suspect."

He nodded his agreement at her and she was soon examining documents. "So you already know the ghost changed your minutes. It also pulled up your report on the adventure at Jill's house last night."

"How could it do that? I deleted it last night a few hours after I wrote it."

"Haven't you heard the phrase 'nothing is ever deleted from the internet'? The ghost likely pulled it up from your trash file. It's usually much more difficult to destroy electronic data versus paper data."

Marie asked, "Do you think that either the Lieutenant's notes or the Palisades Valley Sheriff wrote down in their reports that we were moving to Nathan's house tonight? I'm feeling really uneasy about this. Maybe we should stay in town at a hotel."

"That's a good point, Marie," Jill agreed. "I think we should stay where we planned at Nathan's house, but have a sting operation in place to pick these guys up. Lieutenant, do you have any officers that you could post at my friend's house in case we have any activity tonight?"

"I'll find some officers to post at Nathan's house. If we could find those two killers tonight it would be better for the whole city. If you'll give me the address, I'll have them there by five or six tonight."

Ortiz approached the group obviously having ended her phone call with the Dallas office.

"I should hear back on the location in the next few minutes. The ghost picked a location within two miles of the FBI. I'm just hoping that there is video surveillance on that library. Madeline, can you prevent the information from disappearing if there is video footage of the library?"

"I think so. Give me a minute."

"Madeline, you're a pretty scary person with your incredible internet skills," Ortiz said."I'm glad you're on the good side rather than being partnered with the ghost. The world would be a terrible place with you two free to roam the internet and cause havoc."

Ortiz's cell phone rang and she again stepped away from the group. Jill and Marie finalized their plans for protection provided by the Highway Patrol. The agent stepped back to the group and handed her cell phone to Madeline. She shrugged and said, "Apparently every special agent in charge of a regional office knows about Madeline. They want to talk to her about saving the video feed from the library. They wouldn't accept my saying that Madeline had already fixed that; they wanted talk to her in person over the phone. Sheesh!"

Madeline stepped up to the group and said she would set up a video phone call so that Dallas could share the video footage with Sacramento. She paused for a moment as if thinking about something and then spoke to herself about what she would do. She looked up to see the four people staring at her with puzzled looks on their faces.

"As I was setting up this videoconference call, it occurred to me that the ghost would be able to tap into the video call as anything on a computer seems to be vulnerable. But I figured out a way around that so we won't have to worry that our ghost is listening to every word we say."

Within minutes, the two cities were connected with both locations viewing the library footage. As with most libraries, the free internet use was a popular part of the library. They looked at the users of the library that arrived at a certain time period, presented ID, and then sat down and surfed the internet. During the designated time, there were two people that could be their ghost- one male, one female. Jill debated running both pictures through the facial recognition program, but the ghost was good and would make sure that there weren't any pictures of her or him anywhere on the internet. However it might eliminate one of the two depending on what they found when they did the facial match and so she suggested it to the group. Madeline transferred the two pictures to Jill's laptop and, in no time, a match came up for the male library client. He had a criminal past but nothing amongst those crimes would indicate that he had the skills of the ghost. That led them to believe that the female was the ghost.

"It's going to be me against her and may the diva with the most superior computer skills, win!" Madeline proclaimed.

"No, Madeline we need you to win." Ortiz urged. "You know it's about good overcoming evil."

"I think I've done all that I can here. I'm going to head over to our Sacramento office and set up to watch the ghost for a while, if that's okay with you, Agent Ortiz?"

"Yes that's fine with me and thank you for your help today. I appreciate your flying across country to help us. Let's exchange cell phone numbers so we can get in touch with each other immediately if something is breaking."

In the blink of an eye, she was out the door with her trusty laptop under her arm and a look of excitement over the battle ahead with the mysterious ghost. Jill supposed that for a computer geek like Madeline, it was like she was going to come face-to-face with some avatar that had tormented her in a videogame for the past three years.

Ortiz looked at the remaining group and said, "I think I heard a conversation about the Highway Patrol arranging for security at Nathan Conroy's house tonight. What's the plan?"

"Given that the Palisades Valley Sheriff's office was accessed by our ghost, our killers may know that we have moved Jill to a new location, so we're stationing four Highway Patrol officers there."

"Nathan has a loud audible alarm system. As soon as someone steps on the premises, he has bright lights and obnoxious alarms that come on. I know this because I've been woken up by the noise and lights when some poor rabbit wandered on to his property. He could turn off those features if it will make it easier to capture the two suspects. What do you think?"

Moss looked thoughtful and then said, "I don't know the right answer, let me talk to some colleagues and I'll get back to you in a few hours, but I'm inclined to think it is a good idea to turn the special effects off. If they get away too quickly, we will have lost the opportunity to capture them."

"Okay, I'll wait for your call. I think Marie and I are done assisting you now so we're going to take off unless there is something you would like us to research."

Moss nodded and said, "We're executing our search warrant on our second suspect's employer. If we gain any identifying information that needs searching, I may contact you but otherwise your work is done here and you have a long night ahead of you. It sounds like Special Agent Ortiz is locked in geek mortal combat with her technician chasing the ghost."

With a smile and a "see you later", Jill and Marie exited Highway Patrol Headquarters to the promise of a very warm afternoon developing later that day. They stopped at a sandwich shop to grab sandwiches and water. They used the shop's restroom to change into kayaking clothes and were soon back on the road heading to a place that Jill knew rented kayaks.

Slathering on sunblock, changing into flip flops, they soon had the kayak laden with their food and drink cooler and set off paddling down the lazy river. The kayak company had given them directions of what to look for in order to exit the river and get a van ride back to their car. In the meanwhile, they would float downstream for several hours. Marie left her cellphone behind in the car while Jill's cellphone was wrapped in a water proof bag and stored in the cooler. Normally she didn't carry her phone with her on a river trip like this, but with the case poised to break open in the next twenty-four hours, she wanted to stay connected.

"With our interrupted sleep last night, the heat, and the gentle sway of this river, I could just fall asleep," Marie said on a sigh. "If you see me dozing, take my paddle from me and tie my boat to yours and we'll be fine."

"It is a relaxing place, sort of the antithesis of last night. Watching the monitor to see if someone was about to try and kill us in our sleep- it is hard to unwind from that kind of terror."

"Yeah, I might have nightmares on that experience. Where do you want to pull off and eat? Perhaps that will refuel me and drive the lethargy from my brain."

"We can pull off anywhere, so why don't we move towards shore now?"

With a little effort, they pulled to the side of the river, tugging their kayaks up the bank, and pulling out the food cooler. Spreading the beach towels on the sandy soil, they were soon leaning back against a log in the shade, munching on sandwiches washed down with water.

"Hard to imagine as we sit on this peaceful shoreline, that there are two people planning on trying to kill you tonight," Marie observed.

"I suppose it is kind of weird that we're just enjoying ourselves out on the water without a care in the world. I wonder how Nathan is going to feel when he hears that we're a target tonight?" Jill asked somewhat anxiously. She was insecure in her relationship with Nathan when it came to purposely putting herself in danger.

"He'll probably start stretching his muscles once he gets the news. He'll want to be in shape for the coming battle."

Jill had to laugh at the picture that Marie painted and relaxed a little as she had nailed Nathan exactly, then stopped mid-laugh to look at her friend. "I'm sorry that I'm putting you at risk. I've gotten so used to dragging my friends into combat with me that I don't give you a second thought. I could arrange a hotel for you if you would rather have a good night's sleep and be safe."

"Don't worry about it; between Nathan and the four Highway Patrol Officers, I feel well protected. It should be an exciting night and it will give me some material to tell my assistant about when I return. Remember, she always expects big and exotic stories, so I'm staying at Nathan's for her."

"Thanks for maintaining your sense of humor about the situation."

"What are friends for? Are you ready to get back in the water and paddle some more? The food and water perked me up."

They spent the next two hours on the river. The current could carry the kayak slowly downstream or they could make better speed by paddling. When they approached the designated pick-up location, they paddled over and pulled the kayaks up to a small parking lot. The shuttle van generally stopped every thirty minutes, so they reverted to talking about the case while waiting with no one around to overhear their conversation.

"This has been an interesting case as far as the sovereign citizen movement," Marie noted. "I wonder how many potential employees I have researched that belonged to this organization. I would think they don't do well during background searches as all of their information is missing or inconsistent. I would also think that they would be somewhat anti-social because of their views of the world. It's such an extreme view I would think that you would have a hard time having common conversation with your fellow man."

"It's really an extraordinary view and I wouldn't think there would be common ground with anyone," Jill agreed. "You're either inside the movement and think the rest of the nation follows illegal laws or you're on the outside looking in and you think the movement people are just plain crazy. I hope we get the two suspects tonight, but this ghost skulking in the background, roaming at will and changing major government systems without leaving a trace is a force to be very wary of. This person can wreak havoc with anyone's identity. I also think that once they have these two suspects in custody that there will be two new movement members that step up and cause problems. They could take away a lot of the power of the movement by locating this ghost of computer systems."

With that last comment, the kayak rental company van pulled up and loaded their kayaks. They jumped in the backseat for the ride back to the car. A little over an hour later, they were at Nathan's house with Jill explaining the latest news on the case and the plan for that evening. He looked resigned and even started making subtle stretching moves, and both Jill and Marie burst out laughing.

"What are you laughing at?" he asked.

"We chatted about what your reaction would be to the trouble ahead tonight," Jill said. "Marie won the bet as she said you would start stretching the moment you heard that the suspects might visit your house tonight and that was what you were just doing."

"What did you think I would do?" Nathan asked Jill.

"I just thought you would be mad," said a chagrined Jill.

"I am mad at the two suspects, but not at you. What's the schedule tonight?"

"The four officers are due to arrive by six. They wanted plenty of time to scour your property in daylight. They would also like you to turn off the audible and light effects of your alarm system, but it's your decision whether to comply with that request."

"I can do that, we got sufficient warning from your system yesterday and with police at the house, we have even less to worry about," Nathan said. "That reminds me; you need to do something about your alarms when you're asleep. You need to have an audible alarm at least inside your house. You have that expensive system, but if I hadn't been reading late we would have missed the opportunity to prevent getting murdered in our own beds."

"I agree and I'll call the alarm company tomorrow to get an audible alert in my kitchen, my bedroom, and my lab. Since I seem to have a continuous supply of maniacs intent on murdering me, I need a better alert system."

"Good. Should I plan on making dinner for the police?" Nathan asked, moving on now that he felt confident that Jill would improve her own security. Last night was the third attack on her property and so it was better to be prepared for the next killer trying to get at Jill.

"I don't think so. I mean the lieutenant did not ask us to feed them so I would think they would grab something on the way here. Besides they want time when they first arrive to assess the situation, so we should probably plan on a late dinner and then you could ask them if they want to eat with us."

"Okay. We'll either be having Chilean Sea Bass for dinner or a pasta dish if the officers join us as I don't have enough Sea Bass for seven people. Let me go make the adjustments to my security system before I forget. Is anyone covering your house tonight?"

"No, but I have my system set to notify me if there are intruders, so that will be enough of a warning to get our local sheriff over to my house."

"You know you two are really calm given that sometime in the next twelve hours, two killers are projected to show up and try to murder you," Marie observed.

"I am more worried about what to feed potentially seven people than the two killers. They have no history of knives or guns and the Taser has a fifteen foot range so I think I can win against those odds. After the two attempts on my life in Breck, it's much easier to be prepared for what comes your way; my competence has been tested and I'm around to talk about. If I'm wrong, we will have four Highway Patrol officers here for back-up. A guy doesn't get many opportunities to use the martial arts with the serious purpose of maiming someone. If I get to take these two guys on, it will be better than a competition for my evaluation of my hapkido skills."

Jill just shook her head and said, "I'm going to take Trixie outside to play fetch and the officers should be arriving at any time."

Marie sat in Nathan's kitchen drinking a crisp white wine he had poured for her. "I'm going to miss you guys when I head back to Wisconsin tomorrow. As always, you have been a great chef. I'll also miss the intellectual challenge of gathering data on someone. I do that in my everyday job but it's not life and death like it is on these cases with Jill. Next time I'm here, I want to go back to Yosemite. It's such a beautiful place and I feel like we only saw the smallest part of the park."

"I know what you mean. Jill and I visit the park every four months or so and hike a different part of Yosemite. There's so much beauty in that park," Nathan said as he glanced over at a computer monitor in his kitchen. "It looks like the Highway

Patrol is here. I'm going to go find out how many people are here for dinner."

Marie joined him and went outside to meet the officers.

They arrived in two black Ford Crown Victorias, the kind of car that hid on overpasses waiting to catch unsuspecting speeders. After introductions were made, the three civilians stood looking at the cars with the same concern.

"I don't have any garage space that could hide these cars but I do have two tarps that we could throw over them and then I have some old rusty farm tools that we could lay on top of the tarps so that it looks like the cars have been sitting here for a while," Nathan suggested.

"If necessary we could shovel some dirt on top of the tarps to make it look old," Jill contributed with a gleam in her eye.

"Dr. Quint, it sounds like you don't have much affection for our Highway Patrol cruisers by the fact you want to throw dirt on them," replied one of the officers.

"Please call me Jill and I'm not threatening you. I'm just telling you my fantasy is to swing a sledgehammer at those gum-balls you call police lights on top of your car."

The officers chuckled at that and said to Nathan, "Mr. Conroy, we'd like to tour your property and have a demonstration of your security system. After the tour, we'll borrow those tarps that you mentioned and allow Jill to shovel some dirt on them for therapy."

"First things first gentleman, call me Nathan by the way, are you joining us for dinner or have you already eaten?"

"We have a cooler filled with sub sandwiches that we brought with us, but we haven't eaten yet," replied another one of the officers clearly hopeful of something better.

"Would you like to join us then? I'll be making pasta, salad, and garlic bread, with ice cream for dessert. I also have the perfect wine to go with this food but as you're on duty I suppose you can't drink."

"We would be happy to join you if you have enough food. We'll want to survey this property first if you don't mind."

"I'll take you on a tour and then I'll work on dinner."

An hour later, the tour was complete and Nathan had set up his alarm system to feed into the cell phones that the officers carried. Nathan had also provided the men with a sofa and bedroom where they could stay as they rotated shifts. Nathan loved cooking, so despite his earlier complaints, he enjoyed making dinner for everyone. After dinner was finished, the officers established their posts and duty rotation and they checked in with Lieutenant Moss and updated the local Sheriff who was aware of the operation.

With all the usual routines of eating, cleaning the dishes, and conversing, everyone including the officers settled into a feeling of nervous anticipation. Would the killers attack tonight or would they have to go through this routine for the next week? Was Jill's house vulnerable? Jill and Marie stayed awake until nearly midnight which was beyond their normal bedtime, but finally the lack of sleep from the previous night caught up with them and they went to bed.

CHAPTER 24

*A*llen and Jerome returned from their road trip to look at mailbox companies and target locations with ideas and a need to do more research. Allen studied the science of building explosions and building implosions to deduce what it would take to have a sideways blast at the auditorium. He had decided that leaving a maintenance cart outside the auditorium wall was the only way they could avoid detection.

Jerome was studying the land in and around Nathan Conroy's house. He could vividly picture the road leading up to Conroy's property and they had a few places to park the car. Now looking at the map, he could get a better visual of the pluses and minuses of each of the three locations they had scouted out on their road trip. Jerome settled on the one farthest away as it had bushes they could pull the car behind. It was a farther walk, but it was more about staying undercover than proximity. He had two plans for entering the property depending on whether the gate was open and the nighttime lighting in the area. If it was open they would enter through it as long as the lighting was poor. He also had a plan for the backside of the property as well as a third option if necessary. Consistent with a Spanish style house, there was a six foot stucco wall that gave the image of a Hacienda on three sides and it appeared heavy foliage created the fourth wall. If the gate was closed, they would follow the wall to its end and enter through the trees and bushes and whatever else was growing there. Studying the blueprints of the Conroy house filed with the County building Department, the quickest route to the bedrooms was through the front door and then down a hallway to the right. One problem was determining which bedroom the esteemed Dr. Quint would be asleep in. His first guess was the master suite followed by the next biggest bedroom. He then worked out a game plan to test for an alarm system including cameras that might alert the occupants to their presence. Satisfied with his tactical plan to kill Dr. Quint, he printed out a copy to share with Allen.

"Allen, do you want to go over the kill plan for Dr. Quint and then we can split up and get some sleep before meeting tonight?"

"Sure, I finished my research on the bomb preparation. I know how to build one that will work on the side of the building, so we just need to wait for the components to finish arriving and I'll need to get a maintenance cart for use. I should have enough supplies that I'll be able to build a small practice bomb to try out before the real thing."

"Excellent. I think we would be at risk for discovery if we had to go inside the auditorium after getting through security. I was also dreading the roof approach. Now, about tonight. Here is a map of the property and the house and this is what I think we should do," Jerome explained the plan he worked out and some decision points they would have to make as they went and they both agreed they would worry about security cameras as they got closer to the house as they assumed they had set off a silent alarm when he picked the door lock at Dr. Quint's house. Her vineyard had been so dark that unless they had made the visit under a full moon, they wouldn't have been able to see any security monitors. They split up soon after that.

While Allen tried to retain a cool persona around Jerome, he was in reality deeply passionate and excited about the night's mission. The stupid doctor only thought she had to move her residence elsewhere and she would escape him. She represented much of what was wrong with the current society. She had a license to be a doctor issued by the false government. She then worked for that false government. She had outed the bad politicians in that Northern California town, but everything else that she did worked to limit the powers of good people like Jerome and him. He would have to thank her for making them think of an alternative way to strike at the Department of Revenue because next to killing Dr. Quint, he had the auditorium explosion to be proud of next week. He and Jerome would become legends in the movement for ending the lives of people who were against the principles of sovereign citizens.

At midnight, the two men met up each with their bag of supplies to carry out their mission. Again in all black apparel with black grease marker covering the skin of their faces, they loaded up the car to make the journey to Jill Quint's temporary home. Allen had wanted to tell Jerome to drive faster, but by maintaining the speed limit, they wouldn't be stopped for speeding. They headed for the parking area that they had designated for the night's job. Keeping with the plan to put Dr. Quint to death with nitrogen gas, they had a small full cylinder with a mask and each was armed with a Taser. Like the defibrillator, the two Tasers had started out as what any civilian could purchase, but Allen had modified them to have greater distance reach. While many sovereign citizens believed in the right to bear arms, both Jerome and Allen had an unexplained aversion to killing someone with a knife or gun. They considered their own methods as effective, but humane and bloodless. They didn't need the violence of murder; they just needed the person gone.

They arrived at the property to find the lighting average and the gate closed. The house was shrouded in the darkness of everyone being asleep. The two men walked the side wall which went on for longer than they expected. They reached the end of the wall and it did bump up against heavy foliage, but there was also a wire fence that would keep dogs in and deer out. Putting their hands on top of the wall, they used it as leverage to scale over the wire mesh.

"Let's head for the front door," Jerome directed. "We want to follow the back fence to the left side stucco wall that way when we reach the front of the house our entry is closer to the left side wall. The lighting looks okay and I think we can stay hidden in the shadows."

Allen nodded and did a fist bump with Jerome as they continued to follow the fence walls to their destination. They reached the front door of Conroy's house and Jerome pulled the pick set out of his pocket to unlock the door. They silently moved inside and closed the door. Off to the left, they could see the nightlight in the kitchen. As planned, they silently moved down the hall careful not to make any sounds from footfalls. They headed to the master bedroom, Tasers in their hands for self-protection if they came upon anything unexpected in the silent house. Their eyes were adjusted to seeing in the dark and even without the nightlight they could follow the hall to the bedroom where Jill Quint lay asleep and where she would hopefully die in a few minutes.

Moving silently, Jerome opened the door to the master suite and stood there and listened. He heard no sounds. He looked at the forms in the bed. There appeared to be a man with his head turned away from the door and a woman with long blond hair sleeping on her side with her face tucked into his back.

Jerome looked over at Allen and they each gave the thumbs up signal. Then Allen held his hand out and did a silent 3-2-1 countdown with his fingers to fire the Taser at each person on each side of the bed. They aimed and fired simultaneous streams to both sides of the bed. There was a popping sound followed by the start of flames beginning where the two people had lay in the bed.

CHAPTER 25

arie, Jill, and Nathan sat in their pajamas in Nathan's office watching their two suspects move up the property, through the front door, and down the hall to the master bedroom. There were two officers out of view of the door's entrance into the master bedroom. There were also two officers who had come up behind the suspects after they fired.

The popping noise and distraction caused by the fire covered their movement.

The Highway Patrol had brought two fake blow-up officers with them that they used as decoys in patrol cars to slow down speeders. They placed the dummies in Nathan's bed, with both faces turned away from the door and a blond wig on the second officer. In dim light, on their sides, with the wig, and covered by the bedclothes, they looked very realistic. What they didn't think of was what would happen when the electric current of the Taser hit the dummy. There was a wee bit of a balloon popping sound followed by a bigger ignition of flames as the dummies and their clothing caught fire.

Above the noise, the officers yelled at the suspects to drop their weapons. The two suspects turned to fire at the two officers, but before they could get a stream off, they were jolted from behind by the two rear officers. They dropped to the floor with their bodies shaking with spasms as the officers quickly handcuffed them and pulled them from the burning room by their feet. Nathan and Jill rushed in with buckets of water to throw on the bed, while Marie had stayed behind in the office to call the Fire Department. The flames were soon out after they dumped about six buckets on the bed. The room would have smoke and water damage, the mattress destroyed, and the two dummies would never again serve as decoys.

The Highway Patrol had decided they needed an actual attempt made on Jill's life in order for them to arrest the two suspects, charge them with attempted murder, and deny them bail. Their suspects were too good at vanishing into the vapor and if they had simply arrested them on a burglary charge while the case was sorting itself out, they might have been able to get out on bail.

Ten minutes later, both the fire department and Deputy Davis were on the scene. The mattress was taken outside and hacked into pieces to make sure there were no embers still active inside. The firemen were a little taken aback when they heard what caused the fire. They were finished a short while later and packed up to leave. Deputy Davis had spoken with the Highway Patrol who had waited for an escort to take the two suspects back to Sacramento; she then came over to speak with Jill, Nathan, and Marie.

"Just saying that my shifts go a lot faster when there is action at your property. I also rank high with my fellow deputies since I seem to be the one that is on the scene when someone tries to murder you. Have you thought of just retiring to your vineyard, growing grapes, living a calm non-violent life?"

"Are you kidding? My sole reason for everything I do is to make your shifts go faster and keep your skills sharp with your gun. I bet you never had an opportunity to shoot real people until killers started stalking me."

"I was perfectly happy keeping my skills up by visiting the shooting range."

They were soon interrupted by the Highway Patrol. Their escort had arrived and they were heading back with the suspects to the Sacramento County Jail. They had two additional cruisers as they wanted to make sure they were not accosted by any sovereign citizens on the way. Jill did not envy the officers as these two suspects would be particularly trying to interview.

Things were wrapping up and as Deputy Davis was getting ready to leave, she hesitated for a moment and then asked Jill, "As payback for all these rescues I have to make to save your sorry ass, I wonder if you would do me a favor?"

Jill, without pause said "Yes."

"Wait a moment, I haven't told you what I want yet."

"Doesn't matter; if it is within my power to grant it I'll do it."

"Okay I volunteer with some teens that have found their way into the juvenile justice system. I would like to bring them out to your vineyard for a little career development," Deputy Davis explained. "You're one of the few people I know who could give the kids an explanation of two careers - farming and criminal investigation. If you could find a bloody dummy - maybe if there is anything left of the dummies that got burned, and scare them as to what they will look like with gunshots or knife wounds, that would be great too."

"I'll borrow a dummy from someone and if it goes well, I think we could field trip your kids to the Sacramento Coroner for an even grosser moment to scare them. Give me a date and time and I'll be ready. Seriously, I enjoy stuff like that, bring them as often as you want."

"Good. Thank you. This is important to me," said the deputy and then she left.

It was an hour away from dawn, but they were all exhausted

from two nights of interrupted sleep. Marie headed back to her bed she planned to skip the morning meeting in Sacramento if there was one and Jill and Nathan made do in a third bedroom as the master would be out of commission for a while.

"I'm sorry about the destruction to your house tonight," Jill commented in a worried voice. "I'll reimburse you for whatever it takes to restore your bedroom."

"Now that's a dumb comment, I can more than afford to pay for it myself. Whatever the cost of getting rid of the smell of smoke and a new bed, you're worth it to me. I am very happy that the dummies caught on fire rather than the two of us. Besides I had been thinking about getting a California King bed and now I have a reason to do so."

"I think your bed frame is ok it's just the mattress that is destroyed. You just need a new mattress."

"No, I'm going to claim this on my insurance and get a better bed. Don't try to talk me out of it."

"Okay, if you need an excuse for a new bed, you now have it," Jill agreed. "Thanks for being a good sport and can I just say that I love you but I am really tired and I need to go to sleep."

Just like that, Jill was out cold while Nathan was left with his own thoughts. It had been a wild night and he was very grateful that the officers had put dummies in the bed rather than him and Jill. The little fire in the bed made him want to run out and purchase a few blow-up dummies, for the next time that Jill's life was at risk. With that last thought he settled down in bed curling around Jill, relieved that they had made it unharmed against another one of Jill's murder suspects. Life was certainly never boring with her around he thought as he drifted off to sleep.

CHAPTER 26

*J*ill was up early in light of her middle of the night excitement several hours ago. She gave herself twenty minutes to shower and dress. Then she grabbed a coffee in her to-go mug and make the drive to the meeting in Sacramento. She was curious to find out what new information they had on the two suspects. That curiosity was keeping her alert on the drive to Highway Patrol headquarters despite getting less than four hours sleep.

Lieutenant Moss gave her a broad smile when she entered the conference room and said, "Jill, with your help we've arrested the two deadliest killers of State employees," and he begin clapping which was picked up by everyone else in the conference room.

Jill was embarrassed by this show and said, "Actually it was your officers that were so superb and saved my and my friends' lives last night, so let's have a round of applause for the California Highway Patrol."

After the room quieted down, Moss began the meeting by asking Jill to describe what happened the previous night. Her view was more entertaining than the report he had gotten from his officers. His officers had said simply that there had been a small fire that was extinguished. Jill's description of running in with buckets of water to throw on the two flamed-engulfed dummies and the bed was pretty funny. The committee needed a laugh after the stress and worry about additional murders.

"Lieutenant, have you learned anything during the interview process with these two suspects?" Jill asked as this was what she was really curious about. She also thought the case wasn't really over until the ghost was found.

"We haven't gotten anywhere with these two as they are citing laws from the 18th century related to the constitution that make no sense to our officers or the district attorney. The FBI is interviewing them at the moment to find out more information about the ghost. We have matched their fingerprints to prints on the defibrillator and a few other pieces of evidence we have collected so without them ever making a statement and with the activity at your friend's residence last night, we have enough information to send them to prison for nearly two decades."

"Good, when I sat in another room and watched them fire their Tasers at the dummies that were made up to look like my friend and me, I wanted them to go to jail for their actions. It was funny to watch only because it wasn't really me in the bed."

"It was a good thing we used those dummies; the crime lab examined their Tasers and they both had been modified. They might have killed you or your partner if the stream had struck you, but in case it didn't, they had a nitrogen gas cylinder and mask in a backpack."

There was dead silence in the room at the stark pronouncement of just how desperately the two suspects wanted to kill her until Jill broke it with, "Like I said, many thanks to the CHP!" And then changing the subject, she asked "Have the employees been able to come home now and resume their lives?"

"Yes, we sent a couple of buses to pick them and their families up. It will be business as usual tomorrow, which is good, because the Department of Revenue has nearly shut down over the past week."

The Lieutenant wrapped up this last meeting. With the suspects in custody, there was no need for any further meetings; the case was closed from the Highway Patrol's perspective of solving the murder of its employees. The meeting soon broke up and Jill looked at the time, planning the remainder of her day. She needed to be home by noon to have lunch with Nathan and Marie before taking her to the airport for her return trip to Wisconsin. That gave her another hour to close out her documentation and billing for both the Highway Patrol and for Anna Valencia and then she would contact Special Agent Ortiz to see what was going on with the capture of the ghost.

The agent picked up the phone when Jill called five minutes later, "Hey Special Agent Ortiz, we finished with the task force meetings with the arrest of the two suspects. I was curious as to how you were doing with tracking down the ghost? Madeline sounded like she was close to finding her electronically."

"The Dallas Field Office picked her up about an hour ago. Madeline and I are on our way to the airport to catch a flight to Dallas to interview her and likely return with her to Sacramento as she is an accessory to the attempted murder of yourself and Nathan Conroy. Those are her only charges at the moment, but we're hopeful that we can link her to any number of sovereign citizen malicious activities."

"Can you call me when you interview her in this city, day or night? I would like to observe the interview."

There was a pause and then the agent said, "Well okay. I think I can create a legitimate reason for you to observe. Why would you want to? It might be the middle of tonight or early tomorrow when we interview her, do you still want to observe if it is the middle of the night?"

"I would like to observe her in person as there is something that bothers me about her. You can call me in the middle of the night if that is the way your schedule is going. Here's my cell phone number. Call me."

After Jill ended the call with the agent, she got in her car to head home for lunch with Nathan and Marie. She was sorry to see Marie go, but at least they had found time to hike in Yosemite and kayak the river. Marie was likely glad to go home for a good night's rest after their last two interrupted nights. She would see her friends and teammates in the fall when they went on vacation to the UK. During the drive, she called Anna Valencia to update her on the case. She knew that the police had notified Anna that her husband's suspected killers had been arrested, but Jill wanted to close out the engagement with her client.

After an awesome lunch with wine for Marie and Nathan, they headed out to the airport. Marie was having a hard time staying awake after Nathan served the Chilean Sea Bass for lunch with an excellent wine he paired with the meal. Jill laughed and had her friend put her seat into a reclining position so she could get a quick nap in on the way to the airport. Soon enough they were hugging each other goodbye, knowing they would stay in touch, and see the whole gang in London in a couple of months.

Jill was exhausted driving away from the airport; three hours on the highway already today and that was after, at the most, four hours of sleep last night. Tonight she would be in her own bed at an early hour to try and regain what she had lost. The only missing piece was the identity of the internet ghost. It wasn't part of the investigation for which she had been hired, but it had been easy for the ghost to tap into some very secure websites and wreak havoc. Jill wondered if any of her own websites had been altered. She had a simple website for her consulting business, and a more complex website for her Quixotic Winery describing her winemaking process, Moscato wine and a couple of awards she had picked up. She would check on that when she got home. Hopefully, the cyber-ghost had stayed away from Nathan's website as it was critical to his business.

She checked the websites once she got home to find that her forensic pathologist consulting website was completely sabotaged. A quick look and her winery and Nathan's graphics website appeared to be spared the cyber-ghost's handiwork. She called Nathan to explain what happened with a question on how she could take down the website until it could be repaired. Jill gave Nathan her passcodes but even he couldn't alter it. She debated who to call next. She felt like she had already called on Henrik too much and besides his staff might still be involved with the FBI. She decided she would try David Gomez in Colorado and she dialed his number.

"Hey David, it's Jill Quint. How are you doing?"

"Hello Jill, I am doing okay. I just finished teaching another group of juvenile delinquents that are getting into trouble hacking. I'm afraid I might create a bigger pipeline of reformed delinquents than the FBI can afford to hire."

"I think that is so cool how you are helping to steer them in the right direction. Speaking of hackers let me tell you about my current case, "Jill said as she began to describe the sovereign citizens and their internet ghost.

"What a fascinating case! I would have loved to help with it, but it seems like you solved it without my help."

"Actually, I do need your help. Before the ghost was arrested she got into my forensic pathology consulting website and she posted some gross pictures there. It's everything from porn to gross murder scenes with knives stuck in bodies and maggots eating the skull. Can you just take down the website so no-one can see this material? Fortunately, she left my winery website alone."

"Oh no. I was walking out to my car when you called. Let me go back to my laptop and see what I can do. I'll call you back in ten minutes."

"Thanks David, I really appreciate your help."

As promised, he returned her call less than ten minutes later and stated he had success taking down her website.

"I tried removing the terrible content, but your cyber-ghost had that nicely rigged so that it set off a little miniature virus. It was just faster to close down the website. I could save it if you want but you won't be able to use that domain name again without getting the same material. I could use your damaged website as a teaching activity and see what my young hackers will do with it."

"I would like it sanitized eventually and then be able to use it again. I don't think you want to show them the pictures though."

"I agree. I'll go through and replace the images with pictures of something pleasant, and then have them work to eliminate the pictures and put some safeguards in place so this can't happen again. Give me a month or so and you can have your website back."

"I don't want any new business in that time period so it suits me to have it unavailable."

"Jill, I don't mean to be rude but can we continue this conversation later? I'm late for a meeting that I'm speaking at."

"Yes please go David; I'll catch up with you later."

With her website resolved and the case complete on her end, although not by the FBI, it was time to return to her regular day job as a vintner after she took a nap. She really was exhausted. She fell asleep while creating a mental list in her head of what needed to be done around the vineyard. She awoke an hour later when she heard her phone ringing.

"Hello."

"Is this Jill Quint?"

"Yes"

"Oh hi Jill, I didn't recognize your voice. This is Special Agent Ortiz."

"Oh. Sorry, you woke me out of a deep sleep nap that I needed after my last two disturbed nights. My brain isn't quite in gear yet."

"Okay, sorry about that. Look we are about to board a plane in Dallas with our suspected sovereign citizen internet ghost. We will return to Sacramento by ten so if you want to meet me at the FBI building in Sacramento around 10:30, you can observed the interview."

"Special Agent, thank you for the invite and I'll see you at 10:30."

"Can I ask why you wanted to observe this interview?"

"I have a way out in left field hunch that I want to see validated."

"What's the hunch?"

"Can't tell you, it is so far out there that I'll lose all credibility with the FBI if it doesn't bear out."

"Ok then see you later," and a puzzled Special Agent ended the call. They had arrived in Dallas and given the complexity of the case under way, the Dallas office just wanted the suspect out of their holding and into someone else's. They were thrilled to release her immediately to the Sacramento office - one less nut case to occupy the legal system in Texas. Leticia found herself in the company of two Dallas agents providing additional security with the suspect. Within hours they were in Sacramento and on the way to the FBI office.

It was late and they had a long day, but they wanted to disconcert their suspect. Special Agent Ortiz began with Madeline sitting at her side for any geek translations.

"What is your name?"

There was dead silence to the question much like it had been hours earlier when she was questioned. She had as yet not uttered a single word in their company. Her fingerprints had come back unmatched. Madeline tried a computer question and got no response. They hadn't offered her a lawyer yet but they were getting close to the time when it would have to be offered and the request honored.

Jill was watching through the window and beginning to feel a little more confident in her suspicion. Using Henrik's software she tried a beta feature that wasn't on the market yet. She entered the picture of this woman and matched it to the man Jill thought was her brother - the Caucasian suspect she met in Nathan's house last night. When the computer blinked up an answer, she asked an agent standing near the door to the interview room to send in a note to Ortiz.

She watched her read the note and then look up at the one-way glass, a puzzle on her face. Then deciding that since she had not gotten any other questions answered, she may as well ask Jill's.

"Are you the sister of the man known as Thomas Hull that the Highway Patrol arrested last night for the murder of four Department of Revenue employees? Have you spoken with your brother in the last twenty-four hours? Would you like to?"

The woman raised her eyes to the agent and asked, "What did you say?"

"I think you heard me. We have a preliminary computer match between yourself and your brother which is truly amazing because according to all records, you were killed in a car accident ten years ago, but you weren't in that car were you? You have silently assisted your brother at erasing his identity for years.

"We're doing DNA testing on you and your brother as we speak and the results will be back to us in twenty-four hours. You can continue to sit there mute or if you would like to ever speak to your brother again then you can begin answering questions. Since we already have DNA evidence of your brother's storage area and we have been able to partially connect you to his activities, we'll be charging you as an accessory to four murders."

With these last few sentences, the suspect crumpled and said,

"I'll tell you what you want to know after I have spoken with my brother."

"I'll allow you to speak to your brother after you give me your name. Then you'll have one hour to speak with him and that will be it."

"My name doesn't matter as I am confirmed dead. You can't do anything with it. Nor can you find any evidence of what I chose to call myself now. I am the ghost you have been chasing for several years and it was good while it lasted."

"Do you belong to the sovereign citizen movement?"

"No it's a stupid organization full of whacky ideas."

"But your brother deeply believes in it and you've been helping him for a while."

"So, I helped him because he is my brother, not because I believed in what he is doing. I have felt for years that he was wronged by our parents when they forced him into the military."

All of a sudden, Special Agent Ortiz felt like an elephant was sitting on her body. This woman in front of her had so many layers of complexity and wrong-doing that it might take the FBI years to understand the scope of her damage. She needed some time to think and so she said to her suspect, "I'm going to leave now and arrange for you to visit your brother and then you'll be locked up in the Sacramento County Jail. You have been read your rights multiple times; do you wish to have the assistance of an attorney?"

"No, I do not need an attorney."

The Special Agent and Madeline got up and exited the room, leaving their suspect guarded by other agents.

She walked over to Jill and said, "I can see days and weeks ahead of us as we try to figure out what she did with a computer. She may have eliminated the identities of some people - death in cyberspace. How did you know they were related?"

"I watched her walk and mannerisms on the video from Dallas and thought them related. Since that is a very unproven scientific approach I was hesitant to speak about it to anyone. I wonder if her brother knew of her existence or if she was strictly a ghost to him."

The agent hadn't even thought of that. There were layers in this case that would keep her occupied for weeks to months as she figured out brother and sister - so similar that Dr. Quint saw it but so far apart in many other ways. With that, the two women parted ways. As Jill was leaving, Ortiz said "Hey could you avoid another case in this area? I need time to unravel this one before you pull me into another complicated murder situation."

Jill just gave her a small smile and left. She breathed in the fresh air relieved for the first time in days that she and hers were safe for the foreseeable future until she took the next case and sought justice for a new client. She couldn't bring their loved one back from the dead, but at least she could help identify and stop the person who caused their loss.

The End

ALSO BY ALEC PECHE

Now You Don't See Me

Where Did She Go?

How Did She Get There?

Dog Humor

Eat, Play, Poop: Letters to my parents from camp

New Urban Fantasy Series

The Awakening at Lake Tahoe (short story)

ABOUT THE AUTHOR

I reside in Northern California with my rescue dog and cat. I love to travel, play sports, read, and drink wine and beer. I enjoy the diversity of the world and I'm always watching people and events for story ideas. All of my stories are generated by my imagination, I don't use AI to write books.

If you would like to sign up for my bi-weekly blog and announcement of new books, please follow this link: https://www.AlecPecheBooks.com

While you're waiting for the next story, if you would be so kind as to leave a review for this book, that would be great. I appreciate all the feedback and support. Reviews buoy my spirits and stoke the fires of creativity.

Readers that sign up for my blog receive a free prequel novelette for the Jill Quint Series.

Author Profile on Goodreads

Author Profile on BookBub

AFTERWORD

As a fictional Moscato wine grower in the Jill Quint series, the author thought she would offer readers a recipe in each electronic book going forward of drinks or food to make with Moscato, if sweet white wine straight-up is not to your taste. This recipe is likely equally sweet, but you could substitute diet 7-up and make limeade from scratch with stevia or another sugar substitute.

Mix: 1/4 can of frozen limeade concentrate, defrosted with 1 cup of diced strawberries in a blender and make a puree. Run the puree through a strainer to remove some of the seeds. Add to a pitcher filled with the remainder of the limeade and 1.5L of Moscato wine. Garnish with 1 cup of sliced strawberries and a sliced lime and chill in the refrigerator. When ready to serve, top off each glass with 7-up from a 2L bottle.

www.ingramcontent.com/pod-product-compliance
Lightning Source LLC
Chambersburg PA
CBHW050236110726
47898CB00007B/2176